PROBABLE CLAUS

Probable Claus

Jon L. Breen

FIVE STAR
A part of Gale, Cengage Learning

GALE
CENGAGE Learning™

Detroit • New York • San Francisco • New Haven, Conn • Waterville, Maine • London

GALE
CENGAGE Learning™

LIBRARY OF CONGRESS CATALOGING-IN-PUBLICATION DATA

Breen, Jon L., 1943–
    Probable claus / by Jon L. Breen. — 1st ed.
        p. cm.
    ISBN-13: 978-1-59414-734-0 (alk. paper)
    ISBN-10: 1-59414-734-5 (alk. paper)
    I. Title.
PS3552.R3644P76 2009
813'.54—dc22   2008043422

First Edition. First Printing: February 2009.
Published in 2009 in conjunction with Tekno Books and Ed Gorman.

For Joan and Geoff Gunson

AUTHOR'S NOTE

Every effort has been made to follow criminal justice procedure with the utmost accuracy. However, it should be noted that the city and state depicted in this novel are fictitious; that states vary in their laws and procedures; that at least some seemingly nonsensical laws and procedures are used in nearly every jurisdiction; that judges in the courtroom can do just about anything that enters their sometimes addled heads, though they may be reversed on appeal; and that the writer of fiction is allowed to make stuff up because that's why it's called fiction.

PROLOGUE

Monday, July 24

Wilbur Ricketts, night security man at the Baines Building for nearly three decades, knew everyone who worked in that towering Art Deco edifice, from the Baines brothers themselves to the newest custodian hired last week, and he knew more than a few secrets that he never would divulge. When on this warm July evening, a man in a Santa Claus suit came through the revolving door and waddled toward the security desk, Wilbur was surprised, certainly, but not as surprised as someone unfamiliar with the local scene might have been.

Anyone in the city would recognize the wearer of the white-trimmed red jacket, trousers, and stocking cap, black boots and belt, even with that massive white beard concealing some of his features. With or without the Yuletide regalia, Charlie Baines was a local institution, a symbol of charity and generosity and selfless good will, beloved by all. Where others portrayed Santa for a couple of hours or, in professional cases, for a season, Charlie obviously wanted to inhabit the role 24-7-365. Still, of all the times Wilbur had seen him enter the lobby garbed as Santa, it had never happened in the middle of summer.

"Good evening, Wilbur," St. Nick said through his beard, white teeth gleaming and blue eyes crinkling benevolently. "How are you this fine evening?"

"Good, but, ah—"

"And how is your lovely wife Myrtle?"

9

"Feeling much better, thank you, but ah—aren't you a little warm, Mr. Baines?" Well past eleven p.m., the temperature was still in the high sixties.

"Yes, it is warm, but this suit means more to me than a response to the weather, at least in the meteorological sense. Emotional weather is another matter."

"Uh, what do you mean by that, Mr. Baines?"

"I'll tell you a secret, Wilbur. I sometimes get a little down, a little depressed, a little bent over by the stresses of life, even a little angry."

"Even you, sir?"

"Alas, yes, even me. And when I get that way, even in the heat of the summer, I just put on this Santa Claus suit and let the spirit of Christmas sort of wash over me like a big wave, and I feel better again. Now tell me, is my brother in the building?"

Wilbur peered at the computer screen behind the security desk and verified that Andrew Baines, the elder of the two brothers who were so central to the city's commercial and cultural life, was indeed in his office on the thirtieth floor. "Yep, he's up there. Only person in the building 'cept you and me and a couple of other security guys and a few cleaners."

Charlie Baines, looking over Wilbur's shoulder at a figure in a well-worn tracksuit stretched out behind the security counter, said, "And Oswald, I see."

"You know he's harmless, Mr. Baines. You won't say anything to your brother, will you? He doesn't like to have Oswald around."

"Which is something Oswald and I have in common. Oswald must know more about what goes on in this building than anybody else, including my brother."

"Oh, he does for a fact," Wilbur agreed. Touching a finger to the side of his head, he added, "But his voices tell him things, so he also knows a lot that never happened."

"Yeah, I hear voices," said Oswald, lifting his head. "Too loud voices. Voices that talk about me when I'm asleep like I'm not awake." Pulling himself to a sitting position, he fixed his gaze on Charlie Baines. "Hi, Santa."

"Hi, Oswald."

"You're a few months early."

"I hope I'm not too late." Charlie Baines sneezed suddenly and withdrew a tissue from his pocket.

"Bless you," said Wilbur automatically. "Summer cold?"

"Just allergies," Charlie said, tossing the tissue in a wastebasket. "Always get me this time of year. Log me in, Wilbur, and I shall beam myself up. We need to have a serious discussion, Andy and I."

"I'll take you up in the elevator," Oswald offered, getting to his feet.

"You gotta stay down here, Oswald," Wilbur said firmly. "You know the rules."

"Yeah, yeah, I know the rules. Never go in the lobby in the daytime, and never go to the upper floors at all." He stretched and yawned. "Can't sleep now, though. Guess I'll go out and do some laps around the block." He picked up a cell phone off the counter and, with a wave at Wilbur and Charlie, walked out through the revolving door.

Wilbur said, "If your brother ever sees him, I have to yell at him and make a big production of throwing him out. I think Oswald understands."

"I'm sure Oswald understands more than we imagine."

"Shall I call Mr. Andrew Baines and tell him you're on your way up?"

"No, don't do that," said Charlie with a smile. "I'll surprise him."

Wilbur watched the incongruous figure walk toward the elevator. What exactly his official duties within the firm were Wilbur

11

wasn't certain, but Charlie Baines was the human face of Baines and Company, supporting every cultural and charitable institution in the city. While he had his own large office up on thirty, he appeared there only sporadically. Andrew Baines by contrast was first in the office and last to leave almost every day, rarely attended social functions, never took a vacation, and just about everybody who worked in the building feared and hated him. Wilbur wondered what a meeting between these two, with nobody else in the room, would be like. How did two men, joined by blood and history and financial interests but separated by most every human instinct, manage to communicate with each other? The Baines brothers were everything to the life of the city: Charlie, everything good, and Andrew, everything bad.

Wilbur had noted Charlie Baines's entry at precisely 11:42 p.m. Nearly an hour passed uneventfully. At 12:33 a.m., the elevator door opened and Santa Claus reentered the lobby, every hair of his false beard neatly in place. He walked over to the security desk, appearing calm but uncharacteristically somber. "Wilbur," he said, "something really bad has happened up on thirty. I would have phoned you from up there, but the police will want the crime scene left undisturbed. So I guess you should give them a call."

"Crime scene, Mr. Baines?"

"Yes, I'm afraid so. I have to go now, but the police can reach me at home if they want to talk to me, as I'm sure they will. Sorry if this spoils your evening."

Wilbur Ricketts gaped at him. "Mr. Baines, what's happened?"

"I think my brother Andrew may have had an enemy."

"Lots of them, sir, but what exactly—?"

"You'll have to excuse me, Wilbur, I have to go now. This suit is warm, and I don't need it anymore. Tonight, I mean."

"Mr. Baines, you, ah, really shouldn't leave if—" But Charlie

Baines was through the revolving door and turning up Victory Street at a calm and measured pace. Wilbur Ricketts picked up the phone and started the squeaking wheels of criminal justice in motion.

CHAPTER ONE

Tuesday, September 19

The Baines Building on Victory Street, seven short blocks from the old courthouse, had only one law firm among its high-paying tenants. That firm, however, was so prominent that many thought of the two buildings as the focal points of the city's jurisprudence. The firm had several partners, but the building's directory bore just one name: Gordon Moon, the king of the local defense bar, the highest profile lawyer in the city.

Eve Nyquist, a young blond woman in her early twenties, had been staring at that name for thirty seconds when the security man came out from behind his counter and said, "Can I help you, miss?"

"No, no, I'm a little early, and I'm just drinking it all in, trying to calm my nerves. I can hardly believe I'm actually here."

Wilbur Ricketts said, "I see. But I'm afraid you can't go up to the thirtieth floor without their permission."

Thirtieth floor? But the directory said Gordon Moon's offices were on the twenty-fifth.

"Security's tightened up since the murder," Wilbur went on.

"The murder?"

"I was here that night. They switched me to days so I could field questions from the public."

"I don't have any questions," Eve said with a smile. "At least not about any murder. I have an offer to work for Gordon Moon. I have an interview scheduled with him today. His human resources people said it would just be a formality, but I'm a little nervous anyway. He's a legend in the legal profession in this state. Who was murdered anyway?"

"You aren't from around here, are you, miss?"

"Well, no, I just graduated from the State University law school upstate. I passed my bar exam on the first try, and now I'm ready to tackle the big city."

And it's ready to tackle you, young lady, Wilbur thought, looking at her a little sadly, as he might view a piece of steak heading for the meat grinder.

His expression took the edge off her confidence. Was she coming off as a hick? She said, "If this murder is something I should know about—"

"Well, miss, the victim was only Andrew Baines, the fellow whose family the building's named after."

"Oh. Of course, I've heard about that, but I didn't connect the name with the building. He was murdered here?"

"Thirtieth floor. He was shot, and the police have charged his brother, Charlie Baines, with the crime. I can't imagine Charlie Baines doing it, but it seems like he must have. I can tell you all about it."

She glanced at her watch, somewhat flustered. "Not right now, thank you. I have just three minutes until my appointment, and I want to be on time."

"Okay, but stop by on your way out if you want to hear the story. It was quite a traumatic experience, I can tell you, being in the building when a murder was being committed, and I find it helps me to talk about it."

"Yes, thank you, I'll be sure to do that," she said and walked to the elevator, finding the security man a little creepy and feeling glad to get away from him.

As soon as she stepped off on the twenty-fifth floor, Eve confronted a wide reception desk staffed by three smilingly efficient women of about her age. Potted plants were everywhere, in sufficient profusion that she wondered if someone watered and attended to them as a full-time job. The Moon firm apparently had the whole floor, and a dozen people were in constant motion behind the partition, darting from one office doorway to another, some carrying coffee cups, some carrying law books, some in animated conversation with one another. Which were the partners, which the associates, which the paralegals, which the legal secretaries, which the plant minder, she wondered. And how would the green but ambitious Eve Nyquist fit into this vast organization? She would do whatever it took to succeed, she promised herself again, and to make her success a victory for justice and the highest aspirations of the legal profession.

After a wait of only a few minutes, spent glancing at a recent issue of the glossy city magazine, she was ushered into Gordon Moon's huge office. His walls were covered with plaques and photos of him with dignitaries; his desk, about the size of a ping-pong table, was covered with trophies but uncluttered by paperwork. The window behind the desk offered a breathtaking view of the city skyline. Moon himself, walking around the desk to shake her hand and direct her to a chair, was a small, nattily dressed man in his forties with a huge head and a huge presence.

"Eve, I've been looking forward to meeting you," he said in a rich baritone that obviously was a factor in his legendary success with juries. "Welcome to Gordon Moon. I mean, that is, to Gordon Moon the firm, and I am Gordon Moon the guy."

Back behind the desk, Moon opened a file folder and glanced at it. When he looked up, he said with a smile, "I hope nobody gave you the notion this meeting would be some kind of trial by ordeal. I trust my people to make the right decisions, pick the right people. We know everything about you, Eve."

The penetrating gaze that accompanied the statement made her a little uncomfortable. "Everyone knows about you, Mr. Moon."

"It's Gordon, please, and nobody, including my mother, knows as much about me as we do about you. Thank God. I have way too much baggage to be hired by this firm, so it's lucky for me I'm already here, isn't it?"

Eve smiled weakly, not sure what he wanted her to say.

Fortunately, Gordon Moon hardly paused. "You got good marks on your moot court presentation. More important to me than classroom grades, I have to tell you. They say you can recite statute and case law from memory, a nice party trick but not all that important. Personally, I'm glad to know you don't have any tattoos or body piercings."

"Mr. Moon—"

"Gordon."

"Gordon, I feel that many young women of my generation have made a grave mistake having visible tattoos."

"Forget visible. I happen to know you don't have any at all."

Eve felt herself blushing. How in the world could he know that?

"Not that a tattoo on your derrière would disqualify you, but call me old-fashioned. I like the way you're dressed too. Totally dignified but sexy as hell. I've had new female grads come in here for interviews showing their bellybuttons. Nice for the masculine eye, but distinctly unprofessional for an officer of the court."

"I quite agree," Eve said.

"You're even better-looking than your picture, if you don't mind my saying so."

"Of course not," Eve said, lowering her eyes, but she felt vaguely uncomfortable. Was Gordon the kind of boss she'd been warned about?

"Looking like a super-model will come in handy sometimes. Other times, we will want to play it down a bit. Depends on the client and the charge and the judge and all sorts of things. We have to consider it because, politically correct or not, it's real." He paused for emphasis and fixed his eyes on hers—another jury trick, she imagined. "This is the real world, Eve. Law school is over. So tell me. Just why do you want to be a lawyer? And specifically, why for this firm?"

At last the interview had turned in a direction she was prepared for. She returned her prospective boss's unblinking gaze and said, "I want to bring justice to people."

"Forget that. Our business is to serve our clients."

"Of course it is, Mr. Moon . . . uh, Gordon. I want to defend the innocent."

"Forget that. Our clients are hardly ever innocent. Our business is not serving justice, nor is it helping the system. Serving justice is my wife's business." He smirked again. "My wife doesn't understand me."

Eve stiffened, drew back in her chair.

Gordon Moon laughed. "No, no, you don't get it. If I was going to come on to you, I'd come up with something more creative than that, believe me. I'm famous in courtrooms in this city for my originality. I don't deal in clichés. Haven't said 'incompetent, irrelevant, and immaterial' in years. What I meant was, literally, my wife doesn't understand me. She's a prosecutor, you see, an assistant DA under that preening idiot Prentice Winstead. Their job is to serve justice. They have to think about whether what they're doing is right. We don't. We're pure advocates. So prosecutors rarely understand defense attorneys. My wife and I are different in other ways, too. She's old money, never had to work for a living, looks upon the law like she would a charity gala, in terms of responsibility, I mean. I came up hard, had to work for everything I ever got, a hustler, street person, down and dirty, the kind she'd scrape off her shoe in the normal course of big city life. We met in law school, fell in love, have some great kids together, have a great life. But she doesn't understand me. Not for a second."

"Do you understand her?"

"Men don't expect to understand women, don't even want to maybe. Women are complicated as hell. Women, though, can understand men if they pay proper attention. We're simple. Anyway, don't worry. I don't have to understand you to hire you."

The phone on Gordon Moon's desk buzzed and he picked it up. "Yes? . . . It's who? . . . Eshelman? . . . Yeah, I've been waiting for this."

He winked at Eve, who made a move to leave, but he waved to her to stay.

"Ed, how are you? . . . Yes . . . Yes, of course . . . Yes, I know . . . Good. Call a news conference . . . Of course today . . . Get back to me." He hung up the phone with a smug expression. "It's a biggie, Eve, but I knew it was coming. You heard about what happened up on the thirtieth floor?"

"You mean the murder of Andrew Baines?" she said, glad that serendipity had made her seem well informed.

"We never call it murder." He said it lightly, but she could tell he meant it. "His brother, Charlie Baines, has been charged. Up to now, his civil lawyer, Ed Eshelman, has been handling it, but he had to come to a specialist eventually, and who else but Gordon Moon? This is going to be fun. How'd you like to be third chair on the trial of the century?"

"Trial of the century, really?"

"Well, trial of the year anyway."

"I don't have the kind of experience—"

"And how do you get the experience if nobody gives you a

chance? It's very important in this business to work closely with a mentor."

Again, Eve stiffened and drew back in her chair.

"There you go, misunderstanding me again. I had a mentor, a great old warhorse named Duffy O'Gonigal, God bless him. I'd like to do the same service for you, if you'll let me."

"I have one question first."

"Shoot."

"Is Charlie Baines guilty?"

"Forget that. We don't know if he's guilty. We don't care. To do our job, we don't want to know. And what is our job? It's to get him off. And we have to work fast."

"Can't you ask for a continuance to give you enough time to prepare? Isn't that usual?"

"Oh, that's usual all right. But this case isn't usual. We demand a speedy trial. We waive time every chance we get. Ready or not, we tell the judge and the prosecution we're ready to roll. This one has to wrap by Christmas."

"By Christmas?"

"The closer to Christmas the better, actually. Giving it to the jury Christmas Eve would be perfect."

"But, Mr.—ah, Gordon, this is a major murder trial. And it's already September. Why?"

"You'll see." Gordon Moon stood up. "Come over to the window, Eve."

"All right." She walked around behind the desk, and they looked out over the city.

"You can see the courthouse from here. Hard to spot among all these high rises. When it was first built, it towered over everything else. See it down there?'

"Yes, I do. It looks kind of like a church, doesn't it?" She felt her eyes getting misty.

Moon shrugged. "It's the gothic architecture gives that effect.

21

But, yeah, to people like my wife, it really is almost a house of worship. Not for Prentice Winstead—the DA's purely a political animal—but for most of his prosecutors, I guess it's a sacred place all right. We can't think that way. For us, Eve, the defense bar, it's no church. It's a theatre! And we're the stars!"

CHAPTER TWO

For David Ketchum, making the steep walk up the courthouse steps was more than just a way to confront his acrophobia. Every time he climbed those twenty-eight steps leading to the towering doors of the old building, the assistant district attorney was struck anew by the majesty of the law. He didn't make the walk often—the lines for the security check were usually shorter at the side entrance (or stage door, some called it) reserved for judges, prosecutors, and other officers of the court—but sometimes he needed to be reminded of where he worked and why he worked there, of why he had become a lawyer at a time when light-hitting shortstops made more money and used car salesmen commanded more respect, of why he had allowed a good marriage to crumble under his feet while he was upholding the elusive ideal of a just society.

Here in this marvelous old grime-encrusted edifice, the citizens of this great state—malefactors and victims, defendants and plaintiffs—had been coming to seek or to receive justice for over a hundred years. What stories these scarred and discolored marble columns could tell.

David knew those words over the entryway—"Justice for All; Justice Always"—gave an overly optimistic description of what went on inside. "Approximate Justice for Most of the People Most of the Time" would have been more accurate, but even that well-hedged achievement was a miraculous tribute to the American system of law, given the sad truths of unchanging human nature.

David stopped for a long look up at the pigeon-stained statue of Justice, older than the courthouse, that stood to the left of the entryway. Justice was blind again today. The eye that some mysterious daredevil vandal kept drawing over her blindfold had been cleaned off once again, and the latest repair to the large hole that kept reopening in her blindfold seemed to be holding firm. After the last unsuccessful patching job, an unsecured piece of stone had fallen from the blindfold into the midst of a class of touring school children, who escaped serious injury but were sufficiently traumatized to participate in an elongated personal injury suit against the city and its contractors. Some saw the repeated need for repair of the statue as symbolic of the city and state's corrupt court system. David preferred to see it as a symbol of the constant need to reexamine and adapt the law and its delivery to changing mores and developments.

Most of David's colleagues had not climbed these steps in years. Some of the older and fatter would risk a heart attack if they tried. But on some mornings, he needed an extra reminder of that love of the law and duty to his fellow citizen that had inspired his decision to become a lawyer. He especially needed it on those mornings he was summoned to a meeting with the DA himself, a sure cure for any romantic or idealistic feelings about the law. For once, that security check was a welcome delay, and the long walk down the corridor to the boss's office didn't seem nearly long enough.

Prentice Winstead, in his second term as district attorney, was a busy man. "He's having a big day, David," the great man's secretary, Fawn Ambrosia, confided with a wink. "I had to listen to three versions of his speech to the Civic Improvement League. And he's on his third flower already."

"I guess they wilt under the stress," David said. "Has he

asked you to marry him yet this week?"

"It's been months since his last proposal. I think he's moved on. Thank God."

"He must have figured out you're too valuable in this job, but you'd be a terrific first lady."

"One scandal-plagued term in the state house wouldn't be good enough for me," she said. "I'm holding out for somebody who's presidential timber."

David snickered. "We're lucky he doesn't bug his outer office." He sat down and picked up the entertainment section of the morning paper, then looked up with mock alarm. "He doesn't, does he?"

"I'd be long gone if he did," Fawn said.

David had read through only half a movie review—the second-string critic was complaining once again that Julia Roberts didn't smile enough—when Winstead, immaculate as ever in his dark blue suit, fresh carnation in the lapel, emerged to greet his chief trial deputy.

"David, good morning, good to see you." The standard smile and greeting gave no warning of what was coming. Once they were behind the closed office door, the DA might explode in anger, soliloquize on the failures of the city hall florist to keep him in buttonhole blossoms, or try out a joke he was considering for the day's speaking engagement. There was no telling.

One thing was constant, however. Winstead would scan David's suit as if looking for lint or food stains but say nothing; as always, David had the sense of having failed some obscure sartorial test. Not everyone, maybe no one at all, could measure up to the DA's visual perfection.

Winstead sat behind his huge desk and David took a chair facing him.

"What a morning!" Winstead said. "Just had a call from the *ProPurv.*" This was standard shorthand for the *Provincial Pur-*

veyor, the city's last remaining daily newspaper. "Reporter's coming to talk to me this afternoon. Jack Wong. Sharp fellow. Gotta watch him. Have to be ready. He's a tough, probing interviewer. Inscrutable. Fair, but relentless. Plays hardball."

Jack Wong was a softball pitcher, a *slow pitch* softball pitcher, David thought but did not say. Prentice Winstead had about as much to fear from Wong as from his personal florist.

"I think I have a new response to that standard question about whether I have my eye on the governor's mansion," Winstead said. "Want to hear it?"

"Sure."

"Well, go ahead, ask me."

David cleared his throat. "Mr. District Attorney, is there any truth to the reports that you have your eye on the governor's mansion?"

Winstead paused, as if considering the question. "Yes, it's true. I've always admired that style of architecture, but I can't make an offer on it—it's reserved for the governor. What do you think? Nice? Clever? Thought that up myself. What do I need spin doctors for, I ask you?"

"Do you really like that style of architecture?"

"I don't know. What style is it? Actually, it's an ugly building—don't you think?—but I do have my eye on it, yes, indeed. So do you, David, if you'll admit it, but you're younger. You have to wait a few years."

"Every ADA in the office has his or her eye on the governor's mansion," David agreed. "Why would you want to be a DA otherwise?"

"Right you are. Now, seriously, David, why do you think I called you here?"

"There's always lots to talk about."

"You sly dog. You know damn well why I called you here this morning. There's something else that Jack Wong is sure to ask

26

me about, and I want to be able to give him a good answer. Put on your gloves. I'm about to pass you a hot potato."

"How hot?"

"The hottest. You're my main man, David. You know that. My go-to guy. My chief trial deputy, the one person I know I can trust. The big stuff goes to you."

"Unless it's so big and easy you want to handle it personally."

"This one's big, but it's not easy. I want you to be first chair in the Charlie Baines prosecution."

David had seen it coming but feigned astonishment. "Oh, thanks a lot, Prentice. Do I look like Jerome Cowan to you?"

"Like who?"

"An actor who played a DA who prosecuted Santa Claus. In *Miracle on 34th Street.*"

"This is quite different, David. That guy was a harmless mental patient, and this one's a murderer. Anyway, the case won't come to trial till well after Christmas. They're bound to ask for continuances up the wazoo, right?"

"I'm not so sure. If you were defending Santa Claus, wouldn't you want it to go to the jury on Christmas Eve? I would."

"Look, the people of this city may like Charlie Baines—"

"They love him."

"—but the guy murdered his own brother."

"A guy the public hated as much as they love Charlie."

"I know, I know. But we can't ignore murder, David."

"The statutes don't allow it," David agreed.

"I mean to say, when a guy murders his own brother, the district attorney is expected to do something about it. When the public sees our commitment to blind justice, they'll stand up and applaud the ADA who nails Charlie Baines without regard to public opinion."

"Got it. The public will love it when we disregard public opinion."

"That's not what I said. Or if it is what I said, it's not what I meant. David, don't pull this lawyer shit on me so early in the morning. I have to be on my toes for Jack Wong."

Why? David wanted to ask. *So he won't have to bend over so far to kiss your ass?*

"So how about it, David? Ready to make legal history?"

David knew he had to be firm. Prentice Winstead could (and would) throw a tantrum if he didn't get his way, but he depended too much on his chief trial deputy to make any drastic personnel moves.

"No sale, Prentice. Baines is a dead-end case, a career-buster, and I'm not going to do it. American juries don't like to convict celebrities of serious crimes. Winona Ryder on shoplifting or Martha Stewart on piddling financial fraud are one thing, but murder? If an American jury couldn't bring in a guilty verdict on O.J. Simpson or Robert Blake, what chance do we have of selling Santa Claus as a murderer?"

"Those were California juries. They're all nuts out there."

David shook his head. "No sale, boss. I walked up the courthouse steps today, and Lady Justice looked right down at me—"

"I thought they fixed her."

"—and said, 'Whatever you do, stay away from the Baines case.' "

"You think *I* wouldn't like to stay away from it? We have no choice but to go ahead. If he'd plead to second degree or something, maybe we could cut a deal, but he won't do that. We need a conviction."

"A conviction would be nice, but a scapegoat might be better."

"You want to throw somebody to the wolves over this?" The

glint in Winstead's eye said the idea appealed to him, as David knew it would.

"The ADA who tries this case is ruined, win or lose. If it's botched and Baines walks, we kick the loser out. If Baines is convicted but the public still loves him, the loser is hated. Is that the kind of thing you want to do to me, Prentice, after the way I've supported you all these years?"

"I don't want to do anything to you, David, but I have you to solve these problems, so I can devote my time to—"

For a moment, Prentice seemed stumped. Just what did the district attorney devote his time to? All he could think of was running for governor and auditioning candidates for governor's wife, and he wasn't about to say that.

"—to the onerous but vital administrative duties that come with this office. So if you won't touch Baines, and you agree we have no choice but to prosecute him for murder, what do you suggest?"

Fortunately, David had thought about this ahead of their meeting and was ready with an answer that would appeal to the DA's desire for revenge. "Give it to Melba."

"Melba Wooten?"

"Only Melba in our office."

"Jumping-Jack Wooten? Are you serious?"

"Sure. You know she's a publicity hound."

"That she is." Prentice Winstead shook his head aggrievedly at the idea of any public servant being a publicity hound.

"You know she's a pain in the ass," David reminded him.

"No one knows that better than I."

"And you know she'd like a high-profile case. So let's give her one."

Prentice Winstead's evil smile told David the assignment was a done deal.

"How's her bum knee by the way? Is she planning to leave

the office in the lurch so she can play in the WNBA again next year?"

"It was only a ten-day contract," David pointed out, "and she took her vacation days."

"I don't care. That bitch embarrassed the office. She embarrassed me. Walking away from her responsibilities to play jock. If she were a man, I could understand it. But she's not a man."

"Believe me, I've noticed."

"I'm no hardass, David, you know that. If she did a womanly thing, posed for *Playboy* or something, that I could deal with, but playing pro basketball . . ."

"On TV, too," David pointed out.

"Right. I used to play, you know. I was good, too. Point guard. Look one way, pass the ball the other. Best possible preparation for public life. I don't say I was NBA caliber but neither is Miss Jumping-Jack Wooten. She challenged me to a game of one-on-one, did you know that? No feeling at all for the dignity of my office. I turned her down, though I could have cleaned her clock, of course."

"No doubt about it," David said.

Prentice Winstead wrinkled his brow to simulate deep thought. After a moment, he said, "Okay, it's settled. I tell Wong we are proud to show our confidence in women, in African-Americans, and in the parts of our office that look like our city by entrusting this important prosecution to one of the best-known and most capable litigators in our office. And she can take her eye off the governor's mansion, can't she? I won't tell Wong that part."

"I wouldn't."

"What do you think of this flower, David? Drooping a little, isn't it?"

CHAPTER THREE

Melba Wooten's six-foot-three greyhound body glided between two sweaty defenders for a lay-up. Rebounding the ball herself, she tossed it to a teammate, laughed her throaty laugh, raised her long arms, and said, "Gotta get back to the office, fellas."

One of her opponents, not rendered mute by the embarrassment of being shown up by a woman, said kiddingly, "Why you always quit when you're ahead, Melba?"

"Get me behind sometime, and we'll try something different."

"You could at least have the consideration to sweat a little."

"Makin' me sweat's up to you, or am I wrong?"

"I'll make you sweat in court," said a pudgy, red-faced public defender.

"That'll be the day."

"Come up to my room and I'll make you sweat, baby," said a six-five bailiff.

"Now that's downright crude. You askin' for a sexual harassment suit?"

"I'm just askin' for a ride."

"Like you rode the bench at UCLA? I don't consort with guys with your numbers, loser."

"I'll play some numbers you never heard, baby. I'll put some moves on you. Moves them WNBA chicks never thought about."

"You'd be surprised what them WNBA chicks get up to. And, by the way, you talk like that to me anywhere but the basketball

31

court, and I'll have your balls in a blender. Baby."

Still smiling as she walked toward the women's locker room, Melba reflected how much at home she felt on the basketball court, how she could express her true self. On that kind of court, it was competition that stung and hurt but didn't really matter; in the other kind of court, she was just as skilled but it mattered all too much. On the basketball court, her numbers (in her WNBA stint, ten minutes a game on that fragile knee, she had averaged eight points, five rebounds, four assists, and two blocked shots) told the story; in the criminal courtroom, conviction statistics kept her in the game but didn't really tell the story, the human story, the story of real victims.

Showered, dressed, and behind the wheel of her BMW, Melba reflected on why she identified with victims. It was simple really. She herself was a victim, as she never let anyone forget.

Back in the office, she had a message from Jack Wong of the *Provincial Purveyor.* She knew she'd better call Prentice Winstead's tame columnist back. Sometimes she had to grit her teeth to be nice to him, but it was the right thing politically.

"Melba, congratulations on your new assignment!" Wong said.

"Uh, thank you, and what assignment might that be?"

"First chair prosecuting Charlie Baines."

"I have no comment on that matter at this time, Jack."

"They haven't told you yet, huh?"

"Are you implying a newspaper reporter, even for as prestigious a sheet as the *ProPurv,* has knowledge of my assignments before I do myself? Is that how little you think of the district attorney's office? Look, call me back in a couple hours, huh, and maybe I'll have something to say."

"You always do."

Hanging up the phone, Melba angrily punched out David Ketchum's extension. The chief deputy uncharacteristically answered on the first ring.

"Melba," he said weakly, "I was just about to call you."

"What are you doing to me, David?"

"I'm doing nothing to you, Melba. This is direct from the top. Prentice wants you to handle the Baines prosecution. He thinks it's your kind of case."

"And what exactly is my kind of case?"

"One that gets on the nightly news, what else?"

"And Prentice Winstead is my new press agent, is he? Look, David, I've been victimized often enough."

"You see yourself as a victim, Melba?"

"Are you implying I'm not a victim?"

"I've, ah, never thought of you in that context, no."

"I guess you think because I drive a BMW, have an income from various sources in the high six figures, spend more on my wardrobe than most of the people in this building make in a year, and get asked my opinion on everything that happens in this city from airport bonds to the new symphony hall, I am not a victim? Do I hear you right? Well, think again, buster. Have you ever been a woman, David?"

"Ah, no, Melba, I can't say I have."

"And have you ever been black?"

"No."

"Do you know what it's like in American society to be a woman and black?"

"Well, I think things are getting better—"

"Better and good's two different things, counselor. And another thing. Have you ever been tall?"

"In the words of Humphrey Bogart, I try to be. I'm almost as tall as you."

"I've always been tall. In grade school, I towered over every boy in my class. Do you have any idea what that's like for a girl? And for a young woman? It just gives society another excuse to marginalize you. And marginalize means victimize. I've been marginalized by my gender, my color, my size, my athletic ability, my sexual orientation."

"Your sexual orientation?"

"Yeah, my sexual orientation. Do you have the slightest idea what it's like to be part of the straight minority in the feminist movement? Every place I go, every door I walk through, I'm a minority, and what's a minority but a victim? And to top it all off, I enter a profession everybody hates and makes slighting jokes about!"

"I don't hear nearly as many jokes about women basketball players as I used to."

"I meant lawyers and you know it. Anyway, you take a walk in my heels before you say I'm not a victim, David Ketchum. So you want me first chair in the Charlie Baines case, huh?"

"It's what Prentice wants, but I personally think it's a good fit."

"A good fit, huh? It's a ticket to professional oblivion, prosecuting Santa Claus. You think I'll try to get out of it, don't you? Well, I won't. You give me that case, and I'll run with it. But there's one thing, David."

"What's that?"

"If I'm first chair, I choose my team, don't I?"

"Well, yes, sure. I might have some suggestions, of course . . ."

"Stick your suggestions in the customary orifice, boss man. I won't have some honky redneck sitting by my side at that prosecution table. I want a sister."

"Uh, Melba, I'm afraid you're the only—"

"You think you have to tell me I'm the only African-American woman ADA in this office? You think I haven't noticed that? I said a sister, not a sis-TAH. Only way you're going to put Santa Claus away for murder is with an all-female prosecution team, and I choose the females. You down with that?"

"Sure, Melba."

"And when I ask for investigators and clerical support and extra office space and a wardrobe and makeup allowance and a hotel suite during trial, Mr. DA Prentice Winstead knows enough to give me what I want, doesn't he? Unless he wants to see me on the six o'clock news talking about certain things he doesn't want me to talk about. You down with that?"

"I'm down with that, yeah, sure, down with that."

"Okay, now you'll excuse me, 'cause I gotta get busy. I got a jolly old fat man to put in the slammer."

CHAPTER FOUR

Duffy O'Gonigal, red-faced and portly, sat on his customary barstool at Rumpole's, a trendy courthouse district watering hole named for an icon of hard-drinking barristers everywhere.

Gazing at the television screen over the bar, he said, "Is it me or are those news anchors getting fat?"

Phil Etchebarren looked up from polishing a glass and said, "It's a wide-screen TV and that's not a wide-screen picture."

"Can't you fix it so they don't look that way? When they all stand together, they look like dwarfs."

"The boss says, if we're gonna have a wide-screen TV in the bar, we gotta fill the whole screen. He walks in here and sees little black borders at either side and he'll throw a fit. It's too much trouble to adjust it all the time anyway."

"What's the point of the wide screen?"

"It's great for wide-screen movies."

"And when did you last watch a wide-screen movie in here? When did you watch anything but sports?"

"I hear you, Duff. But the customers expect a big TV in a bar."

"Do people who have those sets at home watch them this way, too?" Duffy wondered.

"Probably."

"Bunch of sheep," Duffy muttered, then wagged his head as if to clear the cobwebs. "Ah, what am I babbling about? Trivialities, that's what. You know, I envy you, Phil."

"Why, Duff?"

" 'Cause they disbarred you."

Phil, who towered over the bar like a sardonic scarecrow, raised bushy eyebrows and said, "Oh, yeah, it's great. So now I pour drinks for the great and powerful and once in a while write 'em briefs on the backs of napkins and give 'em questions to take into courtrooms where I am banned from practicing my profession because of an alleged breach of that rancid oxymoron called legal ethics. That's very enviable, Duff, you're right."

Duffy raised a conciliatory hand. "You mistake my meaning, my friend. Take no offense, and allow me to explain. If we could only trade places, we would both be so much happier. For I, good Phil, am still a member of the honorable bar of this sovereign state and yet I practice not. If I were banned from that bar, I could sit happily at this bar, sharpening my blunted wits with the puzzles in the morning paper and generally enjoying life, without the Irish Catholic guilt that licks at the psyche of a man who cannot do what he does but instead does too much of what he shouldn't do, if you follow me, which I confess I do not." Duffy paused and took a long swallow of his bourbon. "I could practice law again, Phil. My legal brain, pickled in drink and neglected, is better than most men's dry and cultivated. You know that from our conversations; do you not, my friend?"

Phil smiled. "Duff, between us, we could get the wheels of justice spinning again in this city."

"If you were allowed and I were motivated. But you are not, and nor am I. I haven't the energy. I haven't the hunger to go with my thirst. Alas, though, I still have the guilt."

"Try to forget it, Duff. Did you get four down in yesterday's *ProPurv* crossword? It stumped me."

"Never got to it. Too busy trying to get my numbers in a row in that other puzzle they dropped three comic strips to bedevil us with. If my wits started to desert me, you'd tell me, wouldn't you, my friend?"

"Never happen, Duff."

"We have only so much time on this earth. The grim reaper regards us all from a greater or lesser distance. And as he draws closer with his scythe—" Duffy broke off suddenly, looking up at the silent television set over the bar. "Turn up the sound, Phil, please."

"Game's not for another half hour," the bartender muttered but did as his customer requested. When he turned toward the set, he saw the reason for Duffy's interest. The local news showed Gordon Moon, the city's ace defense lawyer, looking like a happily harried dwarf with a half dozen microphones shoved in his face.

"When Edward Eshelman asked me to lead the defense team on behalf of Charlie Baines, I felt honored and a bit humbled. I have the utmost confidence in the people of this city. I know Charlie Baines will be exonerated, and before another Christmas goes by, our official city Santa Claus will be working in his toy-shop and riding on his sleigh, not sitting in a jail cell falsely accused."

The beautiful anchors returned, and Phil turned down the sound.

"That was predictable," Phil said. "A corporate three-piece suit like Eshelman wasn't about to dirty his hands on a murder case. He was bound to call in a heavy hitter."

"And who else but Gordy Moon?" Duffy said. "And a grand job he'll make of it, Phil. I taught him. I was his mentor. Did you know that?"

"The whole city knows that, Duff. The lawyers anyway."

Duffy pushed forward his glass. "Pour me another, and one for yourself. We'll drink to the lad's success. You know what I told Gordy in those days when I was top of the heap and he a mere stripling fresh from the academy, bright of eye and eager to learn from a master? The law is a flower, I told him, and the lawyer is a hummingbird." Duffy took a gulp from his glass as soon as it was filled. "But that little bird best not bend his beak on the stem and get addicted to the wrong kind of nectar. That's the kind of lessons I gave him, Phil. I made that lad what he is today."

"He's sure got a big head these days," Phil said.

"That's your damned TV!" Duffy retorted. "Or were you speaking metaphorically?"

"Take it as you like, Duff."

"Thank you, my man. I like it straight up, with your best draught as a chaser."

CHAPTER FIVE

Gordon Moon, weary but exhilarated, was thinking about Duffy O'Gonigal as he drove home that evening. He often thought of Duffy and everything his mentor had taught him, especially on the eve of a big case.

"The law is a tree," Duffy had said, "and the lawyer is a woodpecker, relentlessly pounding his beak in the name of justice, hammering on the tree in order to save it." Beautiful words, beautiful thoughts from a man who loved the law. Would they ever sit side by side at a defense table again? Sadly, probably not. Such a great legal mind, but Duffy couldn't stay sober enough to exercise it in more than half-hour spurts.

Gordon waved to the gate guard as he drove into Flicker Manor. He hadn't been raised with his wife's advantages, and living in such privileged splendor still felt disorienting. The trees, the lawns were so immaculate, and the world of law and courtrooms was so messy, it was hard to reconcile the two parts of his life. The disparity didn't seem to bother his wife, Agnes Wagstaff Moon, a brilliant lawyer whose family money permitted her to turn her back on the major firms waving offers her way and pursue the kind of law she loved: no, not pro bono law helping the poor fight the system and overcome their disadvantages, as the idealistic young Gordy Moon might have chosen, but prosecutorial law, helping those poor into penitentiary cells.

Gordon glanced at his watch as he turned into his long curving driveway: seven-fifteen. Walking through the front door, he heard the sounds of children's laughter bubbling up from the family room below. Duly warned, he quickly headed in the opposite direction. Not quickly enough.

When he was halfway up the stairs, Agnes confronted him coming down. She had changed from her daytime power suit into a floor-length gown. His wife looked as stunning as ever, not a flowing raven hair out of place.

"Do you know what time it is?" she inquired, turning him around and prodding him down the stairs.

Gordon looked at his watch. "Seven-seventeen. Am I late for something?"

"Are you late for something, Gordon? Oh, no, not late for anything, not for anything important. Maybe late for life, that's all."

"Honey, I'm tired. I've had a tough day. Can't I just go upstairs and get cleaned up?"

"Do you even know your children, Gordon? Do you know their names?" A shrill scream from below punctuated the question.

"Do you want me to recite them for you, Agnes?" he said between clenched teeth, not to avoid the question. He knew the names and the ages and even the genders (not easy, given their androgynous forenames) of his three little ones as well as he knew the local court rules.

"Not necessary," she said sadly. "But, Gordon, even if you do know their names, do you have any concept of what it is to be a parent? Coming home after seven o'clock in the evening, when little Wimmy has a seven-thirty bedtime. Do you know how important a father is to a child's development? Do you have any concept of how important quality time with one's children is in their formative years?"

"It's been a busy day, Agnes." More screams and clatter from below. "Rosita hasn't quit, has she?"

41

"Why would you think that?"

"What are they up to down there anyway?"

"I was just on my way to see. I'm a caring mother, you know. I like to be aware of what my children are doing, and what they're thinking about, and what their hopes and fears are."

"And what they think about being named Wagstaff, Weston, and Wimbledon?"

Agnes lowered her eyes for a moment. "You don't have to tell me they get teased. Children can be cruel."

"So can parents."

Agnes smiled humorlessly. "Keep the clever badinage coming, Gordon. Maybe you won't have to see your children at all. Maybe Rosita can legally adopt them."

"What time did you get home tonight, Agnes?"

"Six forty-five! And what does that have to do with your failures as a parent? Just what are you accusing me of?"

"So you've had half an hour of quality time? Then what were you doing upstairs, huh? Why didn't I find you down in the family room, being family, huh? I'm sure you had some important prosecutorial business to keep you so late, but nothing I could do to save the innocent from you guys could ever be that important. As you may or may not be aware, Ed Eshelman has asked me to defend Charlie Baines."

"I'm aware of that. It's all over the courthouse. Your TV appearance was okay, by the way. Nice tie." Ever so grudgingly, but it was something. "Who's your second chair going to be?"

"Vern, of course. Who else?"

"I'm not having him in this house, Gordon."

"You don't have to. We don't usually hold our meetings at home, do we? Still, the kids would love some quality time with their Uncle Vern."

"You keep my brother away from those children."

"Why? They prefer him to either of us."

42

"That's a despicable thing to say!"

"He's not a child molester, you know."

"I'm very well aware he's not a child molester. But I think the kinds of jokes he tells can be a subtle form of child abuse."

"They're not *Playboy* party jokes, you know. They're potty jokes. Kids that age love potty jokes."

"They're disgusting. His whole manner is a terrible influence."

"Agnes, you know your problems with him have nothing to do with the kids."

"Everything I do has everything to do with the kids!"

"Not coming home till a quarter to seven while a nanny raises them for you?"

"Keeping evil people off the streets, which is more than you do in that sleazy practice of yours!"

"Sleazy? If you're going to call names, I can play that game, too!"

A small child appeared at the top of the stairs that led to the basement family room. "Mommy, Daddy, you're making too much noise."

"We'll be right down to see you, honey," Agnes said sweetly. "Won't we, Daddy?"

"Sure." Gordon tossed his suit jacket on the back of a chair and resigned himself to quality time.

Agnes said between clenched teeth, "Will you please keep your voice down when we're discussing things?"

He hissed back, "It's easy. When we're discussing things."

A cell phone lying on the coffee table emitted its distinctive ring, and Agnes scooped it up. After listening for a moment, she said to Gordon, "I'll take this upstairs. See you later."

Gordon was left to face the family room alone. Agnes could be difficult, but at the end of the day (and this was it), he supposed he was glad they'd stayed together for the sake of the children.

CHAPTER SIX

"We secure, girlfriend?"

"We're secure, Melba."

"Nobody from the defense bar listening in?"

"This is a cell phone, you know, not a land-line extension."

"That's okay then. We're probably broadcastin' on some-body's radio or outa somebody's dental work, but what the hell. Look, I just got the assignment in the Baines case, and I'm pickin' my team. I want you there beside me, girlfriend."

"Well, you know, Melba, it's a little awkward."

"With your husband on the other side, you mean?"

"That's part of it."

"Now look, girlfriend. Word is it you fight all the time anyway, so why not just move it into the courtroom?"

"It's not just Gordon. My brother Vern will probably be second chair."

"So? You want to protect your little brother?"

"I want to kill my little brother. We can't stand to be in the same room."

"That's what I like. I like anger. I like killer instinct. When I played in the WNBA, you know why I was so successful? You know why I averaged thirty-two points, twenty rebounds, sixteen assists, and eight blocks if extrapolated over the full forty minutes I woulda played if my knee woulda stood it?"

"Well, you're talented, Melba."

"That ain't it. Basketball is not just physical. It's mental. I

45

played like a man, not like a girl. And part of playin' like a man is to hate the opposition. We got a tough task, girlfriend. We gotta hate Santa Claus. We gotta hate a guy everybody loves. If we got people we hate on the opposition team, that just makes our hate easier, our hunger easier. It makes it easier to realize the people we represent are victimized by guys like Charlie Baines who smile and smile and be a villain still, like that old honky of Avon said, and if the people are victims, we are victims, and if we are victims, we either knuckle under or stand up, and if we stand up, we stand tall."

"I'm not as tall as you, Melba."

"Yes you are, girlfriend. Call me MJ, call me Magic, call me LeBron or call me Steve Nash if you must. I make my teammates better than they ever thought they could be. I give my teammates six inches they didn't know they had, and that's no sexual reference. Are you ready to be my teammate, Agnes? Are you strong enough? Are you good enough? Did you come to play?"

"I'm with you, Melba."

CHAPTER SEVEN

Friday, September 22

David Ketchum called a meeting with the all-female prosecution team at a conference room in the district attorney's office. He was there five minutes early, and Agnes Moon was the first of the team to arrive.

"So, Agnes," he said lightly, "you and Gordon are doing a Tracy and Hepburn number, eh?"

She looked at him suspiciously. "What does that mean?"

"Well, you know, in *Adam's Rib,* where they play lawyers, a prosecutor and a defender married to each other, and they go to court on opposing sides."

"Oh, I get it. One of your old movie references." She appeared relieved for some reason. Agnes always seemed to be on edge. It came from juggling work, family, and a fortune, he guessed. "So Audrey Hepburn was married to whom?"

Before David was forced to address this, Stacey Bamwanger entered the room and perfunctory good mornings were exchanged. Third chair in the Baines prosecution, Stacey was the bitterest and angriest ADA in the office.

The three of them sat in awkward silence until Melba Wooten breezed into the room, saying to David, "Morning, boss man. Let's get this over with, shall we? I got work to do."

"Right." David cleared his throat. "Now I don't have to tell any of you your job. You're experienced prosecutors, and you know how to handle a murder trial. But this one is going to be

47

different for a number of reasons. As you know by now, the defense gets up and waives time before breakfast every morning. They're pushing Baines's right to a speedy trial for all it's worth. We'd like a delay, of course, but the prosecution doesn't have that luxury."

"Sure, why give rights to the only people serving the public interest?" said Stacey.

"That means we go to court the first of December, and it'll take us right up to Christmas. We'll be asking a jury to convict Santa Claus right around Christmas Eve. What do you think, guys—er, ladies—er, folks?"

"We'll rise to the challenge," Melba said simply. "We gotta keep one thing in mind. I revere Santa Claus as much as anybody. Santa Claus gave me my first basketball, and he was a *white* Santa Claus at that. But the dude we're putting on trial ain't Santa Claus. He's a murderer, a guy who killed his brother in cold blood. It's what they call fratricide, and it's right up there with matricide, patricide, uxoricide, and sororicide. Our job is to nail him and not let any red-nosed reindeer or jingle bells stop us."

"That's the spirit," David said. "Now we've drawn Judge Estrada. I think she's a good choice. Very even, very fair."

"You know what fair means when applied to judges, don't you?" Stacey said. "That's a code word for favoring the defense. You know that, Dave. Why bullshit us?"

"I always thought fair was a good thing, Stacey," Ketchum said with studied mildness. He wished she wouldn't call him Dave, but he wouldn't make an issue of it. "And the local bench is a little short of hanging judges since Roy Bean retired."

"Don't remember him," Stacey muttered, and the rest of the team didn't seem to get the joke either.

"Judge Estrada will be just fine," Melba opined. "I have no problem with her at all."

"Uh, there might be a little problem," Agnes Moon said.

"Wha's 'at?"

"I know Judge Estrada."

"So what? We all know Judge Estrada. We know a lot of judges."

"I, uh, know her a little better than the rest of you. She used to work for my family. In our home. As a domestic."

"A domestic?"

"A maid, okay? Marisol was one of the best we ever had. It was such a waste when she went to law school."

Melba shook her head. "My, my. I knew Judge Estrada came from humble beginnings, but I never dreamed—"

"She wasn't an illegal, was she?" Stacey asked.

"No, no," Agnes said. "Her parents were, but she was born here. She was an American citizen. One of the few we ever— But that's not the point. I've never tried a case in her courtroom. Given our prior relationship, I just wondered if it might be awkward for her."

"We don't care what's awkward for her, girlfriend," Melba said. "How does it work for *us?* Did you get along with Judge Estrada?"

"Oh, we got along fine. She didn't hold things against me. But my brother treated her dreadfully."

"Let me get this straight. This would be that same brother who'll be sitting at the defense table alongside your husband?"

"My brother Vern, yes."

"Well, it seems to me, if she doesn't like Vern, that works in our favor, now doesn't it? I'll be surprised if the defense doesn't try to get another judge."

"Not if they want to go to trial before Christmas," David Ketchum said. "She's their only hope."

Melba rubbed her huge hands together. "Now that's just fine. Could be she'll recuse herself once she gets a load of t cast of characters, and that'll delay us till after the holidays. But if she doesn't, we don't say boo. If anybody asks, Judge Estrada is a model of judicial even-handedness and just dandy with us. Looks like a win-win." She turned to Agnes. "Just how bad is the blood between these two anyway? I mean, did the rich kid just talk mean to her or did he rape her or what?"

Agnes looked down at her hands. "I don't want to get into specifics, and thankfully I don't know all the specifics. Well, I'll take that back. I can give you one example from one day, when we were teenagers. The two of us were alone in the house with just Marisol there. Understand, she wasn't our nanny or anything, but she had instructions from our parents not to take any guff from us. If she gave a bad report, our parents would have taken her side."

"Old school parents," Melba said.

"Anyway, we were always fighting in those days, like brothers and sisters do—you know how it is. Or maybe you don't, but if you had a brother like Vern, you would, believe me. Vern had this cheap little transistor radio. Totally worthless, but it did work. I picked it up that day, without really thinking about it 'cause I wanted to hear a weather report. My crummy brother comes into the room, sees me with his little radio to my ear, and goes in full dog-in-the-manger mode. He was always like that. His toys were his toys. Nobody else could play with them."

As she spoke, Agnes closed her fists, and her knuckles turned white. Her colleagues glanced at each other. Always tightly wound, she was going a couple of turns tighter.

"Take it easy, girlfriend," Melba said lightly.

"You have to hear this. I didn't give a damn about his little radio, but I was sick and tired of his selfish attitude. Anyway, things got out of hand, and we wound up struggling over it physically, rolling around on the floor of the living room, crash-ing into a table and knocking over a vase of flowers, making a real mess. Finally the radio came apart in two pieces. Marisol had heard the commotion and saw us lying on the floor there. At that point, we both stopped thinking about the radio and started thinking about what our parents might do to us. I couldn't stand the prospect of being grounded. I mean, the whole reason I was checking the weather report was—But never mind that. We both begged Marisol to let us help clean it up and not tell our parents what had happened. She agreed, but she said she would take charge of the radio and give it back to us when we could be good children. I didn't really care. The radio meant nothing to me, and I realized she was confiscating it to get at Vern. This is before a lot of other things happened between them. Just take my word for it, Vern Wagstaff and Marisol Estrada don't like each other."

"You don't like him much either, do you, girlfriend?"

"No reason I have to like an opposing lawyer, is there?" she said. "Better if I don't. I mean, of course, that doesn't apply to my husband, but . . ."

"Havin' your brother there gives you somebody to hate. Got it."

Stacey said, "What's so objectionable about Vern Wagstaff anyway?"

"What you sayin', girl?" Melba demanded. "When did Miss ADA Hardass ever have a good word to say for anybody?"

"I don't know. It's just that he always seemed like an okay guy to me. For a defense lawyer, I mean."

"Oh, he's charming all right," said Agnes. "But once you get to know him, the charm wears off fast. He has to control everything and everybody."

"How does he manage as a second chair then?" Melba asked.

Agnes shrugged. "Gordon seems to be able to work with him. He can't boss Gordon any more than he could boss Marisol Estrada. Believe me. She hates his guts."

CHAPTER EIGHT

Vern Wagstaff, a tall and slender man with a perpetually insouci-
ant manner, had been gifted with a smugly masculine version of
his sister's good looks. As he leaned back in the visitor's chair,
he did not have his feet on his brother-in-law's desk and he was
not blowing smoke rings, but he registered that kind of attitude.
"Don't sweat it, Gordy," he said. "Judge Estrada is a plus for
our side."

Gordon Moon shook his oversized head and said, "I don't
like it. It's messy, having somebody on the bench who used to
be a servant to one of the lawyers."

"Two of the lawyers. One on each side. And I always got
along great with Marisol. She, uh, taught me a lot."

"What do you mean by that?"

"Never mind. The point is, she liked me, and I don't think
she ever liked Agnes really."

"What makes you think that?"

"Oh, lots of things. There was this one time, Agnes and I
were fighting over something, and it came apart, and Marisol
took it away from us. She didn't tell our parents—she was nice
that way—but she did keep this thing that came apart, and I
knew she did it just to annoy Agnes. It meant nothing to me. I
mean, with all this sisterhood crap, women don't play together
all that well. They make nice, sure, but it's all a sham. Behind
the smiles, they always have the knives out for each other."

"Uh, Vern, these sexist comments of yours are perfectly okay between us boys, but when Eve joins us, tone it down, will you? She's new to all this, and when I interviewed her the other day, she seemed a little sensitive."

"Well, we'll beat that out of her."

"Seriously, you better watch the cracks until she knows you a little better. I said I wanted to be her mentor, but the Baines case is going to keep me busy day and night, so a lot of the front-line mentoring is going to fall to you. You have to treat her gently. I wouldn't want her to get the wrong idea."

"You know I'm always on my best behavior with the ladies," Vern Wagstaff said, combing his hair. "And if she's all you say, I'm sure we'll get along great. Men and men can get along just fine; men and women can get along in ways to inspire the poets. But women and women, my friend, are always competing with each other, however subtle it is. That's why a woman judge helps us, if it's Marisol or not."

"I still don't know. Her cousin Rosita works for us now. That makes it even more awkward."

"Why? Does your nanny discuss cases in progress with you?"

"Of course not, but—"

"Does she call up her cousin and give her advice on her legal decisions?"

"I seriously doubt it, but—"

"Look, if this is such a problem that Judge Estrada doesn't think she can be fair, let her recuse herself. But if she decides to stay with the case, it's fine with us. You want to get this trial over by Christmas, right? Go to the jury Christmas Eve, you've said?"

"It would mean a lot to Charlie."

"Christmas Eve falls on a Sunday this year. We'd need a wrap by the Friday before at the latest. That makes for a mighty fast trial. So we can't do anything to slow the wheels of justice, like challenging the judge. That's settled, right?"

Gordon shrugged. "I guess so."

"Now to the important stuff, Gordy. How are the kids? Do they miss their Uncle Vern?"

CHAPTER NINE

Eve Nyquist worked as hard as she could in her first few days at Gordon Moon, anxious to justify the great defender's faith in her. So far, she'd been given no work a competent paralegal couldn't handle, but she'd done it fast, done it immaculately, and asked for more. She was so much better at on-line legal research than any of the less recent graduates, she did a job in a third of the time expected. She felt she was becoming a pest asking the various associates and their secretaries for more work. Well, if so, so be it. She was a lawyer, and she was determined not to cheat on her billable hours.

As for the Baines case, she'd met Vern Wagstaff, the second chair, but so far she hadn't been privy to any of his conferences with Gordon about the case, nor had she been assigned any work on it. She admonished herself not to worry about it. If they gave her a job to do, she'd do it well. If they didn't, at least she'd have a good seat to watch great lawyers at work.

One benefit of not being overworked in the big city was being able to see the sights in her free time. Everyone told her the Twister Grill, a revolving restaurant atop the Friendly Neighbor Bank Building, was a must. She would go up there, she decided, but not for lunch. Much too extravagant. Maybe just have a look and then go on to the art museum.

As she stepped into the elevator at street level, a startlingly handsome man in a dark business suit was already there. Apparently he'd got on in the parking garage. He gave her a tight smile. She lowered her eyes demurely. You had to be careful in the city. Everyone had told her that. But she found herself assessing the value of his expensive suit and trying to guess what business he was in. Just so he wasn't a lawyer. But that was fanciful, imagining a relationship on no acquaintance at all, just an elevator ride.

As the elevator rose, the man seemed to stand more and more rigidly, and beads of sweat started to form on his forehead, though it wasn't at all warm.

"Are you okay?" she asked him.

He nodded. "Yes. Touch of claustrophobia. I don't normally do elevators, but it's a long walk to the Twister."

"The lunch must be worth it."

"It is. But that's not why I do this. I think it's important to confront your fears, don't you?"

She smiled. "I confront them every day."

When they stepped out of the elevator, he let out a relieved breath and said, "Wow, that was intense. I feel like I just played a scene out of *Sweet Charity*."

"I'm sorry, you what?"

He smiled broadly. "Never mind. Are you having lunch?"

"Oh, no. I just came to have a look at the view, maybe have a drink."

"Then have lunch with me. I don't normally like to eat alone here. I like company."

Eve wondered what they would think of her back home, getting picked up on an elevator. But getting picked up by an obviously successful man, a man who looked like he belonged on the cover of a romance novel, a man secure enough in his masculinity to confide his claustrophobia to a perfect stranger?

"Thank you. I'd love to have lunch with you. I'm Eve Nyquist."

"David Ketchum."

When they were seated, she drank in the view, spotting some landmarks, asking her companion about others. He pointed out the football stadium and the zoo and the new performing arts complex, but he didn't look out at the city for long.

"Don't you enjoy the view?" she asked.

"I love the view," he said, looking straight at her with penetrating brown eyes.

"I, er, mean of the city."

"Oh, that. Actually I don't, from up here anyway. Touch of acrophobia. Fear of heights. I come up here to confront it head on. I'm getting much better. If I just look at you, I won't even know I'm going around and around in circles seventy stories above the street, constantly moving, moving."

"You don't have motion sickness, too, do you?"

He laughed. "No, I escaped that one, thank God." After a perfunctory glance at the menu, he signaled to the waiter. "Enrique, what's on today?"

"Ah, Mr. Ketchum, you chose the right day to honor us. We have the Chilean sea bass you have enjoyed so much."

Enrique described several of the day's other offerings in glorious detail, but Eve heard not a word. She was becoming fascinated by this open, friendly, funny man with whom she had shared an elevator. She knew they must have ordered because the waiter went away and a bottle of excellent pinot grigio appeared at the table.

"So tell me about yourself, Eve Nyquist," David Ketchum said. "How long have you been in the city?"

"Almost a week. I just graduated from law school, and I've been hired by a big firm, and all I've met in the time I've been here is lawyers, lawyers, lawyers. Most of them are quite pleasant, but they all seem to be so driven, which is fine up to a point, but all they talk about is the law, and I love the law, but there are other things in life besides the law, aren't there? I went into a bar for a drink after work the other night. Not that I normally would do that by myself, you understand, but times have changed, haven't they? And I was telling the bartender it was a pleasure to talk to somebody who wasn't a lawyer, and guess what. The bartender turned out to be a disbarred lawyer. They're everywhere."

David Ketchum had an amused look on his face. Eve said, "I'm babbling, aren't I?"

"You can babble all you want," David said, with transparent sincerity. "But there's something you should know about me. And if you want to run for the down elevator when I tell you, I'll be very sorry, but I'll understand perfectly."

"Yes?"

"I'm chief trial deputy in the DA's office. In short, I'm a lawyer." He spread his hands. "There it is."

Eve looked at him and suddenly realized it didn't matter one little bit. But she had to be cool. She couldn't act like a lovesick schoolgirl.

"By the way," David said casually, "if you want to escape lawyers, I wouldn't go into Rumpole's. I mean, the name itself kind of gives it away."

"How did you know it was Rumpole's I was in?"

"I know that bartender, Phil Etchebarren. It's a sad story. Too sad to tell on such a nice day, especially when we're avoiding law talk."

"I don't know if I should be having lunch with a prosecutor," Eve said, only a little coyly.

David looked into her wide blue eyes and marveled. How could one skate through law school still looking like the greatest pressure she'd ever faced had been cheerleading practice, the ugliest thing she'd ever seen her little brother's skinned knee? He wanted to tell her that for her to have lunch with him, to have all her lunches and breakfasts and dinners with him for the rest of their lives, he would quit the district attorney's office with all its backstabbing and political maneuvering, set up in a store front and give free legal services to the poor and disenfranchised. But that was silly. After all, they'd known each less than fifteen minutes. He couldn't possibly be in love. He'd keep it light.

"Has a prosecutor not eyes, ears, lips, organs?" he intoned. "If you prick us, do we not bleed? If you tickle us, do we not laugh?"

"I don't tickle on the first date," she said, with a girlish giggle.

"If you sandbag us in court, do we not lose?"

"Don't let's talk shop. Tell me about yourself, David."

He shrugged. "There's not much to tell. When I was three, my parents were killed in an accident, and I've always suspected they were murdered. I know I have an identical twin from whom I was separated at birth and I've never met—I understand there may be a third identical triplet, but I can't be sure. I was raised by a kindly aunt and uncle who I'm sure have some secret or secrets they've kept from me for my own good. I have this pathological fear of heights to overcome, which is why I come to places like this. But every woman I meet tells me I have an even more debilitating fear of commitment. What they don't understand is that I've made a commitment in the past, but I got burned badly—after our divorce, my wife disappeared and took our two children with her, and all my efforts to find them have run into dead ends. Since I've been an assistant DA, I've been shot three times and I've killed two people—strictly self-defense but still painful. I have a cat and a dog and I like to cook for myself and for friends. I jog every morning and my hobbies are movies, martial arts and orchid breeding. That's about it."

Was he joking? Eve looked into his kind, sad eyes and decided he couldn't be. She had found her attraction to this unusual man growing with every trauma he described, but she'd keep it light.

"David," she said, "you sound like a series character."

He smiled sadly and shook his head. "They tell me I'd need a sex-change operation for that, and I'm not quite ready yet."

"No, I don't think you are," she said. "And you will check with me before you do?"

Their hands touched across the table.

Feeling a level of involvement beyond one lunch they hadn't even consumed yet, Eve said, "If we see each other, though, David, couldn't there be a conflict of interests? I'm, uh, going to be working with Mr. Moon on a very big case in the very near future."

"You're working for Gordon Moon? Congratulations. You've landed with an excellent firm."

"Yes, thank you, I know, but you see I probably shouldn't be seeing somebody from the district attorney's office, although I realize we aren't really seeing each other. Well, of course, we're seeing each other in the sense that I'm seeing you and you're seeing me right now at this moment, but the very idea you might want to see me again is presumptuous on my part—"

"Stop talking, or I'll dive across this table and kiss you right in front of all these people."

"Part of me wants to keep talking," she said.

"We can see each other all we want and talk all we want and be together all we want, Eve Nyquist. We just can't discuss our cases, that's all."

"Oh, David, I hope it's really that simple."

They looked into each other's eyes, and for that moment, far above the sordid streets of the city, nothing seemed simpler than the awakening of love. When Enrique brought their lunches, both of them had a single thought: good times ahead would be as plentiful and as reliable as Chilean sea bass.

CHAPTER TEN

Friday, September 29

The next morning, Gordon Moon called Eve into his office for their first one-on-one meeting since her entrance interview. She spotted the Friendly Neighbor Bank Building through that fantastic window and had to will her mind to keep from wandering.

"You've been doing an exceptional job, Eve," the great defender said. "My colleagues are getting frustrated trying to keep you busy."

"Thank you, Gordon. I want to prove I'm a real lawyer and not just some wide-eyed small-town girl who aced her exams."

"Oh, you're proving that. Eve, we have a concept in the law called the billable hour. I'm sure you're familiar with the phrase."

"Yes, sir. Billable hours are sacred to me. Oh, maybe not as sacred as the Constitution or the state codes or the Supreme Court reports but still sacred. When I represent billable hours to a client, I want that client to know that every minute of that billable hour I'm bringing the full measure of my legal training and experience to the resolution of that client's problem, whatever it is."

"Certainly. We wouldn't have it any other way." Gordon paused again, as if carefully considering what he would say next. Finally he spoke as if revealing a new concept, a sudden insight, something he'd never thought about before—another jury trick, and a good one. "But that billable hour can include jobs beyond performing the actual research and writing and questioning and conferring involved."

"Can it? Like what?"

"Well, travel, say."

Eve smiled. "Up to now, that hasn't been an issue. All my travel has been between our law library and the associates' offices."

"There's also thinking."

"Thinking?"

"Of course. Part of what you do for the client is to consider the various options, formulate a plan of action, turn things over in your mind. And that takes place not just in the office but on the way to the office, at home over breakfast, in the shower . . ."

"But, Mr. Moon—!"

"Oh, don't get that look again, Eve. I'm making a point. I'm not the big bad wolf, I keep telling you. And call me Gordon."

"Gordon, you misunderstand me. I've been in the city long enough to take references to my showering habits in stride. But it sounds like you're telling me that every hour I'm awake should be billed to the client."

"Not necessarily. I've come up with some of my best legal strategies when I'm asleep. In dreams, I mean. It can happen."

Eve's dream life was her own business, and she certainly wouldn't want to bill a client for the dream she'd had last night abut a certain assistant district attorney. *Put that thought out of your mind, girl, and try to pin down what the boss wants from you.*

"Gordon, has my work been accurate?"

"Absolutely."

"Then am I being reprimanded for doing my work too fast?"

"Eve, you're not being reprimanded at all. The fact that we're billing four hours to the client when we could be billing forty without any eyebrows being raised is a tribute to your industry and devotion. I'd just like you to include some of the work you do for the client that may be intangible but is still real and legitimate."

"Gordon, I'll do whatever you say. Logging my thinking will be difficult, since my mind wanders like everybody else's." If he only knew! "I am human, you know." *Too human for my chosen work?* "Estimating the length of my job-related dreams may be harder to quantify, but I'll certainly give it a try."

Gordon smiled. "You only have to do that if you actually have a dream that bears on the client's case. Now for the real reason I asked you to come in. Do you have anything pressing this morning?"

"I was hoping I might. What they gave me I had finished by nine o'clock."

"Good. Vern and I have decided it's time to involve you more fully in our preparations for the Baines trial."

More fully? Eve thought. *They haven't involved me at all.*

"The three of us are going to visit our client. As a member of the defense bar, Eve, you'll have to get to know your way around the local penal facilities."

CHAPTER ELEVEN

The County Jail was a big, gray, depressing building adjacent to the courthouse. The three lawyers went through an elaborate security procedure, and nothing about the wanding of her body by a jail matron was nearly as offensive to Eve as the comments of her co-counsel Vern Wagstaff.

"Aren't you the Wicked Witch of the West?" Vern said to the matron.

"Yeah, my broom's in the closet, but I can still stick my wand where the sun don't shine."

"You're the highlight of her day, Eve. She likes little girls who are lost in the woods."

Eve exchanged a rueful glance with the matron, who muttered, "What century is he lost in?"

Gordon Moon didn't say anything, but he didn't seem to find his brother-in-law amusing either. He mostly just ignored him. Eve was determined to do the same, at least until she was sure how much of his verbal garbage was just the rough male gallows humor that permeated the world of cops and lawyers and how much was offensive in intent. One had to get along with one's colleagues, and women needed to be strong to succeed in the competitive world of law.

Once they had passed through security, they entered an office-cum-waiting room area where they were greeted by an elderly uniformed guard Gordon introduced as Bill, adding, "He takes good care of our client."

Bill shook her hand and said solemnly, "Very pleased to meet you, miss, that is, counselor. I do my best, and I hope you take good care of Mr. Baines, too. He's a wonderful man. I admire him very much, and many of us here feel the same."

"Then you believe Mr. Baines to be innocent?" she said. Gordon threw her a look that suggested she shouldn't be asking that, but she wanted to know the answer.

Bill shook his head. "I have no opinion on that, miss, and frankly I don't care. As a part of the criminal justice system in this city and county for the past forty years, I probably shouldn't be saying that, and I'm surprised to hear myself. But there's many a man in this city who would be ready to applaud Mr. Baines if he really did kill his brother." The guard gestured to a doorway at the other end of the room. "Now, miss, I need to tell you what you're in for."

"You're supposed to ask the prisoners that, not tell the lawyers," Vern Wagstaff said.

Bill, unsmiling, turned to him. "Counselor, you're real amusing as always. But I believe in preparing new lawyers, especially young ladies like Miss Nyquist, when it's their first time visiting a prisoner. I don't want her to be too shocked by what she sees. And hears." He turned back to Eve. "You'll be visiting your client in his cell, which is in our far wing. You'll all be able to confer with him there in privacy, and I think we've made it reasonably comfortable. But to get there, we have to pass through the main jail population. We're going to be going through that door and walking along the cellblock. It's a kind of a long walk, and the atmosphere can sometimes make it longer. There are men in that cellblock, Miss Nyquist, and not all of them are very nice. I want you to know what to expect."

"I think I do." She imagined the clanging of metal on metal, tired men in close quarters, ugly confining bars, shouted imprecations of innocence, cries for help.

"If you'll permit me, miss, that is counselor, you are quite an attractive young woman and very attractively dressed if I may say so. A female lawyer like yourself has to be inured to the possibility of rude remarks being made by the prisoners as we pass along the cellblock. Obscene remarks even. The fact that you'll be accompanied by me and two male lawyers will not make the slightest difference to some of these men."

"I understand," Eve said.

"She's read *Silence of the Lambs*, Bill," Vern Wagstaff said in an impatient voice.

Eve looked at Vern and said pointedly, "And I've been dealing with men all my life."

She steeled herself as they walked through the big door. At first glance, she found the scene as grim and depressing as she had expected, but once the four of them came into view of the prisoners, the whole cellblock erupted into cheers, along with shouts of "Go get 'em!" and "Save Charlie!" Not one of the prisoners presented an argument on his own behalf.

As they got to the end of the cellblock, Bill said softly, "Call it a Christmas miracle in September if you want, but that's how much Charlie Baines is loved, counselor."

Entering the more secluded wing where Charlie Baines was being held was like passing from Kansas into Oz. His cell, if you could call it that, was decorated for the holiday that was still months away. In one corner was a neatly trimmed Christmas tree with wrapped presents under it. A Santa Claus suit on a hanger, in a bag of clear plastic, had been neatly hung from a hook on one wall.

The prisoner himself was a smallish, round but not precisely fat, man who appeared to be in his middle sixties. His reddish brown hair was only lightly touched by gray. He offered them a broad smile as he rose from his cot, greeting them more like a host welcoming guests into his home than a prisoner in his cell being visited by his lawyers.

"So you're Eve," Charlie Baines said, looking her up and down as men normally did but somehow not in an erotic way. "It's such a pleasure to meet you, and I do appreciate what you're doing for me."

"Mr. Baines," she said, "your decorations are amazing."

"Oh, yes." He glanced around the cell with pride. "Actually it's none of my doing. It was comfortable enough but a little drab and spare when I checked in, so to speak. Bill and his crew came in and put this stuff up last week. Some might say it's rushing the season. I don't think even the malls have their Yuletide stuff up in September, do they? But for my money, Christmas cheer comes in handy any time of the year. Especially in hard times, and I have to admit these past couple of months have not been easy."

Gordon said, "I see the suit came."

"It did, yes, and thanks so much for having it sent over."

"Of course, it's not the one you wore that night. They impounded that one as evidence."

"Yes, I know, but I always have Santa suits in reserve. I do like to have one handy, though I can't think when I'll have a use for it while I'm in here."

"You never know," Gordon said, and Eve wondered if he was plotting some future stratagem.

Bill cleared his throat. "Actually, Charlie, we have this jail employees' Christmas party in December. It's the only time of the year the families get to see the jail, and it's always a nice event for the kids. I know it's a lot to ask—"

"You want me to play Santa Claus! Bill, it will be my pleasure," Charlie said, oozing delight from every pore.

"That is, of course, if you're still in here then."

"Oh, I think I will be. I won't have been tried yet, and I've been denied bail, so it's too much to hope I'll be out by then.

But even if I'm not still in residence, I'll happily come back for your party. Don't you worry."

"I still can't understand why you're not out on bail, solid citizen like you," Bill said. "I mean, you're certainly no flight risk."

"Except on Christmas Eve, of course," Vern Wagstaff said. "You're liable to jump in your sleigh and take off for parts unknown."

Charlie Baines laughed heartily, but nobody joined him.

"We tried to get bail, but the judge's hands were tied by the statute," Gordon explained to Eve. "The law of this state allows no bail on charges of first-degree murder, no matter who the accused is."

"Well now," Bill said, "I know you folks need to get down to business, so I'll leave you to it. But if there's anything you need, anything at all, you just give me a wave." He turned to Eve. "I'll have the cell in full view, but I won't be able to hear anything you say."

"How about a scotch and soda, Bill?" Vern Wagstaff said.

Bill scowled at him. "Counselor, I appreciate your sense of humor as much as ever."

When Bill had retired to a respectful distance outside the cell, the four of them sat down, extra chairs having been provided for their visit, and Gordon turned to their client.

"Charlie, we've been through this a few times, but Eve hasn't heard it, and we need to bring her up to speed."

"Absolutely, Gordon. Anything you'd like."

"Just tell us about the night of your brother's death in your own words."

Charlie said with a wink at Eve, "I'd use Dickens's words if I could, but if I must use my own, they'll have to do." Then he turned serious. "I've been telling people for years that my brother was not as evil a man as people think. We had our disagreements, but usually I was able to bring him around to some sort of compromise. That usually involved him still making out like a robber baron but not destroying too many people along the way. The thing I came to talk to him about that evening may have seemed a small matter, but it had taken on a big symbolic value for the local community. The Majestic Theatre. You won't know it, Eve, because you're new to the city. You've been there, Gordon?"

"Many times, yes."

"And you have, haven't you, Vern?"

"I don't believe so, no. Art houses aren't my thing."

"It wasn't always an art house. Andy and I went there as children, to see the Saturday matinees. In those days, it was a first-run house. When the big multiplexes took over the movie market, it turned to foreign films, revivals, independent productions. Old Sid Monarca, whose family had built the theatre, especially endeared himself to me every Christmas when he booked in classic Christmas movies on the big screen. I still remember his *Christmas Carol* marathon. Imagine! Five or six renderings of Scrooge running in rotation for forty-eight hours. You could see Reginald Owen, the TV version with George C. Scott, the musical with Albert Finney, the updated with Bill Murray, the classic version with Alistair Sim—I always thought he was best screen Scrooge, but others have their own opinions . . ."

Charlie trailed off, seeing the expression on Gordon Moon's face. "Oh, dear, I'm doing it again, aren't I?" He explained to Eve, "Just get me started on Christmas, anything about Christmas, and I forget what I'm supposed to be talking about. Gordon nudges me to get me back on track before I start reciting my wassail recipe. But the Majestic Theatre was important to the city's psychic health. Where else would you see whole evenings devoted to Douglas Fairbanks, Charlie Chaplin,

Harold Lloyd, Buster Keaton, Mary Pickford, Clara Bow, and other pioneers who can still connect with contemporary audiences if given the chance? And the building was an architectural marvel, a living reminder of the great days of movie palaces. For a lot of us, that old, ornate, one-screen theatre became the heart and soul of the community. I was thankful for Sid Monarca's steadfastness in keeping it going, and I never took any notice of the rumors about him."

"Such as what?" Eve asked.

Charlie shrugged. "One of their theatres burned down. One of his brothers died under mysterious circumstances. You can't take seriously the stories you hear about any prominent citizen. Some of the gossip about my brother Andrew was incredibly scurrilous."

"Even worse than the reality?" Vern said.

"That's a good way to put it, yes. To Andrew, real estate deals were like a game. He enjoyed treating the city as his own personal Monopoly board, sometimes acting on his own but other times in the interest of moneyed clients. He profited always and, to give him his due, the community profited sometimes. But this particular development plan would involve razing the Majestic Theatre and adjacent properties to put up another big office tower. Sid Monarca swore he wouldn't sell, but he has always worked on a very narrow profit margin, and he had some silent investors he had to satisfy. As the offers for his building increased, it was getting harder and harder for Sid to justify holding out. Some friends of the Majestic tried, and failed, to get it declared a historical monument and thus protected from destruction. Ultimately, what it came down to was Andrew. My brother had the power to change the development plans and save that beautiful old movie house. He and I had had such great times there together as kids, I was convinced I could persuade him. But every try had failed.

"That night Andy died, I came to the Baines Building in my Santa Claus suit. Did I think dressing like that in the July heat would help to turn my elder brother around? Maybe, a little bit. But it was more because of what the suit did for me. When I get discouraged, putting on that Santa Claus suit gives me a sort of second wind."

"Like Batman," Vern offered.

"Not quite as athletic as that. If the suit didn't augment my powers of persuasion, it had a way of defusing my anger. Let me tell you this, Eve, as I've told these fellows several times already. I'm not perfect. I'm proud of my public image as a jolly old do-gooder, constantly cheerful and generous and all that, but it's not always easy to live up to. I have my dark side. Am I capable of killing another human being? Maybe I am. Was I even capable of killing my own brother? I shudder to think so, but maybe I was." He waved toward the Santa Claus suit hanging on the wall. "But I was surely not capable of such an act while I was wearing that suit, which I would not dishonor by shedding my brother's blood or anyone else's." He smiled ruefully. "Doesn't prove a thing, of course, but I'm telling you a basic truth about myself. And I want to tell that truth to the jury. If your boss will let me testify, that is."

"It's usually not a good idea for the defendant to testify," Gordon said.

"But surely in this case—" Eve said. Gordon's expression told her she was saying too much, and she knew it was dangerous to argue with her boss in front of a client. But if she couldn't give her opinion, even as third chair, what was the point of being a member of the defense team?

"We haven't made a definite decision about that," Gordon said. "We'll have to see how it's going at that point. But as a rule of thumb, I don't like my criminal defendants to testify."

"Because most of your criminal defendants are criminals,"

Vern pointed out. For a moment, Eve thought Vern was supporting her, but his next statement disabused her. "But we still have to be cautious. What skeletons does Charlie have in his closet that could come out on cross-examination?"

"Everybody has them," Gordon said. "Even Charlie. Anyway, go on with your story. Tell Eve exactly what happened between you and your brother that night."

"In a word, nothing," said Charlie Baines.

"You mean he was already dead when you got there?" Eve said.

"That's just what I mean."

"But why did you wait so long before you reported it?"

"You've hit on one of the prosecution's key questions," Vern said.

"And you don't like my answer," Charlie said cheerfully. "But what can I do? It's the truth." He turned back to Eve. "When I got to the thirtieth floor, I didn't go directly to Andy's office. I stopped in my own office first. There was something I wanted to find before I confronted my brother."

"Was it some document related to the real estate deal?" she asked.

"No, I was privy to no such documents. What I was looking for was a cache of old lobby cards Andy and I used to collect as children."

"What are lobby cards?" Eve asked.

Charlie Baines rubbed his hands with the enthusiasm of a child describing a toy. "Something quite unique and wonderful, Eve. You don't see them anymore, except maybe in Europe, but they were an advertising vehicle, smaller than a full-sized poster, that movie theatres used to promote films on exhibit or coming the following week. Usually, they would be posted in the lobby. They commonly came in sets of eight, in a standard size of eleven by fourteen inches. The top card would have the title of the picture and the main credits, and the others would be stills of scenes. They were highly attractive to children as souvenirs, and I might add, they are valuable collectors' items today. When the film being advertised moved on, the manager would give them to Andy and me for our collection."

"That was generous of him," Eve said.

Charlie Baines looked pained. "You understand, we were sons of the richest man in the city. People were constantly catering to us. We were given things we didn't really need or deserve while other children were going without. Looking back, I'm not at all proud of that. But we didn't think about that at the time. We just wanted those lobby cards. Andy lost interest in them when he became a teenager, but I kept them. He wouldn't have seen them or perhaps even thought about them for, oh, forty or fifty years. I was hoping some forgotten chord of nostalgia in him might make him rethink his demolition project."

"And you kept these in your office?"

"Yes. As a Baines brother, I was assigned an absurdly large office, with a walk-in closet, private bathroom and shower, all sorts of amenities I didn't need and rarely used, plus a fair number of nooks and crannies. I'm not a tidy person and a bit of a packrat, and I often use the office for additional places to store the clutter that fills my house."

"You're not married then," Eve ventured.

"No, I never married. Neither did Andrew, apart from one youthful mistake he immediately and rather ruthlessly corrected. There will be no more Baineses to carry on our name, and that fact may have something to do with the people that we became, the things we thought of as important. No use going off on that tangent, though. What was I talking about?"

"The clutter in your office."

"Oh, yes. It had another function. It made me look busy, even though very little of it had anything to do with the business. That night I came to my office, I couldn't remember exactly where I had put the lobby cards, so I spent quite a bit of time looking for them."

"And did you find them?"

"No, I never did. I looked everywhere but the shower. I wouldn't have put them in there. I have no idea what became of them."

"Do you think the fact that they're missing has something to do with your brother's murder?"

Charlie considered. "I suppose they could, but it was quite a while since I looked at them, so I can't say how long they'd been missing."

"How long did you keep looking?"

"I lost track of time. According to what I'm told, it must have been nearly an hour. When I finally gave up looking, I went to my brother's office, which was down the hall on the same floor. There I found him, seated in his office chair, head tossed back, eyes staring at nothing. There was a great deal of blood. He'd been shot, of course."

"Did you touch the body?"

"I took his pulse, and he had none. There was no doubt he was dead. I started to pick up the phone on Andy's desk to call down to Wilbur, the security man, but then I realized I shouldn't disturb the crime scene."

Gordon Moon asked a surprising question. "Charlie, did you sneeze while you were in your brother's office?"

"I might have. I was sneezing all day. I have these allergies, and sometimes when I haven't worn the suit for a while, the dust makes me sneeze."

"But you didn't leave anything behind in the office, did you?"

"No, certainly not."

"You kept your beard on all the time?"

"Yes, I did."

"And you didn't change beards at any time when you were on the thirtieth floor that night?"

"No, there was no reason to."

"Mr. Baines," Eve said, "Wilbur Ricketts found you to be almost unnaturally calm when you came downstairs. Were you in shock at finding your brother's body?"

"No, I don't think so."

"And why did you go home and not wait for the police to question you?"

"The suit was getting hot, and I knew they could find me when they wanted me."

"You must have been devastated by your brother's death, is that right?"

Charlie Baines looked her in the eye and said seriously, "I told you I was human. When I saw my brother, companion of my youth, for whom I had always expressed love despite his faults, I came to realize that in my deepest soul, I hated my brother, and I was both relieved and delighted to see him dead."

Charlie appeared more shaken than anyone else by his outburst, and he visibly drew himself back from it. When he spoke again after a few moments, he said, "That's the real reason I wore my Santa Claus suit that day: to make sure my anger toward my brother did not cause me to do or say anything I would regret." He smiled weakly. "As the weather gets cooler, I may wear it around the cell. I don't think Bill will mind, and it will keep me out of the psychiatric wing."

"Or get you there faster," Vern Wagstaff said. This time not even Charlie Baines laughed.

CHAPTER TWELVE

Standing with his two colleagues in the jailhouse parking lot, Gordon Moon said, "You can see why I don't want him to testify."

"I don't know," Eve said. "He might be very effective telling his side of the story."

Vern said, "His side of the story being that he hated his brother and would have liked to kill him, that he came to his office late on the night his brother was killed, but that his magic suit cast a spell that guaranteed he wouldn't kill anybody. The man's a raving lunatic. In a good way, of course."

"I don't think he's a lunatic," Eve said. "But I can see where his testimony might be a little too honest. Why did you ask him if he'd sneezed, Gordon? And what was that business about changing beards?"

"We'll get into that later." Gordon looked at his watch. "Kids, I have another appointment over in the courthouse. Why don't you guys grab some lunch, and I'll see you back in the office this afternoon. We can kick things around a little more."

"Great," Vern said quickly. "You take the car, boss, and we'll walk."

Eve was frankly apprehensive about having a one-on-one lunch with Vern Wagstaff, but after all, he was a professional colleague. It's not as if it were some kind of a date.

"How about the Twister," Vern suggested when Gordon had left them.

"No, that's much too expensive."

"I'll pay."

She looked at him sharply. "We're not billing a client for this, are we? I won't have Charlie Baines paying for my lunch, however much money he has."

"And he has plenty, with or without his late blown-away brother. But it's not on Charlie, it's on me."

She shook her head. "Colleague lunches we go Dutch, and it's strictly business, right?"

Vern looked hurt. "Baby, you have the wrong idea about me."

"If you call your professional colleagues 'baby,' I think I have exactly the right idea about you."

"No, you don't. The way I talk, the cracks, it's all just a way to deal with the pain."

"Pain?"

"The pain of this job, the misery and sadness I see every day. I use humor as a release. Not always very funny maybe, but you've chuckled once or twice, now admit it."

"Once or twice is about it, yes."

"Here's what you have to understand. People in the system accept that kind of talk as a way of keeping the demons at bay. You may have thought I was rude to that police matron—I saw the look on your face—but we're old friends and she loves it. When you see me with somebody not in the system, which I don't think you have yet, I adjust my manner accordingly."

"And that's how you got the reputation as a womanizing creep?"

With a comical shudder, Vern said, "Now you're getting into the spirit of things. Look, if I have that reputation, it's with people who don't really know me. Gordon has asked me to be your sort of guide to the whole process of the Baines case. He wants your input, certainly, and I know you'll have some good ideas. But this is supposed to be an educational experience for you. If I'm going to be your mentor, you can't hold me at arm's length."

"Look, Yoda, unless you're teaching me martial arts moves, arm's length is plenty close enough."

Vern sighed. "Has all the air gone out of me yet? Am I a deflated balloon spreading out on the sidewalk or a busted piñata that's given up all my candy? I retire to my corner, bloodied and beaten."

"Good. Now we can have some lunch."

"Let's make it Rumpole's, least romantic place I can think of."

"Fine."

They walked a block or two in silence. Half a block from Rumpole's, they saw a familiar figure in a gray tracksuit, walking toward them and talking into a cell phone.

"You've met Oswald?" Vern said softly.

"Yes, I've met Oswald," Eve said. "He's one of the nicer people I've met around here."

"Hello, Mr. Wagstaff," Oswald said cheerily. "Hello, Miss Nyquist. Santa's innocent. Santa didn't do it. You'll get him off."

When the homeless man had passed, Vern said, "Whoever gave him that cell phone had a great idea. Now nobody can tell he's a fruitcake."

"You know, Vern, it's that kind of judgments on people that make you so charming."

"That's it. Throw it back in my face. It feels good. We're going to have a good professional relationship."

As they got to the door of Rumpole's, Eve stopped and said, "Of course, I want a good professional relationship with you, Vern. But you need to know I'm seeing somebody."

"Seeing somebody? You only hit town a week or so ago."

She smiled enigmatically.

When they were seated in Rumpole's, Eve asked in a whisper, "Now what was that sneezing question about?"

"The crime scene people picked up some evidence in Andrew Baines's office that they think ties Charlie to the crime. DNA maybe. Our boss thinks the evidence is too convenient and means somebody is trying to frame Charlie. I prefer the other alternative, which I've already expressed: our client is a fruitcake."

"You must be really fond of fruitcake, Vern. Maybe I'll get you one for Christmas. What about the question about the beard?"

"A Santa Claus beard was found sitting on Andrew Baines's desk. Sitting in his blood."

CHAPTER THIRTEEN

October and November

Even with the official Santa Claus in jail, the city continued its inexorable march toward Christmas. The opening of the trial was set for Monday, December 4, and both sides feverishly planned their cases, deposing witnesses and discussing strategy. Citizens received jury duty summonses, some with cries of delight but most with groans of displeasure. On Halloween, a child who thought a bloodied Santa Claus suit was a suitable costume was sent home from school in disgrace. A poll in the *ProPurv* showed strong citizen disbelief in the guilt of Charlie Baines and a concomitant low approval rating for the district attorney's office. Well before Thanksgiving, the malls were in full commercial Yuletide mode, and the day after that November feast day, one local radio station began its annual twenty-four-seven Christmas music marathon. Their morning disc jockey began a listener survey to name the all-time worst Christmas song. Some listeners found the promotion in questionable taste, even when he announced he would stick to secular offerings and leave the religious carols alone. And of course, the local public television station was gearing up for the holiday version of its four-times-a-year viewer funds appeal.

Meanwhile, in various parts of the city, scenes were played out involving actors in the courtroom drama to come.

"We really shouldn't be seeing each other, you know."

"Why not? We won't talk about the case."

"Okay," said Stacey Bamwanger, snuggling closer to her companion on the sofa. "It's nice to be with somebody and not talk about the case. But it feels weird when it's a lawyer for the other side, somebody who makes his living defending killers, a champion of the dregs of humanity." She sighed. "Strange are the ways of human attraction."

"Right," said Vern Wagstaff. "What's it like working for that jerk Prentice Winstead?"

"I hardly ever see him. As far as I'm concerned, the boss is Dave Ketchum, and he's jerk enough for anybody. Lots of people think he's God's gift, but I think he's basically shallow and frivolous. All those references to old movies. It's enough to make you gag."

"You know, though, there are some kinds of movies that can be very stimulating to the human pleasure centers."

"Oh? Is that right?"

"Yes, I have a large collection of videos I'd like to share with you. You're a great lady, Stacey Bamwanger, but you're too uptight. You need to loosen up, discover the inner Stacey, wild and sexy and up for anything."

"You think so, huh? And you think these videos of yours would help?"

"Trust me."

Duffy O'Gonigal sat at the bar at Rumpole's and said to Phil Etchebarren, "That's quite a challenge young Gordon has taken on, Phil, quite a challenge. I ask you, is that going to be a trial? A classic. One for the books."

"Scuttlebutt is both sides want to finish by Christmas," Phil said. "That's moving awfully fast."

"By current standards maybe. But in Edinburgh in 1889, William Bury was convicted of the bloody murder of his wife in a trial that took only one day. One day, Phil, all the evidence and jury deliberations as well. And why not? If the Scots could cover everything vital to a murder prosecution in one day, even in Twenty-first-Century America, a couple weeks should be ample time."

"Did you ever try a murder case that fast, Duffy?"

"No, but not for want of trying. Look at that fellow there." He pointed at the TV over the bar where a stocky baseball pitcher, made stockier by the distorted picture, was working quickly. "He always plays like he was late for an appointment somewhere else. If he had his way, the game would be over in an hour and a half. Nothing he can do about the TV commercial breaks between innings, of course. I was like that in court, Phil, a quick worker. It was always the prosecution trying to slow things down, not me. But there's so much to remember in a case, so much law to hold in your head, so many facts to keep at your fingertips. You never need it all, but you have to have it all at the ready just in case. You know, I sometimes think the law is like a school of fish, and the lawyer is a pelican who has to carry more in his pouch than his stomach can hold."

"Have another, Duff?"

"Don't mind if I do."

"Oh, I didn't tell you," said David Ketchum. "I'm going to be on TV."

Eve looked at him suspiciously. "Oh? Why?"

"Because I'm photogenic, articulate, and charismatic, I guess."

"David, we've agreed not to talk about the Baines case, but is it about the Baines case?"

He shivered. "Certainly not. Nothing to do with your case and nothing to do with the law. Strictly a fun thing."

She relaxed and smiled. "Great. When are you going to be on?"

"Hello, Judge Estrada speaking."

"Marisol, it's Rosita."

"Hi, cousin. How are things?"

"The children I love, but these gringos I work for are—"

"Rosita, I don't want to hear about it. They'll both be in my courtroom next week, and I want to keep an open mind, okay?"

"Okay. You'd laugh if I told you, but that's not why I called. In *Tia* Juanita's enchilada recipe you gave me, there are too many decisions to make."

"Now there I can help. Easiest decisions I'll make this week."

CHAPTER FOURTEEN

Sunday, December 3

The TV camera panned a huge Christmas tree, a red-robed church choir awaiting their cue, and a bank of phones manned by men and women in Santa Claus hats, before coming to rest on a green-eyed blond beauty in a charmingly short holly-themed dress, standing next to a sweatily frantic man, jacket off, sleeves rolled up, and tie askew in full telethon mode.

As she smiled coolly, he effused warmly, "Your public television station, WORK, channel 77, needs your support so we can continue to bring you the kind of programming you just can't get anywhere else. What am I talking about? How about the Rock of 'Eighties reunion concert coming up later this evening, or the spectacular Reindeer Rap/Hip-hop Chanukah/Quality Kwanzaa extravaganza tomorrow night, or the great program we brought you earlier this afternoon, Oona Swarthman's *Money Advice*—and remember this offer is still open: for a two-hundred dollar pledge you can get a personally dedicated copy of Oona's latest book *Secrets of Personal Money Management You Should Have Been Taught in High School But Weren't,* or for a four-hundred dollar pledge, we'll throw in a copy of her new video *Make Crushing Debt Work for You.* Just as Oona works for you, WORK works for you to bring programs like the one you've just been watching, Dr. Wade Flinders's inspiring and provocative *Self Help Won't Help You if You Won't Help Yourself.* Now we all know at this time of the year, there's a lot of strain on our budgets, what with throwing parties and giving gifts and enjoying ourselves with our friends and families. But please, please, please, spare a little for your public television station so we can go on bringing you this fine programming that you can't get anywhere else, uninterrupted by commercials. Pick up that telephone and talk to one of our hardworking volunteers at 1-800-GOTOWORK."

Now he seemed to notice what every male viewer had been fixating on: the Hitchcock blonde standing next to him. "You all know WORK's own Alison McCready, host of the award-winning *Today in Your City*. Even at this festive time of year, we aren't neglecting our commitment to the best in public affairs programming, and coming next, live, is a special edition of that great program. Hi, Alison."

"Hi, Greg, and hi, everybody." She put a friendly hand on the sweating man's sleeve and did her best to register warmth and concern. "My goodness, Greg, you're putting your heart and soul into this pledge appeal. Why don't you just sit down and relax for a while?"

"I'll relax, Alison, when we've met our goal of fifty thousand dollars in pledges at this break."

"Well, we'll just have to meet it then. I worry about you. But I know how much WORK means to you." She smiled at the camera. "And how much it means to our whole community."

"Thanks, Alison, and you mean a lot to our whole community as well. So tell us: what's the topic of your special show today?"

"Our topic is a local controversy that won't go away: the threatened closing of the venerable Majestic Theatre. And we may have a few surprises." She winked at the camera. "Now, if you'll excuse me, I'm going to head down the hall to our *Today in Your City* studio, and while I'm doing that, I want you all to call 1-800-GOTOWORK and help this poor hard-working man, Greg Beggs, reach his goal before he drops dead of a coronary."

"Thanks again, Alison, and while the East Meets West Memorial Church choir sees us out of this break with their rendition of 'Frosty the Snowman,' please, please, please pick up that phone and make your pledge to one of our jolly operators." Greg Beggs swayed dramatically, as if he really were about to collapse from exhaustion, but the telethon schtick would be lost on the viewers at home: the camera was already following (were this not public television, you might say lasciviously) Alison McCready as she walked past the choir, the phone bank, and the tree, and through a door, turning and giving a coyly smiling wave as she disappeared.

Once she was through the door and safely off camera, Alison erased her TV smile and stalked down the corridor toward another door, behind which her guests waited. Alison's personal assistant Sandra Glickman scurried in her wake, ready to note any orders or bon mots from her mercurial employer. Sandra, herself an astonishing beauty in selected off hours, wore a drab, loose-fitting pants suit and no makeup, her brown hair in a careless ponytail. She had to be careful to dress down enough not to steal any attention from the boss.

"This is such crap," Alison muttered. "I should be doing real TV. PBS is a hotbed of hypocrisy." She stopped in mid-stalk and turned to Sandra. "Note that. I'll use that phrase sometime. Hotbed of hypocrisy—yeah, I like that. I won't use it about PBS, though, at least not while I'm still working here, huh?"

"Why do you call PBS a hotbed of hypocrisy?" Sandra asked, doing her best to approximate the voice of a pilgrim seeking wisdom from a mountaintop guru.

"To start with, they say no commercials, but then they lead into my show with three or four of them. They snatch away ten minutes of my show during pledge appeals, but I probably shouldn't care because they've already scared off my core audience by loading up the pledge appeals with a bunch of infantile self-help garbage. This show today would hit the roof in the ratings if it were on a real station, properly promoted, but we'll be lucky if anybody's watching at all. I ask you. Do I belong on public television?"

"You certainly don't!" Sandra said enthusiastically, relishing the ambiguity.

"Network is good. Cable, depending, can be even better. But UHF is the professional pits. It stands for Unseen, Hopeless, and Futile. Remember that, Sandy."

Yes, yes, I remember, my job is the pits. And please do, knowing how I hate it, keep calling me Sandy.

"Were those movie notes I gave you okay?" Sandra asked.

Stopping before the door to the *Today in Your City* studio, Alison stopped, turned to her assistant and said, "Oh, I'm sure they were. Just like you, Sandy, boring but reliable. I didn't read them all. This show isn't going to be about the movies. The movies are my Trojan horse, and I'll get them off the subject as fast as I can."

"But the panelists think—"

"Panelists don't think. You don't think. It's my show. I think."

Alison reassumed her cool smile as she entered the studio and graciously greeted her four guests, who were seated on deck chairs in a simulated garden, now decorated with holly to complement her dress. She took her seat in the center and arranged her gorgeous legs to best advantage. Early in her career at WORK, she had anchored from behind a desk. When an e-mailer suggested she was hiding what he speculated must be "PBS legs," she insisted on a new set, one that she assured the station manager would create a warmer, friendlier, not to mention more *Today Show*-like ambience.

One of her four all-male guests, David Ketchum, leaned over and said, "Alison, I'm not being ambushed here, am I?"

She widened her eyes in comic innocence. "Why would you

say that, David?"

"I thought this was going to be a discussion of movies and the Majestic Theatre. I expected to see Mr. Monarca here." He gestured to the elderly Sidney Monarca, who was seated to his right. "What I didn't expect to see was another lawyer." He nodded toward Duffy O'Gonigal, beaming at him from the other end of the garden.

"Neither did I. The *ProPurv* movie reviewer dropped out at the last minute, flu bug or something, and we had to find a fill-in." She whispered conspiratorially, "They tell me he's sober. Enough."

"Then you know it wouldn't be proper to talk about—"

She held up a hand to shush him. "We're almost on."

David shook his head. What had he got himself in for? And what happened to the *ProPurv* critic? Had Alison, who usually managed to avoid having other attractive women on her program, sent her a box of poisoned chocolates? But the second-string critic, that admirer of Julia Roberts's smile, was always available.

Well, it was too late to back out now.

Prentice Winstead peered at his primary television screen, which at the touch of a button sprang out from behind a shelf of fake law book spines on his study wall. He always watched *Today in Your City* when he could tear himself away from the demands of his office, but he'd been alerted that this evening's program might be especially edifying.

"Our topic," said the luscious Alison, "is the fate of the Majestic Theatre and my guests, starting on my far right are Duffy O'Gonigal, well-known and well-respected lawyer in this city for many years and, I understand, quite a knowledgeable movie buff. On my immediate right is Jack Wong, reporter and columnist for the *Provincial Purveyor*, who knows more than anybody I can think of about local business and political affairs, including the Majestic controversy, which has elements of both. On my left is David Ketchum, the chief trial deputy in the district attorney's office, who is equally famous for his encyclopedic knowledge of old movies, and on my far left is the owner and manager of the Majestic Theatre, Sidney Monarca."

When the moving camera forced him to look at someone other than Alison McCready, Winstead noted that his chief trial deputy looked distinctly ill at ease, while Duffy O'Gonigal couldn't have been any more relaxed ensconced on his customary Rumpole's bar stool. Wong was too well dressed for a reporter—you'd think he had *his* eye on the governor's mansion—and old Monarca looked like he might pass away before the program was over. The camera returned to Alison, who was posing her traditional low-key, we're-all-friends-here opening question.

"Since we're talking about the movies, let me begin by asking each of my guests a sort of break-the-ice question. Duffy O'Gonigal, what is your all-time favorite movie?"

"Ah, my dear, that has to be *The Quiet Man*. Reminds me of the old sod."

"Were you born in Ireland, Duffy?"

"Never been there, no, but it's in my bones all the same."

"Jack Wong, your favorite movie. No, let me guess. *The Front Page* maybe? *All the President's Men?*"

Winstead wondered what Wong would say. The reporter had once confided that he admired the Charlie Chan movies, but he could never admit it in public.

"*The Godfather*," Jack Wong said. "For its political savvy. Part one, I mean. Didn't like the other two as well."

"David Ketchum, how about it? Your all-time favorite movie."

"It's hard to pick just one. I guess *Citizen Kane* is tough to beat."

"And finally the real expert, Sidney Monarca. You've shown us a lot of movies through the years, Mr. Monarca. Which is your all-time favorite?"

"Well, Alison," Monarca said in a voice that quavered with age or emotion or something, "I'm going to name one in deference to the season and in honor of a respected citizen who can't be with us here tonight. *It's a Wonderful Life.* Charlie Baines isn't having a wonderful life right now, but I know we all hope he will again."

Prentice Winstead leaned back in his chair. Why exactly was he watching this? Any reference to the jailed Santa Claus could only rekindle public anger at the DA. David Ketchum had better be ready to take the heat off his boss.

David was sweating, not entirely due to the hot lights. He had to keep this discussion away from the Baines case, but he knew Alison McCready would bring it up at first opportunity.

For now, though, she was saying to Monarca, "You've been in the movie exhibition business in this city for as long as I can remember."

"Since way before you were born, Alison. My two older brothers and I started out more than half a century ago. I'm coming up on my seventy-fifth birthday, and I never wanted to do anything but run a movie house, show the movies I love to the people of this community."

"But it's a hard business, isn't it?"

"It always was a hard business. Now it's an impossible business. A one-screen movie house is as obsolete as a horse and buggy."

"But you're still open."

"Barely. A few months ago we thought we'd be dodging the wrecking ball, but we got a reprieve when—well, we got a reprieve. We usually get a little bump around Christmas time, but after the first of the year I may have to pack it in, whatever happens."

"Your lavish lobby decorations and your big-screen showings of holiday classics are kind of a tradition with so many local families," Alison said.

"Yes. We serve hot cider, have carolers in the lobby, peppermint sticks for the kids, the whole nine yards. I'm glad we'll be able to do it again, if only for one last time. It won't be quite the same this year for reasons I think we all know."

Alison turned to David and said, "That brings us to an inevitable subject, David Ketchum."

The hell it does! Think fast, David. "It certainly does," he said and turned to Monarca. "What holiday films are you showing this year, Mr. Monarca?"

"Oh, we got John Ford's *Three Godfathers*—haven't had that one in a few years—and *Meet Me in St. Louis*, of course. That's one of our favorites, and it always brings out the families. We also have a double feature of *The Bishop's Wife* and *The Preacher's Wife*, and after the showing a panel from the university film school will be discussing the whole phenomenon of remakes. You'll remember we did the same thing last year, and quite successfully, with *Holiday Inn* and *White Christmas*."

"*Holiday Inn*'s better," Duffy O'Gonigal chimed in. "Unless you prefer Danny Kaye's dancing to Fred Astaire's. You know, when I was a kid I used to usher at the Majestic."

"Really?" said Alison. "I didn't know that."

"Sure, I know that building as well as Sid does. Love it, too. Hey, I thought that was why you invited me. I can't think of any other reason. You know, Sid, I was really moved by your alcoholism festival a few years ago: *The Lost Weekend*, followed by *Days of Wine and Roses*, followed by a *Thin Man* double feature. I was inspired. After the second night I almost thought about quitting drinking, but fortunately William Powell and Myrna Loy straightened me out in time."

David was grateful for Duffy's help. The old has-been must know on the eve of a big trial uninformed talk from those on the sidelines should be avoided.

"Well," Alison said indulgently, "you get a bunch of film buffs together and there's no telling where the conversation will lead. But we need to get back to the fate of the Majestic. Jack Wong, you've been covering the battle to save that grand old theatre in your columns for some time. What's happening on that front?"

"Well, Alison, as most of your viewers know, there was quite a bit of money raised to keep the theatre going, and with the sudden death of Andrew Baines, who was representing a group of investors who wanted to buy the Majestic to tear it down and take on other development projects, things have sort of come to a standstill. The thing is that no one seems to know exactly who those investors were that Andrew Baines was fronting for. If I knew what was going to happen next, you'd see it on the front page of the *Provincial Purveyor,* believe me. Maybe Mr. Monarca can tell us something, eh?"

Monarca shook his head. "I'm as much in the dark as anybody, and I'd rather be in the dark watching a movie. Nobody seems to want to address it during the holiday season, and I think maybe the investors are waiting for the outcome of a certain event before they make their next move. I've said again and again I want to save the Majestic, but I can't do it without help."

"That brings us to an inevitable topic," Alison said, "one that is intimately tied in some ways to the holiday season and possibly to the future of the Majestic." The look she threw at David clearly said, *you won't dodge the question this time.* "David Ketchum, this coming week will see the beginning of what is being called the trial of the century."

David cleared his throat. "That's an interesting phrase, isn't it? I wonder how many trials in the twentieth century were called the trial of the century."

"The Hall-Mills case," said Duffy O'Gonigal helpfully. "The Lindbergh case."

"The Sam Shepard case," David said. "The O.J. Simpson case."

"The Nuremberg trials," Jack Wong offered.

"The Scopes monkey trial," said Duffy.

"Now there's a film you could revive, Mr. Monarca," David said desperately. "*Inherit the Wind.* Very timely with all the talk about Intelligent Design."

"We're drifting off the subject, gentlemen," Alison said, in the tone of a fondly indulgent schoolteacher.

"Right," David said. "We were talking about the trial of the century, but this century is young yet, and I don't think any particular trial could be said to be the trial of the century, and if it were, it wouldn't really be saying much. I mean you had the Michael Jackson trial, and then there's the Saddam Hussein trial."

"Still," Alison said, "the trial of Charlie Baines for the murder of his brother Andrew is probably close enough to the trial of century as far as the life of this city is concerned." She looked at the camera smugly. "There I said it. Have you been trying to avoid the subject, Mr. Ketchum?"

David smiled, willing himself to stay calm. "Frankly, yes. It has nothing to do with what I was asked here to discuss. I was looking forward to some good old movie talk. Anyway, since my office is prosecuting the Baines case, it's not appropriate for me to discuss it."

"I thought lawyers talked to the media about cases in process all the time. Is there some kind of gag order in effect?"

"No, there's no gag order, but I'm not actually prosecuting the case. I'm working in a supervisory capacity."

Jack Wong jumped in then. "But it's true, isn't it, that the DA, Prentice Winstead, has given you, as chief trial deputy, full responsibility for picking the team that will prosecute Charlie Baines?"

"That's right."

"And you have satisfied him that the evidence is strong enough to assure a conviction?"

"Mr. Wong, whenever we bring a case to trial, we believe a guilty verdict is supported by the evidence. Otherwise, we wouldn't bring the case, would we? But *assure* is a risky word where juries are concerned."

"Does this mean that you don't share the district attorney's confidence in the competence of the people of this city to serve as jurors?" Alison asked.

"Not at all. But you never know which way a major trial like this is going to go. And I'm certainly not prepared to discuss the specifics of the case here tonight."

"Charlie Baines," said Jack Wong, "is a beloved figure in this city. Would it be fair to say that Prentice Winstead is placing his reliance on you in his reluctant decision to bring such a serious charge against such a respected man?"

David wanted to ask Wong who at WORK gave him his own show; he wanted to repeat his outrage at being ambushed by this tag-team method; he wanted to quit the district attorney's office and open an art gallery. But all he said was, "The district attorney and everyone in his office believe in the words over the courthouse door: 'Justice for All; Justice Always.' We trust in that statue of the lady Justice. We trust in the process."

"Have they fixed that statue yet?" Duffy asked.

Alison said, "Duffy O'Gonigal, you've been a fixture in the legal community of this city for as long as I can remember."

"Am I supposed to say 'before you were born,' too, my dear? But I don't know when you were born, you see."

"Never mind that, Mr. O'Gonigal. You also, I believe, have been something of a mentor to Gordon Moon, who will be personally appearing in Charlie Baines's defense."

"I'm proud to say so. He's a great lawyer."

"What advice would you be giving him as he enters what may be the biggest case of his career?"

Duffy drew a deep breath. "I'd advise him not to show his hand. The law is like a guy teaching a bird to talk, and the lawyer is like a mynah bird who sometimes talks too much. Not to mention repeats itself. Gordon Moon will do a great job for Charlie Baines."

"And do I understand, David Ketchum, that the wife of Gordon Moon has been assigned to the prosecution team? Some might see this as a way of undermining the defense."

"I can't imagine why that should be so," David said.

"Is it usual for a member of the prosecution team to have that close a relationship to a member of the defense team?"

"They're both highly professional lawyers."

"Are any others on the prosecution team in relationships with advocates on the defense side?" Alison asked archly.

"Not that I'm aware of, no," David said, wondering what this pernicious woman knew while mentally reassuring himself that he was not really part of the team and thus not really lying.

Alison looked at him fixedly, a bit amusedly, for a few seconds, but she didn't pursue the subject. She looked into the camera and said, "We're about out of time. I want to thank our four guests . . ."

Winstead watched the closing credits, backed by a montage of photographs: first of the Majestic theatre; then of Charlie Baines as Santa Claus, posing with various smiling celebrities; finally, and lingered on longest, showing Baines shaking hands with Prentice Winstead himself.

Fifteen minutes later, Alison breezed through the front door and threw herself into his arms. After some enthusiastic facial intimacies, she said, "What did you think?"

"It was a nice show."

"Nice show, Prennie?" She pushed him to arm's length in mock irritation. "Is that all you can say? We positioned you as the dedicated public servant who put aside his personal feelings to let his office run with a case against a beloved figure. We positioned David Ketchum as a scapegoat. We positioned him as a loose cannon. We positioned you as the next governor of this state." She squeezed his bicep. "How would you like to position *me*, Arnold?"

"What do you mean Arnold?"

"Just call me Maria from now on."

"Maria? But your name is still Alison, isn't it? Your professional name, I mean? And your real name as I recall is—"

"Just shut up, Prennie, and take me to bed."

CHAPTER FIFTEEN

Monday, December 4

Judge Marisol Estrada looked down at the array of lawyers at the defense and prosecution tables. She was glad to have the assignment, overwrought publicity or not, holiday season or not. She loved the law, loved the trial process, and relished being in the middle of a firestorm. If either side had asked for recusal because of her history with the Wagstaff family, she would have complied, but no one had asked and she wasn't about to volunteer.

There was Gordon Moon, super-confident little guy with a big head, literally. Dressed in a well-tailored three-piece suit. The king of the local defense bar fancied himself a real-life Perry Mason, a latter-day Clarence Darrow, a white Johnnie Cochran. He'd be fun to watch from the best seat in the house. And there was Vern Wagstaff sitting next to him, also neatly dressed but without quite the same taste and style. *Oh, yeah, I remember you, Vern. As a little prick. Literally.* There was the defendant Charlie Baines, looking somber but cherubic, in a dark suit. His cheeks showed the beginning of a beard. And finally the junior member of the defense team, Eve Nyquist, who dressed with a combination of good taste and sexiness to which less visually gifted women could never hope to aspire. Eve looked the uneasiest of the four at the defense table, though obviously she would have the least to do in the case.

At the prosecution table was Melba Wooten, a formidable

physical presence in subdued cornrows and a means-business power suit. The judge could imagine her picking up Gordon Moon, dribbling him the length of the court, and slam-dunking him. But this was not a game of one-on-one, and Moon would have moves she might not have thought of. Next to Melba, Agnes Wagstaff Moon looked as constantly edgy and keyed up as she had as an over-achieving child. *Just relax, little Agnes. Take a deep breath, honey. I gave Cousin Rosita Tia Juanita's enchilada recipe just for you.* The third member of the team, Stacey Bamwanger, was regarding the world with her usual sour expression. The judge felt sorry for her, not as an unattractive woman—she wasn't—but as the least attractive woman in the room, a situation not helped by her perpetual scowl and dowdy fashion sense. The judge did not include herself in the rankings of female pulchritude—she was above the competition both literally and figuratively, and anyway was carrying quite a few extra pounds under these proud judicial robes.

The fourth person seated at the prosecution table, and the only man, was the investigating officer, Detective Richard Tracy. A good cop, certainly, but not always at his best in court. He had a notoriously short fuse, and opposing lawyers were always looking for a way to light it. He was big and solid without the pointed chin of his comic-strip namesake. His first name, he constantly reminded people, was Richard, his preferred nickname Rich, but to friend and foe alike he had to be a Dick.

Time to get to work.

"Good morning, ladies and gentlemen," she said in a no-nonsense voice with the slightest remnant of a Spanish accent. "The matter before us is the People versus Charles Nicholas Baines, charged with the first-degree murder of Andrew Baines. Let the record show that the defendant, three lawyers each representing the prosecution and the defense, and the investigating officer are all present. We are hoping to begin jury selection this afternoon, but first, we seem to have two motions before us. Both of them are from the prosecution. Nothing from the defense, Mr. Moon?"

Gordon Moon stood up and said, "No, Your Honor. All we ask is that the defendant's right to a speedy trial be honored, and we will do nothing and allow nothing to stand in the way of his exercising that right. We want this ludicrous assault on every ideal of justice to be ended."

"Mr. Moon, I'm sure you will have noticed there's no jury present, so you can save the oration. Now let's deal with Ms. Wooten's first motion. You are asking, Ms. Wooten, that the defendant be prohibited from wearing his Santa Claus suit during the trial."

"We are, Your Honor," Melba Wooten said, rising to her full towering height.

"Your Honor," Gordon Moon said, springing back to his feet. "Mr. Baines, my learned colleague will surely have noticed, is seated here beside me wearing a business suit. At no time has he appeared at any hearing in connection with this case attired in any other way, apart from that hideous orange jail jumpsuit he was obliged to wear at his arraignment. At no time have we suggested his mode of dress would be any different. Ms. Wooten's motion, therefore, is frivolous and serves only as another delaying tactic on the part of the prosecution."

With a faux friendly smile at her opponent, Melba said, "I will readily admit, Your Honor, that this motion is in the nature of a pre-emptive strike. It is the Christmas season. In this city, Mr. Baines is as intimately and inextricably associated with the Christmas season as Bob Cratchit or George Bailey. Dressing as Santa Claus for this morning's hearing would gain him nothing, but later with a jury present, it could be prejudicial to the people's case. We believe it in the best interests of the people of this state to avert such a shameless stunt before it happens."

Gordon Moon registered equally faux umbrage. "Your Honor, I resent my learned colleague's implication that I would engage in any 'shameless stunt.' And in any case, if Mr. Baines were to choose a different style of clothing, assuming it was neat and clean and tasteful, for some of his appearances in this court, I know of no law or court rule that would prevent him from doing so."

Melba Wooten turned directly to her opponent and said triumphantly, "So you admit you intend to have him sitting at the defense table dressed as Santa Claus."

"I have said no such thing. I merely indicated that normal procedural rules would not prevent it if he were to make such a choice on his own. I assure you, I have more important concerns in this case than picking out my client's suits for him."

Melba registered broad astonishment. "Oh, please, Mr. Moon. Since when do you not orchestrate every move your client makes? Didn't the *Law Daily* call you the Frank Lloyd Wright of the defense bar, with the furniture design as important as the floor layout?"

"While I appreciate the compliment, furniture design is not at issue when a man's life is at stake."

Melba turned back to the bench. Judge Estrada was enjoying the exchange too much to intervene.

"Your Honor," Melba said, "a Santa Claus costume, besides being prejudicial, can serve as a disguise. It could serve to confuse witnesses unfairly. It could even result in some other person sitting in the defendant's place at the defense table. One person in a Santa Claus suit looks very much like another. Behind a white beard—"

"Your Honor, my client has no intention of donning a false beard," Gordon said.

Melba pointed at Baines. "But look, Your Honor, look at that stubble. He's growing a beard of his own. By the time the jury is seated, he could have as full a beard as any Santa Claus."

"Ms. Wooten," the judge pointed out, "beards don't grow that fast. And it appears from here that Mr. Baines's beard is coming in reddish brown, not white."

"Then I move he be prohibited from dyeing it white for the duration of the trial. If he wants a beard, let him have a beard, but let it be a natural reddish brown beard. A white beard would be prejudicial to the people's case. With a full white beard, all he would need is a white shirt and red business suit to approximate Santa Claus, and that would be just as prejudicial as full Santa Claus regalia."

Gordon Moon looked at her incredulously. "Am I to understand that the assistant district attorney would prohibit my client from altering his hair color, when members of the prosecution team have had that freedom and in fact have been exercising it for years?"

Agnes Wagstaff Moon rose to her feet. "You bastard!"

Gordon threw up his hands in innocent imprecation. "I mentioned no names."

Judge Estrada pounded her gavel. "That's enough, counselors. This has been most entertaining, but I know you will refrain from personal attacks when the jury is present. For if you won't, you will be cited for contempt of court. I'm ready to rule on the prosecution's motion. No full Santa Claus suit will be allowed to compromise the dignity of this court and the solemnity that must attend a trial for murder. However, the court will place no prohibition on the defendant's beard or its alteration. Attorneys for both sides will be permitted to follow whatever hair care regimen they wish—and unless my eyes deceive me, you've dipped into the Grecian Formula yourself on occasion, Mr. Moon. Now, may we move to the next prosecution motion?"

All combatants took their seats as the judge shuffled papers. "This second motion deals with discovery. Both sides, as any first-year law student knows, are required to provide witness lists to their opponents. You have done this, Ms. Wooten?"

"We certainly have, Your Honor."

"But Mr. Moon has not?"

Gordon rose to his feet, an innocent expression on his face. "Your Honor, I believe we have complied."

"This is the witness list Mr. Moon supplied," Melba said, holding aloft a fat paperbound volume.

"Yes, that is our witness list. Of course, you realize we do not intend to call all of the witnesses listed, but we are obliged to provide the prosecution with a list of those we may call."

"Mr. Moon," Judge Estrada said, "do my eyes deceive me or is that a city telephone directory Ms. Wooten is holding?"

"It is, Your Honor."

"Presenting a telephone book as your witness list is somewhat unorthodox, don't you think? Indeed, dressing the defendant as Santa Claus, were you to do that, would be standard operating procedure by comparison. You constantly express your client's wish for a speedy trial, and then you advance a telephone book as your witness list. Would you care to explain yourself?"

"Certainly. Part of our defense will be to demonstrate the good moral character of our client, and Mr. Baines is known to everyone in that book, indeed everyone in this city, as a philanthropist, a good citizen, and a symbol of all that is positive in the human spirit."

"And you cannot narrow down your list of possible witnesses?"

"I believe we have. There are many persons in the city without telephones or with unlisted numbers or with cell phones only. We will not call any of them as witnesses but will confine ourselves to those listed in the book."

Melba showed the binding of the phone book to the judge, who asked, "White pages and yellow pages?"

"Certainly," Gordon said. "I have no intention of being difficult on this point. If the prosecution will give me a list of possible witnesses they believe we may or may not call, I will happily check off for them those whom we promise not to call. Will that make you happy, Madame District Attorney?"

Seething, Melba turned her face back to Judge Estrada. "I await Your Honor's ruling."

"Counselors," Judge Estrada said, "once this trial is underway, I expect the cheap and forced humor to stop. Unless it comes from the witnesses." She paused thoughtfully. "Or from the bench. Mr. Moon, given your desire for a speedy trial and your obvious cognizance of the inappropriateness of a telephone book as a witness list, I am sure you have your real witness list prepared and ready to turn over to Ms. Wooten. I direct you to produce it immediately."

Though still looking hurt and innocent, Gordon passed a few sheets of paper over to Melba and handed a duplicate copy to the court clerk.

"Are there any more motions, or is this comedy club closed for the day?" Judge Estrada inquired. After a pause, she stated, "Good. Now let's get together this afternoon and pick a jury, shall we?"

CHAPTER SIXTEEN

When Gordon Moon entered the conference room after a quick lunch at his desk, he found Vern and Eve sitting huddled together in close conversation. Wagstaff's reputation as a womanizer ordinarily didn't bother Moon. But if a romance were brewing between his associates, Gordon would have to nip it in the bud, convince them to save it until the end of the trial.

"Hi, Gordon," Vern said. "I was just filling Eve in on some of the axioms of criminal defense."

"Uh-huh," Moon said. "And what have you learned, Eve?"

She smiled. "It's kind of depressing. 'When you eliminate the inadmissible, whatever evidence remains will still hang your client.' "

"Never heard that one. Do you get those out of fortune cookies, Vern?" He slammed down his file at the head of the conference table, signaling that the necessarily short meeting had officially begun. "Now, then, are we all together on what we're looking for in a jury?"

Vern shrugged. "In this city, about anybody. Who wants to see Charlie Baines fry?"

"It's a big city. Somebody probably does. And the Santa Claus angle means we have to gauge how sentimental they are about Christmas, how much power the image of Saint Nick carries for them. Melba Wooten will be looking for people who are cynical about Christmas, even hostile. If Ebenezer Scrooge and the Grinch were in the jury pool, Wooten would want them in the box, and we'd have to do everything we can to keep them out."

"No, we wouldn't," Eve said. "They'd make good jurors for the defense."

Both Gordon and Vern were speechless for a moment. Then Gordon said gently, "Eve, I don't get your point. Scrooge and the Grinch represent a hatred of Christmas traditions."

"But that's so unfair. They both reformed. The Grinch himself carved the Christmas beast, and it was said no one kept Christmas like Scrooge, who became like a second father to Tiny Tim. They'd be perfect jurors for the defense. Now, if it were Mr. Potter, I'd agree with you. He never reformed."

Gordon scratched his head, thankful Scrooge and the Grinch weren't in the jury pool.

"How can we get twelve people who hate Christmas on that jury?" Agnes Wagstaff Moon asked the room at large.

"I hate Christmas," Stacey Bamwanger said. "Can I be on the jury?"

Ignoring her, Melba said, "How we gonna get twelve Christmas haters in that box? Guess what? We can't. So what's the next best thing?"

"Drag the whole thing out till after Christmas," Agnes suggested. "Send them out to bring in a verdict when the bills are coming in and their Yuletide spirit has worn off."

"Wrong," said Melba. "They'll hate us. We have to be as determined as the defense to get this trial over by Christmas. And they want Christmassy, we'll give them Christmassy. We will be more Christmassy than thou. We will rub the Christmas off Charlie Baines and squirt it on ourselves."

"How do we do that?" Stacy asked.

"We could bring the jury cookies and fruitcake," said Agnes.

Melba shook her head. "Wouldn't be allowed to. Prejudicial."

Judge Estrada said, "Bring in the potential jurors, please."

The bailiff opened the doors to the courtroom and several dozen oddly assorted citizens filed in, filling up most of the rows of spectator seats.

"Ladies and gentlemen, good morning," the judge said, with a trace of a smile. "We're selecting jurors today in the matter of the State versus Charles Nicholas Baines." There were a few gasps from the jury pool. "Yes, yes, I know, just what some of you were praying for and others were praying against. The clerk of the court will be calling your names. When you are called, please come forward and take a seat in the jury box. While we are instructing and questioning those chosen, I ask the rest of you who have not been called forward to pay close attention to everything that is said, since some of you will find yourselves in one of those fourteen hot seats later on. Madame clerk?"

The court clerk kept calling from the gathered jury pool until the box was filled with fourteen people.

"I have a few questions to ask you," Judge Estrada said, "and then I'll turn you over to the lawyers representing the state and the defendant to ask you a few more questions. By the time they're through, you may feel like you're on trial instead of the defendant, but you're not. It's just our way of finding a jury of people who can look at the evidence and arrive at a fair verdict. In my experience, some of you who think you can can't, and others of you who might think you can't, can. Some of you would really like to serve as jurors, and others of you would do anything short of fleeing the country to avoid serving. The way these things work, some of you who don't want to serve will, and others of you who do want to serve won't, because that's how our system works. If it drives you nuts, well, it drives me nuts, too, sometimes, but it's all we've got. Now, how many of you have some knowledge of this case, read about it in the paper, seen it on TV, heard about it on the radio, read about it on the Internet, talked about it to friends and family?"

Every hand went up.

"That's what we all expected. But that doesn't disqualify you. Are any of you personally acquainted with the defendant, Charles Nicholas Baines?"

Several shook their heads, but one middle-aged woman raised her hand tentatively.

"Yes, Mrs. Smith?"

"I serve as a docent at the city museum. Mr. Baines serves on the board and has been extremely generous to the museum. I once gave him a personal tour of one of our exhibits."

"Did you meet him on any other occasion?"

"No."

"Do you believe this experience would affect your ability to give Mr. Baines a fair trial?"

"Well, I hope not, but it's very hard to believe as wonderful a man as Mr. Baines could have committed murder. They'd have to prove it to me."

"That is the state's job, Mrs. Smith. Anyone else?"

No more hands went up. Judge Estrada asked if they knew or had dealings with any of the lawyers for either side, if they had relatives in the criminal justice system, if they had been the victims of crime, if they had any reason they could not be fair and impartial, and if for any reason they were unable to serve in a lengthy trial. Only the last question brought any spirited responses, but Judge Estrada knocked down every request to be excused. "It's tough having to work around Christmas season, but we have to, and I'm afraid, so will some of you."

Through this questioning, only two of the fourteen were excused. Two more were added to the box, the same questions repeated, and finally the jury pool was turned over to the lawyers for the prosecution and defense.

"Ladies and gentlemen," Melba Wooten said, "some of you may recognize me from TV. Not dressed quite the way I am now, so maybe you wouldn't. I've spent some time playing basketball in the WNBA. I think we're a good league, and we're gonna go a long way, and if I didn't have a couple of bad knees, I'd play a lot better and a lot longer. Now, it's true they don't pay us like they pay the men, but we all know everything in life isn't fair, don't we?"

Gordon Moon was on his feet with a show of reluctance. "Uh, Your Honor, is this proper? We're picking a jury here. I could tell them all about my weekend golf game, but how would that aid the process?"

"Ms. Wooten," Judge Estrada said, "is there a point to this?"

"Very much so, Your Honor. My strong feelings about victimization of certain segments of our society may have led me to prolong the introductory remarks, but what I have said relates directly to my standards for picking a jury. Mr. Jones," she said, addressing one man in the box, who looked up with a startled expression, "do you watch sports on television?"

"Uh, sometimes, yes."

"If you see two basketball teams take to the court, what determines the winner?"

"Which team scores the most points, I guess."

"Then it's not determined by which team mascot has the cutest suit?"

"No, of course not."

"So if one of the teams had Santa Claus for a mascot, you wouldn't figure that team's gonna win, would you?"

"Is this a sports event?" Jones asked bluntly.

"No, it isn't, but in some ways it's similar. I lead one team, Mr. Moon leads another, the judge up there, she's the ref with the whistle, and you folks, you're the fans in the stands. But whatever you think about the two teams, whether you like the two teams or not, when the game's over and you look at the scoreboard, you'll know which team won, won't you? And if it's not the team you were rooting for, you'll accept that, won't you?"

Judge Estrada said, "Madame District Attorney, forgive me, but I am very near to blowing my whistle. I'm not sure the jurors are getting your metaphor."

"You people all know who Charles Baines is, don't you? And you all know who his brother was. All I'm asking you is this: if you believe from what you see and hear in this courtroom, beyond a reasonable doubt, that Charles Baines murdered his brother, you must be able to say so with one voice regardless of what you think about him or you think about his victim. Can you all do that?"

Vern whispered to Gordon, "Ask them if they'd base their decision on who won the game on the quality of the cheerleaders' legs."

"I don't think so," said Gordon, adding with a wink to Eve, "We'd win that anyway."

By the end of the day Wednesday, a jury had been seated made up of citizens who said they could judge the case fairly and that neither side could find any excuse to object to. Statistics were unremarkable: six male, six female; five Caucasian, three Hispanic, two Asian, two African-American; four retired, eight still in the workforce; ages ranging from twenty-three (a young dental assistant) to seventy-nine (a retired nurse); other occupations including Department of Motor Vehicles manager, advertising account executive, hardware store clerk, plumbing contractor, accountant, construction worker, and school administrator. The two alternates, also split male-female but both Caucasian, were an unemployed laborer and a pre-school teacher. Selection had been prolonged by the determination of both sides to generate holiday warmth.

CHAPTER SEVENTEEN

Wednesday, December 6

It was pure coincidence that the traditional lighting of the city Christmas tree came the night before opening arguments in the Charlie Baines trial. The assembled choirs sang the carols as beautifully as ever, and the lights and ornaments on the towering tree in front of City Hall shined as brightly. Prentice Winstead attended alongside the mayor and other city officials. Alison McCready was there, along with other media celebrities, but the two gave no indication they even knew each other. In one respect, the event was different this year. No Santa Claus was in attendance. The evening's Santa for years had been Charlie Baines, and no one had the heart to ask anyone else.

None of the central actors in the Baines trial attended the tree lighting. The early days of a major trial are always a strain for the opposing advocates, but the tension increases when you're sleeping with the enemy. In the city that night, at least three bedrooms were scenes of lively drama.

Agnes Wagstaff Moon was propped up with a pile of pillows on her side of the Western King Size but still not big enough bed, before her a stack of documents which she periodically muttered over. On his side, Gordon was trying to sleep, but every time he approached the edge of drifting off, Agnes decided she had something to say.

"That was a shabby trick with the telephone book, Gordon."

112

"Agnes, we shouldn't be talking about the case."

"We're not talking about the case. That phone book had nothing to do with the case. Was that Vern's idea by any chance? When he comes up with stuff like that, you really ought to sit on him, Gordon. It lowers your dignity to be pulling stuff like that."

"Never mind whose idea it was. I have to run my case my way, and we should talk about something else. If we have to talk."

"I hope you're keeping Vern away from that sweet young thing you've got in your third chair."

"He's doing a great job of mentoring her."

Agnes snorted. "Mentoring. That's what you call it, huh? And what if my no-good brother tries to take it beyond mentoring?"

"They're adults, Agnes. They don't need a chaperone."

"No? Well, my brother needs more than a chaperone. He needs a keeper. I know your Ms. Nyquist is just too fresh and innocent and perky and cute to be true. I mean, she must have been around the block a few times. She's been to law school, for God's sake. But I know my brother."

"I know him, too. He's a professional. Anyway, I think he's seeing somebody at the moment."

"How do you know that?"

"I don't know how I know. There are signs, that's all."

"You mean he isn't jumping every woman in the office because he's getting what he needs from somebody else?"

"Something like that. Look, Agnes, I've made his role clear to him. He's taken on mentoring Eve because it's something I can't do."

"You'd better not."

"Not because you say I can't, Agnes. Because I'm too busy with everything else connected with the case."

"And without any help. Your co-counsels are too busy mentoring and being mentored to carry any of the load. That's why you hardly see your family."

"We should get some sleep, Agnes."

"I can never sleep the night before trial. You know that."

"So is it your assignment to make sure the lead defense attorney doesn't get any sleep either?"

"There you go again. Lead defense attorney. You have to throw it at me that you're so important and I'm just a second chair. Typical macho competitiveness. The first time you played a game with Waggy—that's your elder son, remember him?—the first time you played a game with him in ages, you had to ruin it, didn't you?"

"How did I ruin it?"

"You had to win. You always have to win, whether it's in court or playing a board game with your children."

"I don't have to win. I have to *try* to win. There's a difference."

"Waggy is a nine-year-old child, Gordon. Couldn't you let him win once in a while?"

"No, I couldn't, because life's not like that. Waggy has to learn to compete, to improve his game until he can beat me. He has to experience losing so he'll appreciate winning. It's preparation for the real world, Agnes." Gordon paused a beat. "When did we play that game?"

"It was last summer, at the mountain place."

"Oh."

"You don't even remember? You should have a look at your children now and then, Gordon. They're beautiful, and they'll be grown up all too soon. You missed Wimmy's first ballet recital. You said you'd be there, but you missed it."

"You were there, were you?"

"No, but Rosita said it was wonderful. Brought tears to her eyes."

"Did she take the video camera?"

"Of course."

"We'll watch the video then. Tell Wimmy how proud we are, make a big fuss about it. After the trial, though."

"After the trial, after the trial. Some trials never end, Gordy. Some trials last a lifetime. Some say life is a trial."

"Agnes, I have to get some sleep."

"So now it's all about you. Before it was *we* have to get some sleep. But now it's you who has to sleep."

"You already said you couldn't. Get up and read a book instead of clucking over those damned court papers. Take a pill. Do whatever you need to do, but let me get some sleep, okay?"

"Well, you're the lead counsel, aren't you? But here it is the night before trial and you can sleep. All the time I've known you, you can sleep anytime, anywhere, Gordon. How I have envied that. The minute I stop talking, you'll be off and snoring."

"I don't believe you."

"You know it's true."

"Let's try a little experiment then. You stop talking, and we'll see if I fall asleep."

"Sure. I'm wasting my time talking to you anyway."

Agnes looked over at her husband. She sometimes thought he lived to torment her. A part of her still loved him, but another part hated everything he stood for. Sure, they'd stayed together for the children, but could they last until the children were grown? And did it really matter if they did or not since Rosita was doing most of the parenting? She returned to the brief she was reading, but when she realized she'd read the same paragraph four times, she turned back to his side of the bed.

"Are you asleep?" she demanded.

Eve and David had come together at her place for the first time so she wouldn't have as far to go to court in the morning. Her tiny city apartment was not as spacious as the big old suburban house he rattled around in, and the feminine surroundings, familiar as they were, made her more self-conscious than ever. Or maybe it was just because it was the eve of trial.

"Was that nice?" David asked.

"David, that was wonderful, glorious. But I feel a little guilty."

"Why?"

"Should I be doing this the night before trial? Shouldn't I be getting some rest or doing some preparation or something?"

"People prepare in different ways."

"But you're the prosecution, David. Maybe we shouldn't see each other until the trial is over."

"I'm not the prosecution, Eve. I'm not involved in this case, except in a sort of supervisory capacity. I won't even be in that courtroom tomorrow."

"That's exactly my point."

"It is? I don't get it."

"You don't have to be in court tomorrow, and I do, and here you are keeping me from getting any rest. It's like I'm being sabotaged."

"Eve, you're the third chair. You probably won't do anything tomorrow but watch."

"I have to be ready to step in if there's an emergency."

"Oh, yeah, I forgot. If Gordon Moon and Vern Wagstaff drop dead on their way to court, the trial has to go on anyway because the strategy is to finish up on Christmas Eve."

"The Friday before. Christmas Eve's a Sunday. But David, we said we wouldn't talk about our cases. We promised each other that."

"Right. Sorry. But my point was, if I wanted to sabotage the trial, I'd be sleeping with Moon or Wagstaff, not you."

"Would you like to sleep with Moon or Wagstaff?" she said,

unable to suppress a giggle.

"No, some things are beyond the call of duty. So how are you getting along with Wagstaff?"

"David, we said we wouldn't talk about the case."

"That's not the case. That's a person involved in the case. He's reputed to be a sort of a loose cannon."

"Loose how?"

"Let me count the ways. Legally, morally, sexually. I'd watch myself with him."

"Vern's misunderstood."

"Misunderstood? He's understood all too well."

"No, really. He's insecure. That's why he puts up that front of cynicism and wisecracking and flirting."

"Flirting, huh?"

"Of course flirting."

"And he flirts with you?"

"He flirts with everybody. Women, I mean."

"And you let him flirt with you?"

"I have to work with him, David. It's nothing serious. A girl gets used to it."

"You have to watch that guy!"

"I tell you he's a pussycat. He's been very nice to me. He's given me a lot of pointers on the law."

"Just so that's all he's giving you pointers on."

"David, you're getting tiresome. Now leave it alone."

"Maybe you were right. Maybe we shouldn't see each other again till the trial's over."

"If that's what you think, I'll go along with you. As long as it's because you want to avoid conflict of interest and not because you're jealous of Vern Wagstaff."

"Jealous? Should I be?"

"Of course not. He's really a nice guy, and surprisingly shy."

★ ★ ★ ★ ★

"Bamwanger! I do love that name. It's made for screwing. Bam, bam, bam, bam, bam, bam!"

"Vicious Vern, spare me and return to your outlaw gang. How could you make me your prisoner? How could you talk dirty to me? How could you draw your gun and fire it at me? I've been very bad, all because of you. Let me go, Vicious Vern, and let me return to virtue."

"Return to virtue? That's no fun. Besides being impossible."

"Let me leave your evil lair, Vicious Vern. But don't let me go just yet. Punish me, Vicious Vern, punish me!"

"Bam, bam, bam, bam, bam, bam!"

"You're evil, Vicious Vern! You're very good but you're very bad. And I'm warning you, Vicious Vern, when I see you in that courtroom, I'll pull out my six-shooter and plug you as sure as look at you. I will. I will. You can kiss me all you want, but I will."

A few moments later, Stacey said, "You ready to go again?"

"Ah, not just yet."

"Would putting in another video help?"

"Yeah, I think it just might."

"How about *The Man Who Shot Liberty Valence* this time?"

CHAPTER EIGHTEEN

Thursday, December 7

At the city's poshest shopping mall, a little girl sitting on Santa's lap, after the usual avaricious conversation and the standard quotient of ho-ho-hoing, pointed to a green ribbon pinned to his bright red suit and inquired, "What's that, Santa?"

"Uh, that's a Charlie Baines ribbon, Cindy."

"What's a Charlie Baines ribbon, Santa?"

"You ask your mommy. She'll know."

In every mall, on every street corner, at every office party, Santa Clauses were united in solidarity with their ribbons in support of Charlie Baines. It was the only outward sign in the city that it was not Christmas as usual.

For even as a light snow began to fall and the voices of carolers filled the city air, there was serious business going on in the old courthouse.

Seated at the defense table in a still nearly empty courtroom, Eve Nyquist asked Vern Wagstaff what she should look for in the opening statements.

"You never know. Melba Wooten is a sly prosecutor whose performance is tailored to the jury. I'm guessing with this group, she'll go very formal and serious, not a lot of the 'girls in the 'hood' manner you might see with a more urban jury. She likes to use sports analogies, which increase in proportion to the number of men on the jury, but with this group she may not do

119

a lot of that."

"And Gordon? What will his opening be like?"

"Kiddo, you are about to see a master at work. We know what he'll say, of course, but how he says it will depend on what Melba does. He tries to get the jury on his side early by being as different from the DA as possible. If she tries to be funny, he'll be dead serious and subtly suggest she's being frivolous about life-and-death matters. But if she's too solemn, he'll crack a joke. If she comes across as uncertain or ill-prepared, which I assure you she won't, he'll be flawless in his delivery but still seem to have some sympathy for his opponent's limitations. If she seems too slick and smooth, he may fumble with his notes and look like an overmatched amateur, get them rooting for him. He always says the jury wants you to seem human, like one of them, not some mysterious all-knowing wizard from another species. Enjoy this morning, Eve. This will be as good as it gets."

In the next twenty minutes, Eve watched the courtroom fill up. With press, with spectators, with the prosecution team. Charlie Baines, with an encouraging smile as if she, not he, were the one on trial, was brought in by uniformed guards. The clerk, the court reporter, the bailiff took their places. The judge came in heralded by the age-old words ("All rise! Oyez, oyez! Court's in session"), then the jury. The formal preliminaries concluded, Judge Estrada nodded to the prosecution table, and the real drama of the trial of Charlie Baines began to unfold before Eve's eager eyes.

Melba Wooten walked over to the jury box, smiled, and looked each juror in the eye individually before she began to speak.

"Good morning, ladies and gentlemen, and thank you for your service to the community, especially at this time of the year when we would all rather be home with our families. In the next few minutes, I'll be telling you what the prosecution expects to prove in this case and a little bit about how we expect to prove it. As the judge has told you, this isn't evidence, but it'll give you a kind of road map to what the evidence will be. I won't take a lot of your time this morning, and I promise I won't use my lawyerly wiles to try to convince you of anything, because I don't have to. The evidence is going to show very clearly that the defendant Charles Nicholas Baines murdered his brother Andrew Baines. It will show why he did it and how he did it.

"First you will hear some testimony about the Baines family and how important they have been to this city over the past century. You will hear how two sons grew to manhood as their father built the Baines Building and expanded the family's influence in the community and the family's fortune. You will hear how, on the death of their father, one son, Andrew Baines, ascended to leadership in a great business empire, while his younger brother, Charles Baines, gravitated to other pursuits, including becoming the city's unofficial Santa Claus. Charles was loved for the good he did, though few in the city really knew him. Andrew did good, too, through employing people and helping to maintain the city's economic health, but he also had to make the kinds of difficult decisions and take the kinds of unpopular positions that caused some people to oppose him, people like union leaders, environmentalists, and historical preservationists. But just as few really know Charles, few in the city really knew Andrew Baines.

"Evidence will show that Charles Baines began to take his Santa Claus role more and more seriously and that his distance from his brother grew. His identification with Christmas began to make him think of Andrew Baines as Scrooge and himself as Nephew Fred, of Andrew as Mr. Potter and himself as George Bailey, of Andrew as the Grinch and himself as, oh I don't

121

know, Cindy Lou Who, maybe." Some of the jurors smiled. "Matters came to a head when Andrew Baines wanted to demolish the old Majestic Theatre on Main Street to put up an office building. Witnesses will tell you Andrew thought the old place was an eyesore, but architectural preservationists and historians thought it a gem. In an extended battle, Charles came down on the side of the preservationists. We will not argue who was right in this conflict, ladies and gentlemen, but merely show you that it was a source of additional tension between the two brothers. Matters became more and more heated last July as the deadline approached for making a final determination about the fate of the Majestic, with accusations of wrongdoing flying on both sides of the controversy. It was on the evening before the deadline that Andrew Baines died.

"Evidence will show that on the night of July twenty-fourth, Andrew Baines was working in his office on the thirtieth floor of the Baines building. This was frequently the case, for Andrew was constantly aware of and involved in every activity of his business empire. Charles Baines, wearing his Santa Claus suit despite the summer heat, entered the building and signed in with the security officer on duty. We will show that Charles Baines, known to the security guard, was neither searched nor asked if he was carrying any weapons, though we will demonstrate that his Santa Claus suit provided ample opportunity to conceal any number of implements of death. You will see security records showing no one else working on the thirtieth floor that night, and in fact no one else in the building at all apart from security and custodial personnel. The security man stationed in the lobby will tell you that Charles Baines took the elevator to the thirtieth floor and returned calmly to the lobby almost an hour later. Showing no trace of sorrow or remorse, he told the security guard something had happened up on the thirtieth floor and that he would be at home if needed, then went home and awaited the inevitable call from the police. Subsequently, members of the building security force found Andrew Baines shot to death on the thirtieth floor. Police witnesses will tell you that Charles Baines reported finding his brother dead when he arrived at the thirtieth floor office but offered no reasonable explanation for the gap in time between finding the body and reporting it, leaving the question of what Charles Baines was doing on the thirtieth floor in all that time. Ladies and gentlemen, the evidence will show that Andrew Baines was alive when his brother confronted him in his office, that they quarreled, that at the height of their quarrel Charles Baines drew out a handgun and shot his brother to death. Evidence will show that the handgun that killed Andrew Baines was subsequently found in Charles Baines's desk. Forensic evidence, including DNA comparison, will be presented to prove that Charles Baines was present in his brother's office for a longer time than the few moments he claims it took to find the body of his brother.

"Ladies and gentlemen of the jury, you will hear a lot about Christmas during this trial, about peace on earth and good will toward men, and my learned opponents will try to show you a saintly Charles Baines at one with the Three Wise Men and a district attorney bent on spoiling everybody's holiday by putting jolly old Saint Nick in the slammer. But this is a more serious business than that and more central to the moral and spiritual core of this city. Cold-blooded murder is no part of the Christmas story, ladies and gentlemen, and we will prove to you that is what Charles Baines committed against his brother and against the people of this state with the full knowledge of what he was doing. If there's coal in your stocking, folks, Charles Baines put it there. That's all for now, and you have as nice a day as you can under the circumstances."

Melba Wooten strolled back to her seat at the prosecution

table and sat down.

"Mr. Moon?" Judge Estrada said.

Gordon Moon looked up, as if from a daydream. "Yes, Your Honor?"

"Do you wish to make an opening statement to the jury?"

"Oh, is it my turn? Yes, certainly." As he fumbled with his papers, a pen fell to the floor and he bent over to retrieve it. His client, Charlie Baines, looked benign and unconcerned. Vern Wagstaff winked at Eve Nyquist.

Gordon Moon walked to stand before the jury box, smiled somewhat shyly, and cleared his throat. "Good morning, ladies and gentlemen, and I join my esteemed sister in law, I mean sister in the law, we're not related, not that it would bother me if we were, you understand. She sure can shoot that three-pointer, can't she?" He smiled sheepishly. "I think I'd better start over, huh? I'm a little nervous. I always get nervous at the start of a trial. My job's kind of important. I mean, important to my client, sure, but important to my fellow citizens. Important to justice." He shuffled his notes a little, appearing flustered. "I join Ms. Wooten in thanking you for accepting one of the privileges of citizenship and helping us all to service justice, that is, to serve the cause of justice, at this difficult time of the year.

"Well, now, Ms. Wooten said she'd be brief and she sure was brief, wasn't she? For me, maybe a little too brief. Like you, I was hoping to hear exactly how she intended to prove my client, Charlie Baines, was guilty of first-degree murder, but she kind of glossed over all that, didn't she? And I'm sure glad she didn't argue." He smiled and shuffled his notes again. "So when I tell you what the evidence will show, I can be brief, too, even briefer than Ms. Wooten. The prosecution has no compelling evidence of Charlie Baines's guilt. He was in the building that night, and he admits it. But when we start looking at the security measures of the Baines Building, we'll see they were porous as a sponge. When we start looking at the image of Andrew Baines in the community, we'll see he had a lot more bitter enemies with a lot better motive to kill him than his brother, who evidence will show is as harmless and benign as he looks. When we start looking at the DNA evidence, we'll find less there than meets the eye. I won't say any more, because I want this trial to be short, just like you do. So I leave you with this: Charlie didn't do it, and when you've heard all the evidence, you'll say so. Again, thank you for your service."

When Gordon resumed his seat at the defense table, Vern leaned over and whispered in his ear, "Nice job, Gordy, but . . . porous as a sponge?"

Gordon shrugged. "We're working on it."

Over lunch, Eve said, "Vern, can Gordon really expect to get this trial finished by Christmas? I mean, the issues are so complicated. How can we go fast without confusing the jurors?"

"I think he can do it," Vern said. "Ever watch *Perry Mason?* Or, if that's before your time, ever watch *L.A. Law* or *Law and Order* or *Boston Legal?*"

"Sure, I've seen all those, including *Perry Mason*. There was a course on them in law school."

"You're kidding, right?"

"No, really, there was this one professor who specialized in law in fiction and film."

"What's this world coming to? Anyway, when you watched those shows, did you ever get confused by the evidence in the courtroom scenes?"

"Well, no, but—"

"Every big trial, including this one, the judge and all the lawyers fall over themselves assuring the jury it's nothing like TV. But if you make it like TV, if you make it fun, you'll have them in your corner. We don't need to drag things out to make our point. If we're keeping it simple and entertaining and the prosecution is slowing it down and making it confusing, the jury will turn against the prosecution. Gordon will present our case as fast as he can with one exception: irrelevant testimony is okay if it doesn't hurt the defense and if it's entertaining. Comic relief is good, and Gordon will know just how to provide it. Eve, you're seeing a master at work."

CHAPTER NINETEEN

Friday, December 8
The first afternoon's witnesses having been devoted to Baines's family background as Melba Wooten had promised, her first witness the next day addressed the crime itself. He was a small, pale man in a cheap gray suit who looked unaccustomed to being out in the daytime.

"State your name for the record."

"Arthur Griswold. Uh, they call me Artie."

"And what is your occupation, Mr. Griswold?"

"I'm a night security man in the Baines Building."

"And were you on the job the evening of July twenty-fourth of this year?"

"Uh, yeah, I was on the job."

"And did anything unusual occur on that evening?"

"Well, yeah. I mean I found the boss dead, is all. I guess that's unusual."

"You're referring to Andrew Baines?"

"That's right."

"And where did you find him?"

"In his office, on the thirtieth floor, sitting in his chair."

"Was it normally part of your duties to check Andrew Baines's office."

"No. Well, I mean, yes, it was, sure, ordinarily, but not when I knew he was in there. I mean, I wouldn't disturb him if he was in there, but if he wasn't in there, I wouldn't disturb him."

"How did you happen to check Andrew Baines's office that night?"

"I got this call on my cell phone from Wilbur Ricketts down in the lobby, and he told me—"

"There's no need to tell us what he said, Mr. Griswold. Just tell us what you did as a result of what he said."

"I went and checked Mr. Baines's office is what I did, so I suppose you can guess what he said."

"There's no need to guess, Mr. Griswold, but you must testify only what you know of your own knowledge."

"All I know is what I know of my own knowledge. I mean I don't know nothing of nobody else's knowledge, now do I? But I do know what he said."

"That's fine. Now, what was the condition of Mr. Baines when you checked his office?"

"His condition was dead was what his condition was."

"How did you know that?"

"Well now, let me see. Maybe it was the amount of blood all over the front of his shirt and all over his desk and the way his eyes were wide open and staring at me."

"Did you enter the office?"

"No, I sure did not, and I didn't touch anything either."

"Were the lights on in the office?"

"Yeah, on full. I could see better than I wanted to."

"Did you observe anything unusual on the desk?"

"Other than the blood you mean?"

"Other than the blood, yes."

"There was a false beard lying there. White beard. Looked like a Santa Claus beard. Had blood all over it."

"Anything else?"

"No."

"What did you do next?"

"I called down to Wilbur to tell him what I found and I called nine-one-one on my cell."

"No further questions."

When Melba returned to the prosecution table, Agnes whispered to her, "Why did you let him get away with all those smart-ass responses?"

"His testimony's not that important," she whispered back. "We have to pick our battles."

Gordon Moon got up to cross-examine.

"Mr. Griswold, how's the security in the Baines Building?"

"It's great. I mean, it's okay."

"Well, which is it, great or okay?"

"It's very well organized. It's systematic. We do our jobs. Well."

"Did you see anyone on the thirtieth floor when you were checking Andrew Baines's office?"

"No, I mean, if I had, I'd have detained 'em, is what I would've done."

"No custodial staff?"

"Oh, there might have been in some of the other offices."

"But you're not sure? You didn't check?"

"I might have checked. I don't remember. I usually check."

"But you're not sure you checked that night?"

"The nights all run together."

"Including nights you find the boss dead in his office?"

Griswold turned to the bench with an aggrieved expression. "Judge, do I have to answer sarcastic questions?"

"If there is no objection from counsel, you have to answer the questions you are asked, Mr. Griswold," said Judge Estrada. "And given the number of sarcastic answers you've given, I'm surprised you object to sarcastic questions. Would you repeat your last question, Mr. Moon?"

"I'll withdraw it. No more questions." Gordon Moon sat down.

"Ms. Wooten, any redirect?" the judge asked.

"No, Your Honor. We call Richard Tracy to the stand."

The investigating cop got up from the prosecution table, strode to the witness stand, and took the oath. Melba had cautioned the quick-tempered Tracy to be very precise in his direct testimony and keep his cool on cross-examination. She was confident he'd be able to follow the first advice, not so much the second.

"State your name and occupation for the record."

"Richard Tracy, Detective First Grade, city police, ma'am."

"Were you on duty the evening of July twenty-fourth of this year?"

"Yes, ma'am, my partner Detective Joseph Freedy and I were catching homicide calls at the Fifth Precinct station house."

"And could you explain to the jury exactly what is involved in catching homicide calls, Detective?"

Detective Tracy cleared his throat and straightened up in the witness chair. "I can indeed, ma'am, and my apologies to the court and to you and to the jury for any inadvertent deployment of arcane or unfamiliar law enforcement jargon. I shall henceforth attempt to be as clear and jargon-free in my testimony as humanly possible, ma'am." He turned to the jury. "Catching homicide calls refers to the common police practice of placing detectives in a state of readiness in their office environment in order to facilitate their prompt, expeditious, and maximally effective response to any reports from the public of citizen deaths of an apparent unnatural or suspicious nature."

"And did you receive such a call on the evening of July twenty-fourth of this year?"

"No, ma'am."

"No?" Melba Wooten's surprise appeared feigned.

"It was after midnight, so it was technically the morning of July twenty-fifth. Details that may seem insignificant are most important in police work."

"I'm sure all the citizens of this city applaud your attention to detail, Detective. What did you do as a result of the call received early on the morning of July twenty-fifth?"

"Pursuant to a call from the private security forces at the Baines Building reporting the discovery of a deceased member of the public in suspicious circumstances, we proceeded in our unmarked police vehicle to the Baines Building. Upon being briefed by the private security operative occupying the first-stage security point in the lobby of said building, we proceeded to the thirtieth floor of said building by means of the elevator. Upon our arrival on said floor, we proceeded to the office of Mr. Andrew Baines, who proved to be the decedent. We observed Mr. Baines sitting at his office desk, facing the doorway."

"What did you do then, Detective?"

"We then sealed off the entire thirtieth floor pursuant to and in preparation for the advent of the criminalist team that would be charged with collecting and identifying evidence at the scene, which might have pertinence to the events effecting the decedent's decease and lead to identification and apprehension of the suspect or suspects."

"Was there anything on the desk that you believed might potentially assist you in identifying that person or those persons?"

"Yes, ma'am, there was. A white false beard heavily stained with what appeared, based on visual and olfactory evidence, to be blood. There was also a wadded-up tissue on the desk which would also be bagged by the scene of crimes team and sent for analysis."

"What other actions did you take?"

"Pursuant to our discussion with Mr. Ricketts, the private security operative stationed in the lobby, we concluded that the decedent's brother, Mr. Charles Baines, had visited him that evening. Acting on such information, my partner, Detective Freedy, obtained a search warrant by telephone and fax from your colleague Judge Fuchs, pursuant to which we proceeded to search the office of Mr. Charles Baines, located on the same floor as the office of Mr. Andrew Baines. In the course of said search, a .38-calibre Colt Super handgun was found in the drawer of Mr. Charles Baines's desk. This, too, was bagged as evidence."

"Did you subsequently check the registration of this gun, Detective?"

"We did."

"And had it been duly registered?"

"It had been registered to a Mrs. Clarabelle Algonquin, a widow whose domicile out in East Westport had been burglarized six months previous. In the course of said burglary, the handgun was reportedly stolen. Despite the best investigative efforts of our colleagues in the East Westport Police Department, the suspect in that burglary was never apprehended."

"Was it your impression, Detective Tracy, that Charles Baines had fled the scene of the crime on the evening of July twenty-fourth?"

"Objection," said Moon. "Leading."

"Withdrawn, Your Honor. Detective, according to your questioning of those in the building, who did you conclude had first discovered the body of Andrew Baines?"

"Charles Baines, ma'am."

"And was Charles Baines on the scene when you arrived at the Baines Building?"

"No, ma'am, he was not."

"Detective, I have no more questions for now. Your Honor, we would reserve the right to recall the detective later in our case in chief."

"Noted, counselor. I guess he'll be here. You may cross-examine, Mr. Moon."

"Good afternoon, Detective Tracy," Gordon Moon said.

"Good afternoon, counselor," the detective said coolly.

"What did you say your partner's name was?"

"Detective Freedy."

"And what's his first name?"

"Joseph."

"Joe Friday?"

"No, counselor. Joseph Freedy."

"Dick Tracy and Joe Friday? Partners?"

"It's Richard Tracy and Joseph Freedy."

Melba Wooten was on her feet. "Your Honor, I object to counsel ridiculing the witness."

"I'm not ridiculing the witness," Moon said innocently. "I'm merely trying to make sure I have his name and that of his partner straight, and to note the amusing coincidence that he and his partner share their names with two famed paragons of law enforcement."

"There's no coincidence," the witness insisted. "We're Richard Tracy and Joseph Freedy."

"Get off this, Mr. Moon," the judge said wearily. Turning to the jury, she added, "I would direct you to disregard this byplay, ladies and gentlemen, except that there's really nothing there to disregard. You may or may not have found the exchange you've just heard amusing, but it has nothing to do with the case. And I'm sure counsel for the defense is merely trying to lighten the mood of an inevitably somber occasion and is not expressing any contempt for the witness or for this court." With the last words, she stared daggers at Moon, the unspoken threat eloquently conveyed. "Now proceed, Mr. Moon."

"Thank you, Your Honor," Gordon Moon said, following the time-honored custom of lawyers to gratefully receive a rebuke from the bench. He looked back at the witness who, just as he'd hoped, was quietly fuming. "Detective, when you and your partner, to use your expression, catch a homicide, what is your ultimate goal?"

Tracy looked suspicious. "What do you mean?"

"It's a simple question. What is it you're trying to do?"

"Catch the suspect, bring him in."

"Catch a homicide, then catch a suspect. Yes, I see. Detective, when you searched Charles Baines's office, did you find anything of interest in his closet?"

Melba was on her feet. "Objection, Your Honor. The question is too vague. How is the witness expected to know what Mr. Moon considers to be of interest?"

Gordon shrugged. "Closets aren't that big, and some things stand out, but I'll rephrase the question. Did you find several Santa Claus suits hanging in Mr. Baines's closet?"

"Yes, we did find several Santa Claus suits, yes."

"Several pairs of red trousers, several red jackets?"

"Yes."

"Several pairs of black boots?"

"One pair, I think."

"Several red stocking caps with white pom-poms on the end."

"A couple of those, yes."

"Several false beards?"

"A couple maybe. I didn't count them."

"Detective, did you subsequently visit Mr. Charles Baines that evening?"

"We visited the defendant that evening, yes."

"Did you proceed there in your vehicle?"

"Yes, we proceeded there in our vehicle. We didn't walk."

"Pursuant to your visit as result of proceeding there in your vehicle, did Mr. Baines proceed to in any way impede the forward progress of your investigation?"

"No, he didn't."

"Did he proceed to evade your questioning by proceeding in his own vehicle away from his domicile?"

"No, he didn't."

"When you proceeded by means of your plainclothes footwear to the door of subject Baines's personal domicile, did you proceed to ring the doorbell?"

"Yeah, we—Your Honor, can you make him stop doing that?"

"Stop doing what, Detective?" Moon asked.

"You know damn well what."

The whack of Judge Estrada's gavel got their attention. "Mr. Moon, the witness asked me a question, and you will please refrain from further speech until I proceed—until I answer it! And you, Detective Tracy, will do the same. Detective, there has been no objection from the prosecution to the form of Mr. Moon's questions. I simply note that as a fact. Do not take it as a statement of whether objection would be appropriate. All I can say is this: both of you are professionals; both of you have previous experience in courtrooms; and I expect both of you to proceed—that is, to conduct yourselves in a professional manner and get on with this examination without playing silly games with each other. Now get on with it before I lose patience with you both."

"Thank you, Your Honor," Gordon said. "Detective, did Charles Baines flee?"

"No, the suspect did not flee."

"Was he reluctant to welcome you into his home?"

"Well, he wasn't happy."

"His brother being dead, I wouldn't expect him to be happy, would you?"

"I don't know, counselor. I guess that depends on how he felt about his brother, doesn't it?"

"Did Mr. Baines offer any resistance to your entering his

home to question him?"

"No, he didn't."

"Did he offer you any hospitality?"

"He let us in. I told you."

"Forgive me, Detective, I see I haven't been specific enough. Did he invite you to sit down?"

"Yes, we sat down."

"Did he offer you any sustenance? Anything to eat or drink?"

"We don't drink on duty, Mr. Moon."

"Oh, do I take it then that he offered you alcoholic beverages?"

"Uh, no, he didn't."

"Did he seem unaware of the inappropriateness of such an offer?"

"No."

"Did he in fact apologize for not being able to offer you alcoholic beverages, since you were on duty?"

"He might have."

"And are police officers allowed to drink non-alcoholic beverages while on duty?"

"Yes, sure."

"What, if you recall, did Mr. Baines offer you?"

"Uh, tea, I believe. Or coffee."

"Anything else?"

"Uh, cookies. Christmas cookies. I think they must have been frozen."

"I see. And did you accept them?"

"Uh, yeah, I think we did."

"Were they good?"

"Sure, I guess so. We were hungry."

"When you questioned Mr. Baines, was he cooperative?"

"He didn't tell us he did it."

"He didn't confess?"

"No, the suspect didn't confess."

"Is the lack of a confession necessarily an indication of an uncooperative attitude?"

"It would have helped if the suspect had confessed."

"Oh, undoubtedly. But could it be, Detective Tracy, the suspect didn't confess because the suspect didn't do it?"

"Objection, Your Honor," Melba Wooten said. "Calls for a conclusion."

"And who else should make such a conclusion than a police detective experienced in homicide investigation?"

"Objection overruled. You may answer, Detective."

"What was the question?"

"I'll withdraw it," Gordon Moon said. "Did you arrest Charles Baines that night?"

"No, we did not."

"Was Charles Baines a suspect in the burglary of Mrs. Clarabelle Algonquin's East Westport domicile?"

"I don't know."

"Don't know if he did it or don't know if he was a suspect?"

"What's the difference?"

"Did you receive the impression that the East Westport police regarded Charles Baines as a suspect in the burglary of Widow Algonquin?"

"Not to my knowledge, no."

"No more questions, Dick."

"My name's not Dick!"

"Sorry, Detective. Sorry, Your Honor. Slip of the tongue."

CHAPTER TWENTY

Wilbur Ricketts took the stand for the prosecution that afternoon. Melba took him through the events of the evening Andrew Baines died. In doing so, she sought to do what she had failed to do with his colleague Artie Griswold: preemptively reply to a possible defense ploy.

"Mr. Ricketts, around this time of year, we see quite a few people dressed as Santa Claus, don't we, on street corners and so forth and in department stores?"

"Uh, yes, ma'am, we sure do."

"Do you find it's sometimes hard to tell them apart?"

"This time of year, yes, ma'am, they all sort of blend together."

"When Mr. Baines entered the lobby that night, he was wearing a white beard that covered most of his face, was he not?"

"Yes, ma'am."

"Then how can you be certain it was him and not someone else in a Santa Claus suit?"

Ricketts looked mournful, as if he saw an opportunity to help Charlie Baines but couldn't in all good conscience take it. "Well, he talked to me, ma'am. He asked about my wife and made little jokes."

"You'd spoken to the defendant many times before?"

"Many times, yes, ma'am."

"So there was no question in your mind that this was in fact Charles Baines who entered the lobby that night and no one else dressed in a Santa Claus suit in July?"

"No, ma'am," Wilbur Ricketts said sadly, "it was Charlie Baines, all right."

"And when the Santa Claus figure returned to the lobby, after the murder of his brother—"

"Objection, Your Honor," said Gordon Moon. "Prejudicial, argumentative, assumes facts not in evidence."

"Sustained."

"When the Santa Claus figure returned to the lobby some time later, did you again have a conversation with him?"

"Yes, I did."

"And is there any doubt in your mind that this was still Charles Baines, that he hadn't handed off the Santa Claus suit to somebody else or that some other Santa Claus wasn't skulking around the Baines Building that night?"

"I don't know about that, ma'am."

"Sorry? You don't know about what?"

"If some other Santa Claus was in the building that night. I don't know."

"But you didn't see another Santa Claus, did you?"

"No, ma'am, but I still couldn't say that there was or wasn't another Santa Claus. For all I know, there very well could have been." Wilbur had turned cheerful, seeing a chance to help the defense, smiling over toward Charlie Baines, who beamed back from the defense table.

"Mr. Ricketts, in that whole month of July, how many other Santa Clauses did you see in the Baines Building lobby? I mean, did you keep a count, like a birdwatcher?"

"Objection, Your Honor," said Gordon Moon. "Counsel appears to be arguing with, indeed ridiculing, her own witness."

"I'll withdraw the question. Mr. Ricketts, what I asked you was, is there any doubt in your mind that the Santa Claus who returned to the lobby was the same Santa Claus who entered the lobby initially, that is, the defendant, Charles Baines?"

"No, but—"

"That answers the question. And what did the defendant say to you when he returned to the lobby?"

"He said he thought his brother had an enemy and that the police might want to talk to him and if they did, he'd be at home."

"Did he tell you his brother had been murdered?"

"Not directly, no, ma'am, but he said something bad had happened up on thirty."

"You have testified that Charles Baines was recorded as having entered the lobby at eleven forty-two p.m. on July twenty-fourth and that he returned to the lobby at 12:33 a.m. on July twenty-fifth, is that correct?"

"Yes, ma'am."

"Did Charles Baines give you any account of what he had been doing in that time?"

"No, ma'am."

"Did you ask him?"

"No reason to."

"Did he suggest you call an ambulance or paramedics?"

"No, ma'am."

"Whom did you call?"

"I called the police."

"After the defendant had left the building?"

"Yes, ma'am."

"You made no attempt to prevent him from leaving the building?"

"No, ma'am. Why would I do that?"

"No more questions. Your witness, Mr. Moon."

"Mr. Ricketts, good morning. When Charlie Baines returned to the lobby that night, did he appear to you unusually agitated?"

"No, sir. He was a little less lively than usual maybe, but I wouldn't say agitated."

"Did he say he had killed his brother?"

"No, he sure didn't. He said his brother had an enemy, but he didn't say the enemy was him. And we all knew Andrew Baines had plenty of enemies."

"Objection," Melba said. "Your Honor, please instruct the witness to confine himself to answering the question that has been asked."

"The jury will disregard the last part of the witness's statement," Judge Estrada said. "Mr. Ricketts, don't tell us things you believe to be true but only those things you know for a fact, and confine yourself to answering the question asked."

"Sure, Your Honor," Wilbur said, but he looked unrepentant.

Gordon went on, "After the defendant said his brother had an enemy, did he suggest you call the police?"

"Well, sort of. He sure knew the police would be called and would want to talk to him."

"Mr. Ricketts, you've testified that Charlie Baines was still wearing his Santa Claus beard when he returned to the lobby, is that correct?"

"Yes, he sure was."

"So I guess he didn't lose his beard in the act of murdering his brother?"

"Objection. Calls for speculation."

"Sustained."

"Thank you, Mr. Ricketts. No more questions."

CHAPTER TWENTY-ONE

At the end of the day, marking the end of the trial's first week, Eve told herself she wanted nothing more than to return to her apartment and enjoy a respite from the demands of the case. Standing on the courthouse steps, shivering in the late-afternoon chill, she saw how the snow, so pretty and white when it had first fallen, had been plowed to the edges of Victory Street and had turned a dirty gray, symbolic of her mood. And when she thought about her apartment, so cheery in its furnishings and decorations, she was distressed to find the prospect no more inspiring. It had become a lonely place without David.

They had got past their minor tiff the night before the trial began, but David insisted on more and more discretion about their relationship, at least until the trial was over. Not only could they not be seen together, they could not get together in private if it would cause either of them to become conspicuous by their absence in some other expected venue.

This Friday night, for example, David had a Christmas party to go to—there were a bunch of them this time of year, Santa Claus on trial or not: prosecution parties, defense bar parties, corporate bar parties, probate bar parties, the annual Ambulance Chasers' Holiday-in-Drag Revue (always fun but hard to score an invitation to), all culminating in Prentice Winstead's huge party for virtually every lawyer in the city. She and David would both be in attendance at that one but would have to pretend they barely knew each other.

When David did come to her apartment, he insisted on an elaborate ritual to make sure no one saw them together. As far as the doorman of her building knew, David was a friend of a guy who lived on her floor, an elderly collector of baseball cards and beer bottles who was willing to serve as a decoy.

Vern interrupted her reverie. "I know you're an ice maiden, but if you stand there much longer, you'll freeze to death."

She managed a smile. "You're right. I'll go home and brood in comfort."

"Or you could join me at Rumpole's for a drink, commemorating the end of our first week of trial. I'll keep it dignified and professional all the way."

"No, really, I—" She stopped herself. She was determined to soak up every bit of legal know-how she could from her attentive mentor, and she was gradually getting used to him. She was well aware she had contributed nothing of any significance so far to the defense of Charlie Baines, but she wanted to be ready if and when. "All right," she said. "Sure. Why not?"

She had begun to find Rumpole's quite pleasant. It was high-class as barrooms went, and the holiday display of wreaths, bells, a package-laden Christmas tree, stockings hung on the fireplace, mistletoe, and other symbols of the season made it uncommonly cheerful and cozy. Just inside the front door were framed photographs of John Mortimer and Leo McKern, both autographed to someone named Marty, who was clearly a Rumpole buff but otherwise unidentified. The house wines were listed by such names as Pommeroy's Plonk, Chateau Fleet Street, and Chateau Thames Embankment, and married men who frequented the place often offered grave toasts to "She Who Must Be Obeyed."

This particular evening would prove memorable for her first meeting with one of Rumpole's most celebrated habitués. She recognized Duffy O'Gonigal and was predisposed to like him from his appearance with David on that embarrassing television show she had suffered through. He waved to Vern and came strolling over.

"Young Vernon, compliments of the season to you, lad!" he said. "And who pray tell is your lovely companion?"

Vern grinned at her. "Not my companion, alas, my colleague. Eve Nyquist, meet Duffy O'Gonigal, one of the great lawyers of this city."

"Aye and a legend in his own mind!" Duffy said. "So, if this is a professional association, if I insert myself, three will be less of a crowd than ordinarily, or am I wrong?"

"You're perfectly right, Mr. O'Gonigal," Eve said. "Do please join us."

"What are you drinking, Duffy?" Vern said.

"Ah, my lad, on that I am very particular. I refuse to drink anything that isn't set before me. Preferably in a glass, but a bottle will do. However, this round is on me. So what are *you* drinking?"

"Draft Hefeweisen for me, and Eve's chosen tipple is tonic water on the rocks."

"Oh, dear lady! Can't I tempt you with something more festive?"

"She only likes drinks with little umbrellas in them."

"That's right," Eve said. "And when the bartender said he couldn't find any little umbrellas, I decided to stick to tonic water."

Duffy winked at Vern and strolled over to the bar, where he briefly conferred with Phil Etchebarren. Then he returned to his seat at their table.

"Now, I won't ask you young people to talk about the trial in which you are assisting my favorite protégé Gordon Moon. No, I won't ask you at all." Pause. "But tell me, how's it going?"

"Well enough, I think," Vern said.

"You know, kids, I sometimes think the law is a huge Antarctic ice flow, and the lawyer is an Emperor Penguin who must walk for miles and miles to get where he wants to go. He must be patient. He can't hurry. Sometimes he can slide along on his tummy, but mostly he must trudge and trudge and keep on trudging till he gets where he's going. You people have a long way to go to the end of this trial, and I hope you're not rushing things because you want it done by Christmas."

Vern shrugged. "The prosecution seems to be cooperating. They're moving things right along."

"Beware of prosecutors bearing gifts. Charlie Baines deserves the best defense possible. I don't want anything to be forgotten."

Phil Etchebarren came to their table at that point, placing a large glass of bourbon and a beer chaser in front of Duffy, a pint glass of beer with a slice of lemon floating in it in front of Vern, and a tall glass of something-or-other with an umbrella sticking out of it in front of Eve.

Looking at the bartender in good-humored accusation, Eve said, "I see you got in some umbrellas."

"Anything for an esteemed member of the bar," Phil said.

"What is in this concoction exactly?"

"Drink some and see if you like it first."

She took a sip. "It's great. Can't have much alcohol content, can it?"

"No." Phil disappeared before he could be asked for a further recipe.

Vern Wagstaff said, "I have the feeling you'd like to get back in the game, Duffy."

Duffy O'Gonigal shook his head with a sad smile. "No, lad, my time is past."

"Gordon always speaks highly of you," Eve said. "He'd probably welcome your help."

"No, alas, Gordon has a drinking problem." Enjoying her surprised look, he clarified, "By which I mean he has a problem with my drinking. He has this odd idea an advocate needs to be sober."

Eve took another sip of her drink. "Then remind me not to have one of these for lunch. It is good, though."

Eve surprised herself by still being in the bar, more accurately at the bar, when her two companions and most of the rest of the evening crowd had already left.

"Are you okay, Eve?" Phil asked her.

"Sure," she said, half truthfully. "I'm just not used to drinking this much, that's all. I shouldn't be doing this. I have to be in court tomorrow."

"I have a good recipe for a hangover remedy," he offered. "Just in case." He peeled it off a pad under the bar and handed it across to her.

"Thanks." She took it gratefully and stuck it in her purse.

"Should I toss the rest of the little umbrellas or save them for another night?"

"I'll let you know, okay? Can't decide tonight. Phil, do a girl two more favors, will you?"

"Sure."

"Number one, make me some coffee. Black. Strong."

"Easy."

"Number two, and I wouldn't have the nerve to ask this if I were completely sober, how did you get disbarred?"

"That is a long and fairly tedious story, but I'll give you the short version. I was representing a local small businessman, an independent druggist, and you can imagine how few of those there are around. The late Andrew Baines wanted his building, for much the same kind of development deal that made him go after the Majestic Theatre. A guy brought a slip-and-fall personal injury suit against the druggist, a nuisance suit without merit and, I've always thought, engineered by Baines. The case was going against the plaintiff, but I suddenly found myself accused of trying to bribe a juror. No reason I would do that when I was winning, but the guy was convincing enough to lose me my license. I've always figured Baines was behind that juror, but I was never able to prove it." He shrugged. "So, you see, I am yet another citizen of our fair city who has no reason to mourn the late Andrew Baines."

Eve shook her head sympathetically. "Have you tried to get reinstated?"

"Not lately. I kind of like what I'm doing here. Now that Baines is dead, I may give it another try." He smiled. "Unless somebody realizes I had a motive for killing Baines and tries to frame me for that, too."

"Sad, sad story," Eve said. "One other question. Who is Marty?"

"Marty?"

"The guy those pictures are autographed to. Does he own the place or what?"

"He did." Phil poured her a cup of coffee. "Careful, it's hot."

"Thanks. So this Marty sold Rumpole's but left his pictures behind?"

"That was a requirement of the deal. The pictures are part of the ambience."

"Did he ever get permission from John Mortimer to call this place Rumpole's?"

"No idea."

"And has the new owner got permission?"

"No. But I don't think Mortimer would mind, do you?"

"Hard to say. Who does own this place anyway?"

Phil winked. "The boss."

"Right, and does he have a name?"

"I still call him Marty sometimes, 'cause it goes with the photos. He's the guy I blame when anybody says they don't like anything. Everybody just accepts it. Never ask to talk to him or anything. So far anyway."

Eve looked at Phil accusingly. "You own the place yourself, don't you?"

"The boss owns the place," Phil said, winking again. "But it's easier to talk to the boss than people think."

Chapter Twenty-Two

Monday, December 11

On her way to court on Monday morning, Eve switched on her car radio, hoping to hear some uplifting holiday music. Instead, she got that irritating morning DJ trying to select the worst Christmas song. "And that's seven more votes for 'All I Want for Christmas is My Two Front Teeth,' which is really moving up the charts. Now please note that the judges have officially disqualified 'Grandma Got Run Over by a Reindeer' on the grounds of insincerity. We want songs that are unintentionally offensive, not satires that are offensive by design. Now, for your consideration, let's hear that dreadful old favorite 'I Saw Mommy Kissing Santa Claus'!" She was relieved to reach the courthouse.

The second week of the People versus Charles Nicholas Baines began with the direct testimony of the medical examiner. Dr. Frederic Worthington was crisp and efficient. Yes, he had personally performed the autopsy on the decedent, Andrew Baines. He opined that death was caused by a .38-calibre bullet, which had entered Andrew Baines's body through the chest, piercing the bottom left quadrant of his heart, and had been stopped and misshapen by collision with a vertebra. The slug had remained lodged in the body and had been found, removed, and bagged as evidence during the autopsy. Dr. Worthington reported that Baines had apparently been in good health, with no gross abnormalities, and if he had not been shot would have lived for many more years. Direct examination was brief, and on the face of it, no more than perfunctory cross-examination seemed to be indicated, but the defense knew something that had not come out on direct.

"Why didn't they bring it up themselves?" Eve whispered to Vern. "Wouldn't it be less damaging that way?"

Vern shrugged. "Maybe they don't know we know. It sure wasn't covered in the documents they gave us on discovery. Watch this. It's going to be fun."

"You may cross-examine, Mr. Moon," Judge Estrada said.

Gordon Moon gave a friendly nod to the witness. "Good morning, Dr. Worthington. And thank you for giving up your golf game to be with us this morning."

Worthington smiled amiably and nodded, but Melba Wooten shot angrily to her feet. "Objection, Your Honor. Dr. Worthington's schedule is not relevant to his testimony in this case. His alleged golf game is not in evidence, and Mr. Moon's reference to said golf game is prejudicial."

Judge Estrada turned to Gordon. "Mr. Moon?"

"I don't see why it's prejudicial, Your Honor. The game of golf appeals to many of our finest citizens. Many professionals take off and play golf on a weekday morning. Even a Monday morning, extending the weekend. No different from a pick-up basketball game on city time, is it?"

"Your Honor, this is outrageous!" Melba Wooten said.

Judge Estrada turned to the witness. "Dr. Worthington, did you in fact cancel a golf game to be with us this morning?"

"Well, yes, Your Honor, I did, but a medical examiner's hours have to be flexible. We don't always work a nine-to-five schedule."

"Nor do judges, Doctor, nor I would venture do prosecutors or defense attorneys, but I see all categories on the golf course. Thank you for joining us this morning." She turned to the jury.

"Ladies and gentlemen, Dr. Worthington's schedule and when he plays golf are not relevant to this trial and won't be mentioned again. Will they, Mr. Moon?"

"No, Your Honor."

"Please proceed."

"Certainly. Dr. Worthington, how long have you been the medical examiner of this city?"

"Ah, it's nearly seven months now."

"And who was your predecessor in that role?"

"Dr. Yamamoto."

"And who preceded him?"

"Uh, I believe it was Dr. Chang."

"And who is your chief deputy medical examiner?"

"Dr. Nguyen."

"Dr. Worthington, how is the medical examiner of this city selected?"

"He or, ah, she is appointed by the mayor with the advice and consent of the city counsel."

"So you were appointed by Mayor Ginzberg?"

"That is correct."

"Is Mayor Ginzberg a friend of yours, Dr. Worthington?"

"We've, ah, known each other for a number of years. Casually. Socially. I wouldn't say we were close friends."

"So it wasn't the mayor you were scheduled to play golf with this morning?"

Melba Wooten was on her feet. "Your Honor, I object to this line of questioning as irrelevant, and I believe you ruled Dr. Worthington's golf game a closed matter."

"I know what I ruled. Counsel will come to the sidebar please."

All the lawyers came to the sidebar, and Judge Estrada leaned in their direction. "All right, Ms. Wooten, say your piece. But not loud enough for the jury to hear."

"He's playing the race card, Your Honor," Melba Wooten said in a clenched-teeth whisper. "In every movie and every TV show for as long as I can remember, coroners and medical examiners are stereotyped as being of Asian ancestry. He's taking advantage of the jury's expectations that people who do autopsies are supposed to be Asians, and he's trying to imply that Dr. Worthington as a white male is somehow unqualified for the job."

"Did I mention race?" Gordon Moon said innocently.

"Next he'll be bringing up the discrimination suit Dr. Nguyen brought against the city when she was passed over, a matter, I might add, that is still under review."

"Then it was Dr. Nguyen who played the race card?" Gordon said.

"It wasn't the race card. It was the gender card."

"Actually," said the judge, "I believe she played both cards, but we're not playing cards in this courtroom. Mr. Moon, if you wish to impugn Dr. Worthington's qualifications, you are entitled to do so, but I advise you to leave the mayor, the mayor's golf game, and the appropriate racial makeup for pathologists out of it. Is that clear?"

"Certainly, Your Honor."

The sidebar ended and Moon returned to the witness. "Dr. Worthington, do you keep a reference library in your office?"

"Uh, yes, I do keep a few books there that I refer to in the course of my work."

Moon walked to the defense table and picked up a paperback volume. He handed it to the witness.

"Is this one of the books you have in your collection?"

"Well, uh, yes it is."

"Please tell the jury the name of that book."

"It's called *Autopsies for Dummies,*" he said. "But you have to understand—"

"And do you also have a book with the title *The Complete Idiot's Guide to Forensic Pathology?*"

"Yes, as it happens I do. But these are quite sound and useful references. They aren't really for idiots or dummies. Those are just selling titles. They are really quite well done."

"Dr. Worthington, where did you graduate from medical school?"

"I am proud to be an alumnus of our state university campus right here in the city." He smiled. "Go, Hedgehogs!"

"Indeed. And where exactly did you rank in your graduating class?"

"Mr. Moon, forgive me, but in medical training, class rank is not an important factor. Graduates either meet the very high and extremely rigorous standards required for the practice of medicine or they do not. I met those standards."

"Then am I to understand the state university medical school does not have class rankings?"

"That's not what I said. What I meant to say—"

"I think we understood what you meant to say."

Melba Wooten was on her feet again. "Your Honor, I object to counsel interrupting the witness. I ask that counsel be directed to permit the witness to complete his answer."

"And I," Moon countered, whirling on his opponent, "ask that the witness be directed to answer the question I asked. When the witness is evading answering a question, I reserve the right to interrupt him."

The judge turned to the witness. "Please answer the questions you are asked, Dr. Worthington. Or if you don't know the answer, you may say so. Proceed, Mr. Moon."

"Dr. Worthington, how many students were in your medical school graduating class?"

"I don't know the exact number. Around a hundred."

"And where did you rank in the class?"

Jon L. Breen

"I don't remember. It was a matter of no importance to me since I met the standard successfully."

Moon picked up a document from the defense table. "Perhaps this will refresh the witness's memory—"

"Ninety-eighth!" Worthington snapped.

"Then you do remember?"

"It just came to me."

"In your role as medical examiner, Dr. Worthington, how many autopsies have you performed?"

"Oh, quite a few. I don't know the exact number."

"A hundred?"

"Not that many."

"Fifty?"

"Not that many."

"More than ten?"

"I'm not certain."

"Again, I may refresh your memory. Records from your office indicate that the autopsy on Andrew Baines was only the fifth autopsy you performed personally."

"That's possible. If you say so."

"Why so few?"

"The office of medical examiner is largely administrative and supervisory. I have a large staff of very capable pathologists who perform most of the autopsies."

"And why did it fall on you to perform this one?"

"It was considered particularly important. Andrew Baines was an important man in the city. I believed it was not an autopsy I could in good conscience trust to a subordinate."

"Why? Because of your greater experience?"

"I felt it was my duty as the head man, er, person."

"So it wasn't because Dr. Nguyen called in sick that day and there was pressure on your office to get the job done?"

"Certainly not."

"Did Dr. Nguyen in fact call in sick that day?"

"Possibly. I don't recall."

"Dr. Worthington, how many of those four previous autopsies involved gunshot wounds?"

"I think one other."

"And in that other case, did you remove the bullet from the body as you did in the case of Andrew Baines?"

"No, I believe in that other case the bullet had passed through the body."

"Did you observe proper procedure in the handling of that recovered bullet, Dr. Worthington?"

"Certainly. I knew where it was at all times."

"You knew where it was? You mean you didn't immediately bag it and identify it to be turned over to the detectives?"

"It was, of course, bagged and turned over to them."

"But not immediately?"

"I knew where it was at all times."

"It was in your sight at all times?"

"No, but I knew where it was."

"Isn't it a fact, Dr. Worthington, that the bullet sat on a tray in the empty autopsy room for half an hour before it was bagged and identified?"

"I doubt if it was that long."

"But it was left in the autopsy room?"

"Yes."

"Why was it left in the autopsy room?"

"On removal of the bullet, I dropped it on the floor."

"And did you immediately pick it up?"

"No, I did not."

"Why not?"

"It rolled away somewhere."

"And you couldn't find it?"

"I knew where it was."

"Then why didn't you immediately pick it up?"

"I knew where it was generally. I just didn't know where it was exactly."

"So did you look for it?"

"I assigned one of my technicians to look for it."

"It wasn't a job for the medical examiner himself?"

"I didn't think it required a medical degree, no."

"And to your knowledge, did the technician find it?"

"He did."

"And what did he do with it?"

"He placed it on the tray by the autopsy table."

"And did he then leave the room?"

"He came to tell me he'd found it, yes."

"How long did it sit on that tray, Dr. Worthington?"

"I don't know exactly."

"More than fifteen minutes?"

"Maybe."

"Half an hour?"

"I don't think that long, no."

"And did others have access to it in that time?"

"A few. No one I do not trust completely."

"How many people, Dr. Worthington?"

"A dozen perhaps."

"And how did it happen to finally get bagged for the police?"

"Uh, I remembered that it should be. That is, someone remembered. I'm not sure who it was."

"So then it was bagged. How many people were present at the autopsy, Dr. Worthington?"

"Two."

"That is counting yourself and—"

"My technician, Alice Comstock. Not counting Mr. Baines." He offered a brief, pained smile, then said, "Poor joke. Sorry."

"And was your technician in the room throughout the autopsy?"

"She was taken ill at one point and left the room for a few moments. Then she returned."

"Inexperienced with autopsies, was she?"

"She'd assisted at them before. It happens. It's unpredictable."

"Was she in the room when you dropped the fatal bullet?"

"Ah, no."

"And was she the technician you sent to look for it?"

"Ah, no. I sent another technician. Mohammed Lincoln. He found the bullet."

"Had the bullet been damaged?"

"Somewhat by its course through the victim's body, yes. Not by falling on the floor, I assure you."

"Dr. Worthington, isn't it usual for the investigating police officers to attend the autopsy?"

"It's common. I don't think it's required."

"And isn't it usual for the officers to take possession of any evidence, such as bullets, at the time of the autopsy?"

"Yes, that would be the most typical scenario."

"And yet in this case, neither Detective Tracy nor Detective Friday—sorry, Freedy—was in attendance?"

"Ah, no."

"Can you tell us why? If you know?"

Dr. Worthington cast a guilty look at Detective Tracy, who was quietly seething at the prosecution table. "As I understand it, Detective Tracy believed Detective Freedy would be attending, and Detective Freedy believed Detective Tracy would be attending. They, ah, got their wires crossed so to speak. It happens."

"No more questions." Gordon Moon sat down.

On redirect, Melba Wooten asked, "Dr. Worthington, you saw

that bullet when you took it out of Andrew Baines?"

"Of course."

"You noted its appearance, how it had been misshapen by its impact?"

"Certainly."

"And you saw it again at the time it was bagged as evidence?"

"I did."

"Dr. Worthington, as an experienced medical examiner, is there any doubt in your mind that it was the same bullet?"

"None at all."

"No more questions."

CHAPTER TWENTY-THREE

Detective Richard Tracy recognized the next prosecution witness when he met her in the courtroom corridor only after a classic double take.

"Ramirez, is that you?"

The young woman, dressed in a very short dress of bright red and precariously high stiletto heels, looked like she might be going to a party after court. "Yeah, it's me, Detective," she said with a grin. "Want to make something out of it?"

"You look great."

"Why, thank you."

"I never knew you had such good, uh, hair. But I don't usually see you dressed this way."

"Well, when I'm not poking around a crime scene on my hands and knees, I like to shed the jeans and dress the way I feel. Are you complaining?"

"Uh, no, not at all. But have you talked to the ADA about this? I mean, that's not how expert witnesses usually dress for court."

She lowered her voice and said confidentially, "I know, I know. I've done this before, okay? This is how Wooten told me to dress. She gave me some other funny instructions, too."

"What was that?"

"You'll see."

"State your name please," Melba Wooten said.

"Angela Ramirez."

"And your occupation."

"I am a criminalist for the city police department."

"Then you are a police officer?"

"No. I'm a civilian employee. I have no powers to arrest."

"Do you have a particular specialty, Ms. Ramirez?"

"Yes, I'm the department's chief ballistics expert."

"How long have you been in that job?"

"Six months."

"And what was your previous experience?"

"I had a similar job for five years in Cleveland."

Melba Wooten briefly took the witness through the training she had received in ballistics.

"Ms. Ramirez, this past July, did Detectives Tracy and Freedy ask you to examine a .38 caliber handgun in connection with an ongoing investigation?"

"They did."

"And did they also ask you to examine a misshapen bullet?"

"They did."

"For what purpose?"

"The idea was to determine if the bullet had been fired from the gun."

Melba took the gun that had been found in Charlie Baines's office from the exhibit table, where it had already been marked for evidence and showed it to Angela Ramirez.

"Is this the gun you examined?"

"It is, yes."

"And is this the bullet?"

"Yes, that's the bullet."

"Let the record show that the witness has identified the gun found in the drawer of Charles Baines's desk and the misshapen bullet taken from Andrew Baines's body. Did you fire another bullet from this gun for comparison purposes?"

"Yes, I did."

"And is this that bullet?" Melba Wooten said, displaying another exhibit to the witness.

"Yes, it is."

"Ms. Ramirez, as a result of your examination of these exhibits, what did you determine?"

"That the bullet was fired from the gun."

"And on what basis did you make that determination?"

"The lands and grooves matched."

"Thank you. No more questions. Your witness, Mr. Moon."

Gordon Moon rose from his chair. "Your Honor, the lunch hour is near and the cross-examination may be somewhat lengthy. May I suggest we take the lunchtime recess now?"

"Any objection to that?" Judge Estrada said.

Melba Wooten smiled broadly at the jury. "We never object to lunch, Your Honor."

"We'll resume promptly at two o'clock, Court is adjourned."

"She wasn't very impressive, was she?" Eve said, when the three attorneys were hunched over sandwiches in the courthouse cafeteria.

"On the contrary," said Vern Wagstaff. "She impressed the hell out of me."

"I mean as an expert witness," Eve said, "not as a pin-up."

"She doesn't hold a candle to you, babe."

"I don't understand why Wooten didn't ask her for more detail. I mean, what do the jurors know about, what was it, lines and graphs?"

"Lands and grooves," Vern said.

"Have you ever seen her before?"

"I don't think so. She's relatively new to the city, and if I have seen her, she sure wasn't dressed like that."

Gordon Moon spoke for the first time. "You get what's going

on here, don't you?"

"What?" said Eve.

"They're laying a trap for me, that's what. They think because she's a beautiful woman and doesn't have the usual demeanor of an expert witness and I've never taken her on before, I'll assume she's fresh meat like the medical examiner and go after her with my knife and fork on cross-examination. She, of course, will prove to know her stuff backwards and forwards and clean my clock. The result will be the prosecution makes its point, and I antagonize the jury. The female half because I would seem to be impugning a witness on account of her gender, the male half because, well, I don't suppose I have to explain that, do I?"

"Not to me," Vern said. "Be mean to that fox and I'll take a swing at you myself."

"There's only one thing for it. Eve, your moment has come."

"What do you mean?"

"You have to handle the cross-examination of Ramirez."

"Me?"

"Yes, you. It's the only way to counter this ridiculous ploy of theirs."

"But . . . but, I'm not prepared, and I don't know anything about ballistics."

"We'll tell you exactly what to ask. You'll be perfect, and the jury will love it."

"Well, okay. I mean, I'll be glad to contribute something finally."

"Eve, you're going into that courtroom a third chair and coming out—"

"A fifth wheel," said Vern.

Gordon glared at him, but Eve grinned. She couldn't help it. She thought he was funny.

★ ★ ★ ★ ★

Her knees shaking, Eve approached the witness box. Besides learning her lines, she had taken part of the lunch break to put on a sexier outfit, at Gordon's instruction. Veteran courthouse observers had never seen anything like it: one *Playboy* centerfold quizzing another on ballistics.

"Good afternoon, Ms. Ramirez," Eve said.

"Good afternoon, counselor."

"Your direct examination was rather brief. You made reference to a bullet found in the body of the decedent Andrew Baines. I understand the use of bullet as a layman's term, but would the proper ballistic designation not be a slug?"

"Yes, that's correct. We'd call it a slug."

"You used the words *lands* and *grooves* that members of the jury may not be familiar with. Could you define those terms?"

"Yes. Every slug fired from a particular weapon will pick up marks from its trip through the barrel of the weapon. As it spins, it picks up these marks, which are called lands, the raised areas, and grooves, the depressions."

"And these are formed as a result of the rifling in the bore of the weapon, that is, the spiral marks that permit the weapon to be fired with a greater degree of accuracy. Is that correct?"

Ramirez looked somewhat surprised. "Yes, that's right."

"But the term rifling does not indicate that the weapon was a rifle. Rifles and handguns have this rifling, but shotguns do not. Is that correct in your experience?"

"Yes, always."

"Can you tell us more about the specific handgun you tested, the one that is now in evidence?"

"Certainly. What would you like to know?"

"The manufacturer, for example."

"The firearm in question is a Colt .38 Super."

"Is it an old gun then?"

"No."

"Isn't it true that the Colt .38 Super was introduced in 1929, at which time it was considered the most powerful handgun on the market, but was subsequently discontinued?"

"Yes, that's correct. But they started making it again in 2003."

"And the handgun in evidence is a new model?"

"Yes."

"Is this an expensive gun?"

"Yes, relatively."

Eve picked up the murder weapon from the exhibit table and weighed it in her hand. "Would you agree with me that this is a wooden grip?"

"Yes. It's rosewood, I believe."

"The rosewood grip with the double-diamond pattern would retail for over a thousand dollars, wouldn't it?"

"I believe so, yes."

"Do you think someone with no particular aesthetic sense and wanting to save a few dollars might have settled for the stainless steel version with the checkered rubber pattern? Or even the blue carbon steel model, which is cheaper still?"

"Yes, quite possibly."

"Do you think a woman could have fired this weapon?"

"Certainly. Why not?"

"And do you think a woman would have been more likely attracted to the more expensive wooden model?"

"Not necessarily."

"What else can you tell us about the specifications of this weapon?"

"The Colt .38 Super is an auto-loading, single-action pistol with three-dot sights, nine-round magazine, beveled magazine well, and standard thumb safety."

"Does it also have the Beavertail grip safety, combat hammer, and aluminum trigger?"

"That's right."

"What about the barrel length?"

"Five inches."

"Then that would be about eight and a half inches overall length?"

"Yes, that's correct."

At the prosecution table, Agnes Moon whispered to Melba Wooten, "This stuff is all irrelevant. You should object."

Melba shook her head. "No. The sisters are both having fun, and it's not hurting us any. Our trap for your hubby didn't work, but if they want to waste time, that's their lookout."

"Ms. Ramirez," Eve was saying, "when you were given the handgun for examination, which of the officers gave it to you?"

"They were both there, but I believe it was Detective Freedy who gave it to me."

"When you were examining the firearm, did you place anything in the barrel to handle it, such as a pen or pencil, for example?"

"Certainly not."

"Why not?"

"Well, for one thing, it had already been tested for fingerprints, so there was no need to take such special precautions."

"And were you also concerned about the alterations to the rifling that could result from handling the weapon in that way, leading to possible alterations to the lands and grooves on the test slug you would fire for comparison?"

"I'd certainly have been concerned if I had handled it that way."

"Did you ask Detectives Tracy and Freedy if they had handled it that way in the course of their investigation?"

"No. I didn't believe it was necessary. I would expect experienced detectives to know the proper way to handle a weapon to preserve both fingerprints and ballistic evidence."

"How would you handle it if you needed to preserve both?"

"A pencil behind the trigger guard would be safe enough."

"Ms. Ramirez, were you aware of the steps in the possession of the slug taken from the body of Andrew Baines?"

"My only concern is that it was handed to me and the change of possession was duly noted and that the change of possession was also duly noted when I returned the slug with my report. What happened to it before or after is not my concern, though I assume it was carried out in a professional manner."

"Were you aware that the slug had rolled around the floor of the autopsy room and not been found until much later?"

"Objection, Your Honor," Melba Wooten said. "Outside the scope of the witness's testimony and knowledge."

"Sustained."

"Thank you, Your Honor," Eve said. "Ms. Ramirez, I will now ask you a hypothetical question. Purely hypothetically, if a bullet were to roll around the floor of the autopsy room and not be found until much later, could it affect the markings on the bullet in such a way as to effect a mistaken identification?"

"I don't see how, no. It could conceivably make the identification more difficult, but it could hardly add misleading markings."

"But again, speaking purely hypothetically, could a substitution of one bullet for another be made in the hypothetical circumstances I have described?"

"Hypothetically, I suppose it could, yes."

"I have no more questions."

Melba rose for a short redirect. "Ms. Ramirez, hypothetically speaking, if pigs had wings, could they fly?"

"Objection, Your Honor," Eve said.

"Sustained."

"I have no more questions," Melba said.

★ ★ ★ ★ ★

"State your name for the record please," Melba Wooten said.

"Edgar McCandless." He was a six-foot-eight African American who knew Melba as well from the basketball court as from previous witness stand encounters.

"Mr. McCandless, what is your occupation?"

"Criminalist, city police department. I'm a civilian employee."

"And do you have a particular specialty in the city police department?"

"Several, ma'am. One of them is identifying fingerprints."

"Do you recognize this weapon?" Melba passed him the handgun that had been placed in evidence.

"Yes, ma'am, this is a .38-caliber Colt Super which was given to me to examine for fingerprints."

"And did you find identifiable fingerprints?"

"Yes, I did."

"Whose fingerprints were they?"

"The defendant, Charles Baines, ma'am."

"And did you find any other identifiable prints on the gun?"

"No, I did not."

"I have no more questions."

"Go get him, Eve," Gordon said. "You're on a roll."

More confidently, after the successful cross-examination of the ballistics expert, Eve approached the witness and smiled.

"Mr. McCandless, when you find fingerprints on a handgun, does the placement of the fingerprints give you an indication of how the gun was held?"

"Uh, yes, ma'am, it gives you an idea, depending on where the fingerprints were found."

"How about the trigger? Did you find one of Charles Baines's prints on the trigger?"

"Yes, ma'am, I did."

"Which finger was it?"

"It was his thumb, ma'am."

"Forgive my ignorance, since I don't know very much about guns." Eve threw a modest smile at the jury. The statement was truthful, but she knew they would assume she was underplaying her own recently demonstrated expertise. "Is it usual for a person to fire a .38-caliber handgun like this one with one's thumb on the trigger?"

"No, ma'am, not in my experience," the witness said with a smile.

"Would it even be possible to fire a handgun with your thumb on the trigger?"

"It might be possible, ma'am, but I wouldn't want to be anywhere in the vicinity of the guy who tried it."

"Would it be more likely that someone else fired the handgun in the normal way, using the index finger, and that someone who did not fire the gun picked it up after the fact?"

"Objection. Calls for speculation."

"Your Honor, it goes to the witness's area of expertise."

"Overruled. Witness may answer."

"That's certainly possible, yes, ma'am."

"Thank you. I have no more questions."

CHAPTER TWENTY-FOUR

Tuesday, December 12

Eve was spending more and more time at the courthouse, less and less in her office in the Baines Building. But today, an hour before court would resume at ten a.m., she had come back to retrieve a document and was accosted by Oswald as she strode toward the entrance.

"Miss Nyquist," he said, "good morning."

"Good morning, Oswald," she said.

"I have to talk to you. This is very important."

"Oh, Oswald, I'm awfully busy. You'll have to make it quick. Would you like to ride up to my office with me?"

"It's daytime, and I'm not supposed to be in the building. On the upper floors. Any time."

"It's okay if you're with me," she said.

His face brightened. "And Mr. Baines is dead. I keep forgetting. I don't mean I forget he's dead, but I forget he's the only one really cared if I came in the building. I'll ride up with you. We can talk in the elevator. Won't take much time."

As the elevator ascended, Oswald said, "Santa didn't do it, Miss Nyquist."

"Yes, I know you believe that. So do I, and that's what we're trying to prove in court."

"But I don't just believe it. I know it. I heard the real murderer talking that night. He was hiding, and he thought no one was around, and he was talking." Reading her expression, he said, "I know what you think. It was one of my voices. But I know more about my voices than you do. Because I'm the one who hears them. And this wasn't one of my voices. This was real."

They'd reached the twenty-fifth floor. Eve said, "Come to my office, Oswald." The pair of them got some stares as they walked through the reception area.

She asked Oswald to sit down and tell her what he'd heard.

"I was up there that night, Miss Nyquist. I know I wasn't supposed to be, but I come to the upper floors sometimes at night. There are lots of ways to get up here without anybody knowing. If I got caught, I'd get in trouble, so I'm careful I never get caught. I saw Santa Claus come out of old Mr. Baines's office. I saw him walk to the elevator. He didn't see me. Then I walked in the office, and I saw Mr. Baines dead. Then I walked back along the corridor, and I heard a voice coming from one of the closets. It was a kind of a muffled voice, not as clear as the voices in my head that the doctors say aren't real but to me they are. But this voice was outside my head, it was in the closet. You gotta believe me."

"I believe you, Oswald. Go on. What did the voice say?"

"I'm not quite sure. It was a kind of angry voice, and it said something like 'Damned Subaru' or something like that."

"Subaru? The car?"

"It might have been that. Or it might have been something else. I've tried to remember. If it wasn't the car, it might have been a Japanese last name that sounded like the car. That's what it sounded like."

"A Japanese last name," Eve repeated.

"I'm sorry I can't remember better, but that's how I know it wasn't a voice in my head. It would have been clearer if it was. It wasn't clear, so I know it was real. And I know it was the real murderer. Who else would be hiding in there, waiting for a chance to get out?"

Before court, Eve told Vern about her conversation with Oswald. He wasn't encouraging.

"Eve, if we're not going to let our client testify because we're unsure of his mental state, we're sure as hell not going to let that homeless nut testify. What he said means nothing."

"He seemed so sure."

"Only crazy people are that sure."

"And this business of the Japanese surname. Could it have been the name of one of the former medical examiners? Could Andrew Baines's death have something to do with the controversy over the appointment of a non-Asian to the post?"

"Why would it? This is a dead end, Eve. Face it. I wouldn't even mention it to Gordon if I were you."

And when Gordon Moon joined them at the defense table, she didn't tell him about her meeting with Oswald. But she couldn't put it out of her mind.

CHAPTER TWENTY-FIVE

"State your name for the record please," Melba Wooten said.

"Michael Goodspeed." The first witness of the morning was bright, cheery, brisk, smug, self-satisfied, just the sort lawyers like to bring down on cross-examination.

"And your occupation."

"Criminalist with the city police department."

"And do you have a particular specialty in the department?"

"Yes, ma'am. I analyze for DNA."

Melba smiled. "Mr. Goodspeed, some of us immediately begin to nod off at the slightest mention of DNA. I assume we're all aware of this great advance in the field of crime detection and how it works, so I'll leave it to Mr. Moon to ask you for any boring science lectures."

"Objection, Your Honor," said Gordon Moon, rising to his feet good-humoredly. "I will in turn leave it to the jury to decide whose case is the more boring, but I would remind my learned friend that the function of examination is to ask questions, not to make speeches or cast aspersions on her learned friends."

"And may I remind you, counselor," Judge Estrada said, "that these are also not functions of making an objection? Anyway, it's sustained. Proceed, Ms. Wooten, and please don't testify."

"Thank you, Your Honor. Mr. Goodspeed, tell us in the simplest possible layman's terms what DNA is."

"It is the unique genetic code found in the cells of our body."

"And this genetic code is different for each of us?"

"Unless someone else has the identical genetic makeup."

"And who might have one's same genetic makeup?"

"Oh, an identical twin maybe. Or a triplet. Or a clone." Goodspeed smiled. "Not many of them around."

"So to make sure we all understand, leaving aside for the moment identical siblings, DNA typing of the kind you do allows you to make a distinction between any individual living now and any other individual living now anywhere in the world?"

"That's the idea, yes. Any person living now and, I might add, any person that ever lived."

"And through what vehicles may this DNA be found to study?"

"It can be isolated from just about anything we leave behind. Saliva, blood, urine, perspiration, feces, mucus, bits of skin."

"In the course of your employment, did you examine for traces of DNA certain items found at the scene of Andrew Baines's death?"

"I did, yes."

"And what were these items?"

"A facial tissue and a false beard."

"Beginning with the facial tissue, what did you find?"

"Mucus from the nose."

"And this finding was consistent with someone sneezing or blowing his or her nose into this facial tissue?"

"Yes."

"And did you find DNA in this mucus?"

"It would be unique snot if I did not." The courtroom tittered, and Goodspeed smiled. "I didn't mean to be funny."

"Oh, sure, you did," said the judge. "But if the urge strikes you again, Mr. Goodspeed, resist it."

"Yes, Your Honor."

"Mr. Goodspeed," Melba Wooten continued, "did you have a

sample of DNA taken from the blood of the defendant, Charles Baines?"

"I did, yes."

"And did you compare that sample with the sample taken from the facial tissue?"

"I did, yes."

"And what was your conclusion?"

"That Mr. Charles Baines had sneezed into or blown his nose into that tissue that was found on his brother's desk."

"The other item you were asked to analyze was a Santa Claus beard?"

"It was."

"And what did you find on the beard that might include DNA?"

"There was quite a lot of blood, to begin with."

"And did you test that blood for DNA?"

"I did, though under the circumstances it hardly seemed necessary."

"Why wouldn't it be necessary?"

"Well, it was lying in a pool of blood on Andrew Baines's desk, and it seemed likely it was Andrew Baines's blood."

"And yet you tested it anyway?"

"It was always possible that someone else had bled at the scene of the crime and that the blood would reveal someone else's DNA. A long shot to be sure, but we had to test it out. We took several samples of the blood from various places on the beard."

"And what did you find?"

"All the blood tested, like the blood pooled on the desk, was that of the victim, Andrew Baines."

"And was there anything else on the beard that could be tested for DNA?"

"At the point that the beard would meet the face of the

person wearing it, I found particles of skin, which I presumed to be from a person who had worn it."

"Whose DNA was that?"

"It was consistent with the DNA of the defendant, Charles Baines."

"No further questions."

Gordon Moon approached the witness. "Mr. Goodspeed, did Charlie Baines willingly provide a blood sample to be tested for DNA?"

"Yes, he did."

"Can you tell when a particular item gathered DNA traces from a wearer?"

"Not generally, no."

"So it would be fair to say that if Charlie Baines had worn that Santa Claus beard on another occasion, weeks or even months before, traces of his DNA would be on the beard?"

"That's certainly possible."

"Apart from the blood of Andrew Baines, did you find any DNA on the beard that did not come from Charlie Baines?"

"No, I did not."

"So no one else had worn the beard as far as you could tell?"

"That's correct, as far as I could tell."

"But is it not possible that someone could have planted the Santa Claus beard in Andrew Baines's office to implicate his brother, knowing that his skin particles and no others would be found on the beard?"

"Yes, that is possible, of course."

"Thank you, Mr. Goodspeed. I have no further questions. If there is to be a boring science lecture, Ms. Wooten will have to ask for it on redirect."

"No need," Melba said. "You are excused, Mr. Goodspeed."

CHAPTER TWENTY-SIX

At the afternoon session, Melba Wooten said, "The state calls Sidney Monarca," and the elderly exhibitor made his way to the witness box with deliberate dignity.

"Good morning, Mr. Monarca. Please tell the jury your occupation."

"I operate a motion picture theatre here in the city, the Majestic."

"And how is business these days, Mr. Monarca?"

"Terrible, thanks," the witness said with a rueful smile. "The multiplexes are driving the independents out of the business. When my two brothers and I started in business more than fifty years ago, it was a lot different."

"Are your two brothers still involved in the business?"

"No. Carmine moved to New Jersey twenty years ago and sold out his interest. Frank died ten years ago."

"Is the Majestic the only theatre you've operated in the city?"

"Oh, no, we used to have three. The Oriental was our first. I sold that five years ago—the land was just too valuable. Then we opened the Majestic, then the Royal. That was the nicest of the lot, but it burned down just a couple years after we opened."

"Are you acquainted with the defendant Charles Baines?"

"I certainly am."

"When did you most recently speak with the defendant?"

Monarca looked uneasy. "It was the day before his brother died."

"That would be July twenty-third of this year?"

"I believe so, yes."

"And what did you talk about?"

"The Majestic. I told him I was losing money and might have to sell out. He'd been part of a committee to save the building for its historic and architectural value, and he also was trying to do something to keep me in business."

"What was Charles Baines's demeanor on that occasion?"

"He was angry, the angriest I've ever seen him."

"Whom was he angry at, Mr. Monarca, if you know?"

"His brother mainly. Andrew Baines was representing the developers who wanted the land where the Majestic stands. It's very valuable."

"Thank you. No more questions."

Gordon Moon got up and walked toward the witness box.

"Good morning, Mr. Monarca. When you spoke with Charlie Baines that day, did he make any threat toward his brother?"

"No."

"He didn't say he was so angry he wanted to kill his brother?"

"Hell, no! Ah, sorry, Your Honor, but Charlie Baines wouldn't kill anybody. Everybody in this city knows that."

"No more questions," Gordon said, before Melba could speak her objection.

Stacey Bamwanger whispered to Agnes, "He's not asking many questions."

"He wants to get through before Christmas Eve, remember," Agnes pointed out.

Melba said, "And so do we. This jury's in a hurry, and we won't prolong this any more than we have to. We don't have to. We've got the evidence to hang Santa Claus, girls, and we're going to do it." She rose to her six-foot-three height and said, "Thank you, Mr. Monarca. I have no more questions. Your Honor, the state rests."

177

Jon L. Breen

Judge Estrada looked at her watch. "Mr. Moon, will you be ready to begin the case for the defense at ten o'clock tomorrow morning?"

"Certainly, Your Honor," Gordon Moon replied, "as shopping days dwindle and the little ones await the visit from St. Nick."

Melba Wooten almost objected but settled for an eye roll.

CHAPTER TWENTY-SEVEN

Wednesday, December 13

The first day of the defense was a parade of character witnesses, who were not hard to find for a figure as beloved as Charlie Baines. By the end of the day, though, Gordon sensed that the love-fest was getting tiresome, and he knew that the next day he would have to come up with something more substantial. He was weighing his options that evening when a telephone call from Duffy O'Gonigal summoned him to a meeting. Duffy claimed he had something that could be the turning point in the defense of Charlie Baines. Gordon was on his way out when Agnes confronted him on the stairs, she going up and he down. It seemed so many of their discussions took place on this stairway.

"Our kids are getting a Mexican Christmas," Agnes said. "You go in the family room, and they'll all wish you *Feliz Navidad.*"

"What?" Gordon said distractedly. "Who's she?"

"Don't you ever listen to me? The children are turning into little Mexicans. They all want to know when the piñata's going up."

"It's good for them to be exposed to a variety of cultures, Agnes," Gordon said.

"Oh, I agree, and maybe we should expose them to our own culture once in a while. Are you going down to see them?"

"Uh, later. I have to go out. I have to meet somebody."

"Who?"

"I shouldn't say."

"It's about the case?"

"Certainly it's about the case. If it were anything else, I could tell you. What do you think, I'm meeting my mistress?"

She sighed dramatically. "I almost wish you were. Don't you have people working for you to meet with witnesses or informants or whomever? Doesn't being lead counsel at least have the advantage of not having to do everything yourself? Just go down and spend some quality time with the children. While you still can. Before they grow up and leave us. Please. Fifteen minutes."

"Is that my parental quota? Is that how long you spent? I'll see them when I come home."

"They'll be in bed when you come home."

"All right, all right. Fifteen minutes."

When Gordon got to his car, he realized he had spent twenty minutes with the children. He hadn't even looked at his watch as he listened to their bilingual chatter and heard the Spanish Christmas song Rosita had taught them. In the midst of the chaos and pressure of a major murder trial, on the verge of discovering something important, he had made time for his children, and the knowledge gave him a warm family feeling. The sacrifices he and Agnes made for their brood were all worth it.

What she had said was true. He could delegate a lot of routine duties. But not this one. Duffy O'Gonigal, to whom he owed so much, he had to deal with personally. That Duffy asked Gordon to meet him not at Rumpole's but at a hotel bar not frequented by the local legal crowd increased the feeling that this must be something important and confidential.

Duffy rose from a barstool to greet Gordon with a smile and

an embrace. "Grand to see you, lad. We'll repair to a quiet table. What are you drinking?"

"You should know I don't drink during a trial, Duffy," Gordon said.

"What? Did you think I was suggesting something alcoholic? Perish the thought." Duffy turned to the bartender. "A tonic water for my friend. And another of the same for me, please."

"Two tonic waters?" the bartender said sleepily.

Duffy said patiently, "No, lad, one tonic water and another of what I have been drinking."

"Yes, sir."

As they carried their drinks to a corner table, Duffy muttered about the sad state of bartending in the city. When they sat down, Gordon saw his mentor's face lined with concern.

"Not going well, is it?" Duffy said.

Gordon shrugged. "It's early yet. That DNA testimony is tough, but I have a few things up my sleeve."

"There's a lot to juggle when you're in trial, a lot of evidence and a lot of law and your professional standards to uphold. You know what I was just saying to Phil Etchebarren the other day, lad? The law is like a beach, and the lawyer is a shorebird who runs as close to the edge of the water as he can without getting his feet wet in the tide of legal ethics."

"You talked to Phil Etchebarren about ethics?"

"Don't disappoint me, lad. Phil did nothing wrong to lose his license. He was framed."

"Duffy, you know I love you, and I'd be glad to hear some time all about how your buddy at Rumpole's was framed. I don't hear nearly enough stories like that from my clients. But you called me out tonight because you said you had something important for me. Then you give me a little metaphor about legal ethics. What are you up to? Are you about to suggest I do something unethical?"

"Certainly not. Gordy, I can't help you on the DNA. That's beyond my competence. But I can offer you something on the so-called Baines Building security. You said it was porous, and you're right. I'm going to show you just how porous." He pulled a battered document out of his back pocket and passed it across the table. "What you have there is a summary of sixteen different ways someone could get into the Baines Building and beat the security as of last July."

Gordon looked at the list. "That many?"

"That many."

"And here I've always checked in with security and entered through the lobby."

"Ah, but you haven't gone there to commit murder, have you? You want to get Wilbur Ricketts back on the stand and go through this list with him. He'll have to admit what I say is true. Some of these they've closed up since the murder, but most of them are still valid today. The building is a security sieve. Hit that hard, Gordy, and they'll forget about the DNA for a while."

Gordon smiled. "Duffy, this is great. It's like old times."

"Well, I'm not totally useless yet. I like something to exercise my brain besides the puzzles in the paper."

"Do you ever think about getting back into practice?"

"Well, sure. I think about it every day. Like I think about scoring the winning goal for Ireland or eloping with Parker Posey. I think about a lot of things I'll never do."

"It would mean a great deal to me, and to Charlie Baines, too, to have you sitting there with us at the defense table for the rest of this trial."

Duffy's eyes looked moist. "My boy, I am tempted to take you up on that offer. I am indeed."

"But there's just one thing," Gordon said.

"Just one?"

"And I'll bet you know it without my telling you."

"Let me guess. I have to be sure not to dress better than the lead counsel?"

"That's not it."

Duffy looked at his old student for a moment, then nodded his head purposefully and roared across the room, "Barkeep! Another tonic water for my friend, and another of the same for me."

When the bartender came with the drinks, Duffy said, "No, no, didn't you hear me order two tonic waters? I don't drink when I'm on trial."

CHAPTER TWENTY-EIGHT

Thursday, December 14

Having properly introduced Duffy O'Gonigal as an addition to the defense team, with a genuinely warm welcome from the judge and a blatantly insincere warm welcome from the prosecution, Gordon Moon asked that Wilbur Ricketts be recalled to the stand.

"Mr. Ricketts, the security in the Baines Building isn't very good, is it?"

Wilbur bristled a little. "Sure, it is."

"When you told Ms. Wooten you didn't know if there were other Santa Clauses running around the Baines Building that night, weren't you implying there were other ways to get in the building without being seen?"

"I guess I was."

"So the security isn't very good, is it?"

"We do the best we can. We make adjustments when we need to."

"You made a lot of adjustments after the death of Andrew Baines, didn't you?"

"We made a few, yes. Nothing like that had ever happened before, and we want to make sure nothing like that happens again."

"But the budget for security before Andrew Baines's death didn't permit a system that was exactly state-of-the-art, did it?"

"Well, no, I guess not. Like I say, we did the best we could."

"And why was the budget for the security so low?"

"Objection, Your Honor," Melba Wooten said. "Beyond the witness's competence."

"The witness may answer," Judge Estrada said. "If you know the answer, Mr. Ricketts."

"I know the answer all right. Andrew Baines wouldn't pay for it. He thought if we had enough bells and whistles in the lobby, it would look like we had tight security, and that would be good enough."

"The upshot being," Gordon Moon went on, "that despite your sign-in log and other security accoutrements, you don't really know how many people were in the building the night of Baines's death, do you?"

"Well, no, not exactly."

"Isn't it true, in fact, that there were numerous ways to get into that building unseen at that time?"

"Well, a few maybe."

"And wouldn't anyone familiar with the building be aware of those means of entry?"

"A few of them, probably."

"And wasn't the defendant Charlie Baines knowledgeable enough about the various features of the building that he could enter unseen if he chose to?"

"He never did, sir. I mean, when he came, he was always friendly. He wanted to talk."

"But, Mr. Ricketts, if Charlie Baines came to the Baines Building that night with the murder of his brother in mind, would he really have entered through the lobby and let you know he was there?"

"Objection. Calls for speculation."

"Sustained."

"I withdraw the question, Your Honor. No more questions."

Melba Wooten asked, "Mr. Ricketts, if the building security is as porous as Mr. Moon suggests, couldn't Charles Baines have entered the building earlier in the evening without your knowledge?"

"I guess he could, but he didn't."

"How do you know that?"

"Well, why would he?"

"As a subtle piece of misdirection. Couldn't he have entered by one of those other methods, gone to the thirtieth floor and killed his brother, left the building in the same way, then reentered through the lobby in the normal way and only pretended to discover his brother dead?"

"I don't know if he could, but if he did, he'd've done a better job of it."

"No more questions."

Gordon Moon followed Ricketts with three more security guards employed in the Baines Building who essentially backed up Wilbur's testimony. This brought the proceedings to the lunch break and a big decision for the defense.

CHAPTER TWENTY-NINE

Instead of going out for lunch, the defense team ordered sandwiches from a nearby deli so they could meet with a well-guarded Charlie Baines in a courthouse conference room during the break.

"Gordon," the defendant said, "I have to testify."

"Charlie, I don't think it's necessary," Gordon Moon insisted. "Or prudent either. Thanks to Duffy here, we've opened up a whole new line of inquiry. Who knows how many people might have been swarming around the thirtieth floor that night? And if somebody wanted to frame you by planting the tissue and the beard, they could."

"That's called reasonable doubt," Vern said. "It's all we need."

"Maybe I want more than just reasonable doubt," Charlie said. "I want the jury to know I'm innocent, not just think the prosecution can't prove I'm guilty."

"They'll know you're innocent, Charlie," Gordon said. "We can probably find a willing witness for every one of those sixteen ways to access the building without going through security. By the time we're done, the jury will never convict you of anything."

"They don't want to anyway," Vern said. "But if you testify, who knows what the prosecution might come up with on cross, valid or not? It just isn't smart."

"Yes, I understand all that," Charlie said. "But not testifying seems so cowardly. If I don't testify, even if I'm acquitted, people will always have that question in their minds. Why didn't we hear from Charlie Baines? Why didn't he look us in the eye and tell us the truth? What is Santa Claus hiding that's not wrapped up in Christmas paper?" Charlie looked at each of his four defense lawyers in turn. "Well, I've heard plenty from Gordon and Vern. What do you think, Eve? What do you think, Duffy?"

"I think the defense team speaks with a single voice," Gordon said.

"Gordon's right," Vern said. "How many high profile celebrity cases do you know where the defendant testified? It's just asking for trouble."

"Right," said Duffy O'Gonigal, adding with a wink, "And they don't hold it against O.J. Simpson, do they?"

"Whose side are you on?" Vern said. "Anyway, the two cases aren't parallel at all."

"They both involve defendants the public loved and didn't want to see convicted," Eve pointed out in a small voice.

Vern shook his head. "If Simpson had testified, the prosecution might have nailed him, and if he'd testified and still got off, he'd be toast in the public mind anyway."

Eve said, her voice stronger now, "I think if it's important to Charlie to testify, he should testify. Maybe the jury and the public are starting to doubt he's the lovable old Saint Nick they've known all these years. Maybe they need to be reminded."

"Tell me, Gordon," Charlie Baines asked, "who makes the final decision on this anyway?"

Gordon sighed theatrically. "Lead counsel makes the final recommendation, and I recommend you don't testify. The final decision, however, belongs to the client. So it's your call, Charlie."

The four defense lawyers looked at Charlie expectantly. He looked back at them benignly, blue eyes twinkling. Finally Vern said, "Charlie, will you at least leave out the part about how you hated your brother?"

CHAPTER THIRTY

"Your Honor, the defense calls the defendant Charles Nicholas Baines to the stand."

As an almost inaudible murmur ran through the courtroom, Charlie went forward and took the oath in a quiet voice. He took his place in the witness box, looking relaxed, even somewhat relieved, and absolutely benevolent.

Gordon took Charlie through his early life, his family's contributions to the city, and his own emergence as the official municipal Santa Claus. Gordon seemed determined to include every good deed Charlie had ever done, every heart he had ever brightened, to the point that his witness began to appear embarrassed. Finally, they got to the night of the murder.

"Mr. Baines, why did you go to the Baines Building on the night of July twenty-fourth?"

"I hoped to reason with my brother about the plans for the Majestic Theatre, make him see how important it was to preserve this monument to cinematic culture, to twentieth-century architecture, and also to—this is where I truly wanted to reach him—to our childhood."

"Why not see him during the day?"

"I preferred a time when there was no one else around, when we wouldn't be interrupted by telephone calls and pressing matters of business. I wanted to recreate a mood of brothers sharing confidences. I wanted us to be boys again."

"Mr. Baines, you chose to go to the Baines Building dressed

as Santa Claus. Do you often put on your Santa Claus garb in the heat of summer?"

"Occasionally I do, yes. But usually in the privacy of my own home."

At the defense table, Vern whispered to Eve, "Great. He's a Christmassy cross-dresser."

"Shut up, Vern," Duffy murmured.

"Why do you do that?" Gordon asked.

"To reenergize myself. When I'm in a blue mood, it helps me remember my reason for living, to recapture my role in the life of the city, and to remind me of my duties to my fellow human creatures. Around Christmas time, it's easy to stay upbeat. The rest of the year, it's more of a challenge."

"And why don't you dress as Santa in public outside the holiday season?"

Charlie smiled. "People might think I was crazy. I don't want the Christmas spirit to be associated in the public mind with mental illness."

"Was it warm that night, Mr. Baines?"

"Quite warm, yes."

"Wasn't the suit uncomfortable?"

"The psychic comfort it gives me to wear it outweighs any discomfort I might get from the heat."

"Why on that particular night did you choose to go out in public dressed as Santa Claus?"

"I didn't want to lose my temper, do or say anything I might regret. As long as I am dressed as Santa Claus, there is no danger that my baser instincts will take control of me."

"Father Christmas and Mr. Hyde," Vern whispered. Eve didn't crack a smile.

"Would being dressed as Santa Claus in some way influence your brother?"

Charlie laughed. "No, the suit wouldn't gain me any points

with Andrew. Wearing it was for my own benefit. I had other ways of trying to make my point with Andrew."

"When you reached the Baines Building, what did you do?"

"What I always do. I went to the security desk on the ground floor and checked in with my friend Wilbur Ricketts, who keeps track of who is in the building. I also chatted with Wilbur a bit, asked him about his family."

"Mr. Baines, do you know of any other ways of entering the Baines Building, without checking in at the security desk?"

"Several. There's the freight elevator from the parking structure, which I have a key for. A couple of side doors off the alley are often kept unlocked on summer nights. There are other ways."

"Why didn't you enter the building by one of those?"

"There was no reason to."

"Were you carrying a weapon with you that night?"

"Certainly not."

"And did you keep a weapon of any kind in the building?"

"No. Why would I?"

"Did you see anyone else in the reception area of the building that night besides Wilbur Ricketts?"

"Yes. Oswald, a homeless man who sometimes sleeps in the lobby. I don't know his last name."

"How did you get to the thirtieth floor?"

"By the elevator."

"And when you came out of the elevator on the thirtieth floor, did you see anyone else on the floor?"

"No. But I had the feeling I was not alone. It's hard to explain."

"Of course, you knew your brother Andrew was working on the floor, in his office, didn't you?"

"Yes, but I didn't mean him."

"Did you go directly to your brother's office when you got to the thirtieth floor?"

"No."

"Where did you go?"

"To my own office."

"Why?"

"When my brother Andrew and I were young, we collected lobby cards. They advertised motion pictures and were sent to exhibitors who were going to show the films. I thought I had left some of them in my office, and I wanted to take a few to my meeting with Andrew. I thought reminding him of our old hobby might recapture the feeling of being boys together."

"Where did you look for them?"

"Oh, just about everywhere."

"And did you find them?"

"No, I did not."

"How long did this search take you?"

"It must have been nearly an hour. My office is very cluttered."

"Do you keep extra Santa Claus suits in your office closet, Mr. Baines?"

"Yes, several. It's amazing how one goes through them in the holiday season, and I sometimes loan them to others who wish to take on the role."

"So you have extra beards, boots, trousers, belts, jackets, caps?"

"Oh, yes, the whole ensemble."

"Did you at any point that evening change beards?"

"No."

"Or any other part of your Santa Claus costume?"

"No, I did not."

"Was anything missing from among the Santa Claus suits in your closet?"

"I have no idea. I didn't count them. I had no idea it would be important."

"Were you sneezing that night, Mr. Baines?"

"I was, yes. I have some allergies, and searching the dusty corners of my office didn't help any."

"Did you blow your nose during the time you were in your office searching for the lobby cards?"

"Probably several times."

"Did you use a handkerchief?"

"No, paper tissues."

"And what did you do with them?"

"Probably threw them in the waste basket."

"What made you decide to stop your search?"

"I found something that should not have been there, and it alarmed me."

"And what was that?"

"A gun. In the drawer of my desk."

"And did you usually keep a gun there?"

"No, never."

"Have you ever owned a firearm, Mr. Baines?"

"No. When I was drafted into the U.S. Army, I had a rifle assigned to me, but I neither owned it nor felt any particular kinship with it. And since leaving the service, I've never used or even handled a firearm for any purpose."

"Did you touch the gun you found in your desk?"

"I picked it up to look at it more closely, yes. A foolish thing for me to do, I realize now."

"How did you pick it up? Perhaps you could demonstrate."

Gordon walked to the exhibit table, picked up the gun, and held it out to Charlie Baines, who looked at it apprehensively.

"This isn't loaded, is it?" Charlie asked.

"No, it's perfectly safe."

"Something like this, I should imagine." He picked the gun up with his thumb on the trigger and the rest of his hand around the butt. He held his hand up so that the jury could see while Gordon Moon described it orally for the record. Then Charlie returned the gun to Gordon, who restored it to the exhibit table.

"What did you do then?"

"I put the gun back in the desk drawer and went immediately to my brother Andrew's office."

"And what did you find there?"

"My brother's dead body."

"Where were you when you first saw the body?"

"In the doorway. I could see my brother's staring eyes and a great deal of blood."

"Did you touch the body?"

"I checked for a pulse. It was obvious to me he was dead."

"Mr. Baines, did you see a bloodstained Santa Claus beard on your brother's desk when you found the body?"

"No, and I think I would have noticed."

"Did you sneeze while you were in your brother's office?"

"No."

"Did you blow your nose while you were in your brother's office?"

"I did not."

"Did you leave behind a used tissue in your brother's office?"

"No."

"Are you sure of that?"

"Absolutely. Those moments are vivid in my memory."

"What did you do when you were certain your brother was dead?"

"I started to reach for the telephone on his desk, but then I realized it was part of a crime scene and should not be disturbed. I went out into the corridor to see if there was anyone on the floor."

"Did you see anyone?"

"No, but I had the odd feeling I was being watched. I'd felt that way most of the time I was up there, even in my own office. So I took the elevator down to the lobby and informed Wilbur of what had happened and advised him to call the police."

"Did you stay to await the arrival of the police?"

"No."

"Why not?"

"I wanted to get home and out of my Santa Claus suit. It was inappropriate to the occasion. I couldn't imagine being questioned by the police while dressed that way."

"So you went home?"

"Yes."

"And did you tell Wilbur Ricketts that was where you would be if the police wished to talk to you?"

"Yes, I did."

"And did the police in fact visit you that night?"

"They did."

"And did you cooperate with their investigation?"

"In every way I could."

"Mr. Baines, did you kill your brother Andrew?"

"No, I did not."

"I have no more questions for this witness, Your Honor," Gordon said, and returned to the defense table. Melba Wooten rose to cross-examine.

"Mr. Baines, this Santa Claus suit you wear. Does it have pockets?"

"Yes. In the jacket and the trousers."

"Rather large pockets?"

"The ones in the jacket are good-sized certainly. It's important to the work of a Santa to be able to carry small gifts to surprise the young ones when he doesn't have his full sack with him. The full sack is rather hard on the back."

"I see. Then you weren't carrying your sack that night?"

"Well, no. But it was July. It wasn't Christmas."

"Would the jacket pocket be large enough to carry the murder weapon?"

"Maybe, but it wasn't used in that way."

"But if you had wanted to conceal the weapon there, you could?"

"It's heavy and might have made me list a little to one side, so an experienced person might have noticed it. But I suppose I could have concealed it there."

"Mr. Baines, you said when you picked up the gun out of your desk drawer, you held it with your thumb on the trigger. Is that correct?"

"Yes, I did."

"Isn't that an odd way to hold a gun?"

"I'm not accustomed to holding guns. It seemed quite natural to me at the time."

"Is that the way you would hold the gun if you were fire it?"

"Quite likely not. But as I've said, I'm not used to handling guns."

"Does your Santa Claus regalia include gloves?"

"Why, yes, certainly. That is, it normally does."

"But not always?"

"No, not always."

"Were you wearing gloves that night?"

"No, as I recall, I was not. It was quite warm, you know."

"Too warm for gloves but not too warm for a heavy red jacket and beard?"

"I've explained my attire that night."

"Were you wearing gloves when you shot your brother?"

"I didn't shoot my brother."

"After shooting your brother did you remove your gloves and then carelessly handle the gun, leaving your fingerprints on it?"

196

"No, I did not."

"Then perhaps you left the prints deliberately, to make it appear to be a clumsy attempt at framing you for the crime."

"I like to read detective novels, too, Ms. Wooten. I like Agatha Christie. Who is your favorite?"

"Your Honor, please instruct the witness to answer the question."

Judge Estrada, looking slightly amused, said, "Mr. Baines, this is a serious matter, especially serious for you. I'm sure in your own mind, you answered the question, and I'm equally sure most of us inferred your answer accurately, but you might frame your response in a more conventional way."

"My apologies, Your Honor, and Ms. Wooten, for my sarcasm. If I were in my Santa Claus suit, I would never respond so rudely." This got him a few smiles from the spectators and the jury box. "The answer to the question is no. No, I did not wear gloves that night. No, I did not shoot my brother. No, I did not deliberately put my prints on the gun in a complicated effort to frame myself for murder. No."

"Thank you, Mr. Baines," Melba said, more than a touch of sarcasm in her own tone. "If I may move on to another part of your testimony, you said you had the feeling you were not alone on the thirtieth floor that night. Is that correct?"

Charlie shrugged. "It was just a feeling. Nothing I could put my finger on precisely."

"You saw no one else on the floor that night?"

"No living person, no."

"And yet you had this feeling someone else was there."

"Yes, I did. I'm sure you must have had feelings like that."

"Whether I have or I haven't, it was a rather convenient feeling in this case, wasn't it?"

"I don't know why you would say it was convenient. It was just a feeling that I wasn't alone."

197

"Do you often have feelings like that?"

"No, but when I do, they often prove to be accurate."

"But you do understand, don't you, that the jury cannot regard feelings as evidence?"

Gordon Moon rose. "Objection, Your Honor. It is not my learned colleague's place to instruct the jury on what is evidence."

"Sustained," said the judge. "Ladies and gentlemen, what you find persuasive or not is up to you to decide."

"Thank you, Your Honor," Melba said. "Mr. Baines, we've heard from a number of people who were in contact with you the evening of your brother's death, and none of them have testified to any sign of apparent remorse on your part."

"Remorse? Why would I feel remorse?"

"Did you feel no sorrow at your brother's death?"

"Sorrow, certainly. But remorse, as I recall it, is defined as regret for a wrong committed. I committed no wrong to my brother that night."

"Perhaps remorse was the wrong word. Did you show any signs of grief at your brother's death?"

"I was stunned by it. True, I did not collapse or weep. Perhaps I came to a realization that the brother I knew and loved had been dead to me for years. It's difficult to explain. A person never knows how he will react to a traumatic event until it happens, does he?"

"One way you reacted was to flee the murder scene, wasn't it?"

"Not precisely flee, no. I went home, but I made it clear where I would be if the police wanted to talk to me, and when they did, I was where I said I would be."

"Didn't it occur to you that leaving the scene would throw added suspicion on someone who was the logical suspect to begin with?"

"It doesn't seem natural to me that an innocent person would envision himself being suspected of a murder, whatever others might think. I didn't see myself as the logical suspect or even an illogical suspect. I knew I hadn't done it, and it didn't occur to me anyone would believe that I did."

"Mr. Baines, did you leave the building that night because you knew the suit you were wearing could have carried additional evidence of your guilt?"

"No. The suit I was wearing was turned over to the police at their request, and to my understanding it yielded no evidence against me."

"You said you kept several Santa Claus suits in your office, Mr. Baines."

"That's right."

"Did you also keep extra suits at your home?"

"Yes."

"How does anyone know the suit you turned over to the police was actually the one you wore that night? I mean, they all do look alike, don't they?"

"I knew which one it was."

"Certainly you knew. But you had the opportunity to make a substitution. How do we know the one you wore and the one you turned over were the same suit?"

"I suppose you'll have to take my word for it."

"Why were you in such a hurry to get out of that Santa Claus suit?"

"I testified why already. It was warm and inappropriate to the occasion."

"Inappropriate to murder?"

"Inappropriate to assisting the police."

"No further questions."

The defense breathed a collective sigh of relief. After court was adjourned, Eve said to Gordon, "I guess it was a good idea for Charlie to testify after all."

Gordon, not particularly upbeat, said, "I won't go quite that far. But he didn't hurt himself any."

"Were you surprised Melba Wooten didn't go after him more?"

"I was," Vern offered. "If she'd pushed the right buttons, he might have gone really nutty on her. And we're not pleading insanity."

Gordon shook his head. "She didn't want to appear to attack him and antagonize the jury. But she figures she didn't need to. The prosecution thinks the DNA evidence, together with the circumstantial evidence of his being on the floor that night, is so strong that the jury will have to convict."

And Eve feared that Gordon's body language and general mood meant he thought exactly the same thing.

CHAPTER THIRTY-ONE

Friday, December 15

"Did you see Jack Wong's column in the *ProPurv* this morning?" Vern Wagstaff asked over a fast pre-court breakfast in the courthouse cafeteria.

"No," Gordon said. "Haven't seen the paper."

Vern handed it across and Gordon read:

> *Every big case brings them out, and when a beloved figure is on trial for his life, they're even more plentiful. Whether citizens who want to help or nuts who just want attention, whether anonymous voices on the other end of the phone line or visitors to your office, it's something the police have to deal with and so does your humble scribe. Most of these you never hear about because they don't check out or they're absurd on their faces. But this particular one was just too entertaining to keep to myself.*
>
> *The call came not to my desk here at the Provincial Purveyor or to my cell phone but late at night to my home number, information not many people have and which I won't soon be publishing in this space. (I may have to get it changed anyway.) The rasping whisper on the other end informed me that Charlie Baines was innocent.*
>
> *"How do you know that?" I asked him, logically enough.*
>
> *"Because I did it. I killed Andrew Baines."*
>
> *"Who is this?" I said.*

"Call me Deep Snow if you have to call me anything."

"If you want to confess to murder, you should go to the police."

"Maybe I should. Maybe I will, but only as a last resort. I can't stand to have an innocent person punished for my crime, especially if that person is someone like Charlie Baines. But I don't particularly want to be punished for it myself, especially because I think it was an act of civic responsibility and public charity. The people of this city will be quite happy to have the Baines case in the books as an unsolved murder. But first we have to get Charlie off. He didn't do it. I did it. I'm not a killer, and I'll never kill again, so it would serve no useful purpose to come forward unless there were no other way."

"So what do you expect me to do, Deep Snow? I'm just a newspaperman."

"Just get the word out."

"You need to give me some clue, something more to go on than your word alone."

But that was all he'd say. Instead of speaking again, the voice on the other end began humming. The caller could barely carry a tune, but I was able to recognize the melody. It was that most familiar of Christmas carols, "Silent Night." Then he hung up.

Do I think I was speaking to the real murderer of Andrew Baines? Not for a second. But it was one of the most inventive and memorable, not to say creepy, crank calls I've ever received. Maybe I won't change my home phone number just yet. Call again, Deep Snow.

"Cute," said Gordon. He handed it on to Eve, who read through it quickly and passed it on to Duffy.

"Is there some way we can use this to our advantage?" Eve wondered.

"There could be," said Duffy. "What do you think that song he hums means?"

"Means he's another anonymous screwball," said Vern.

"Let's not get sidetracked," Gordon said, whose level of optimism seemed to have risen overnight. "We need to concentrate on convincing the jury that DNA evidence could have been planted. If we can do that, this case is over, Deep Snow or no Deep Snow."

"But maybe this Jack Wong knows something more that might help us," Eve persisted.

"Got to be careful. Jack Wong's the DA's lapdog reporter. There may be a trap in here for us, something that will help the prosecution in an indirect way."

Eve shook her head. "I don't get it. How could this help the prosecution?"

"I don't know, but they work in mysterious ways," Vern said. "I'll bet Melba Wooten's calling Wong right now to congratulate him."

Melba Wooten, who moments before had been calmly turning the pages of the *ProPurv* as accompaniment to her morning coffee, punched the buttons on her cell phone angrily.

"You have reached the *Provincial Purveyor*, one of America's great newspapers," said the brightly robotic recorded voice. "Your call is important to us. If you are calling about an existing subscription, press one."

Melba interrupted the litany of options by entering Jack Wong's extension. Wong answered with his name on the first ring.

"Wong, what you doin' in this column of yours this morning?"

"Good morning, Melba. How are you? Oh, I'm fine thanks."

"Aren't you supposed to be a friend to the district attorney's office?"

"I think I'm supposed to be an objective journalist, but I

value my contacts in the district attorney's office, sure. What's your problem with my column?"

"To start with, if you have information related to a current case, as a citizen you should bring it to us before you put it in everybody's driveway."

"You really think that's important information? The column's not really about the Baines trial. It's about the kind of crank callers that come out of the woodwork in any major case. Conspiracy theorists. People who want to confess. We get 'em here at the paper, the cops get 'em, and I'm sure you folks do, too."

"It didn't read that way to me. Jack, you have to keep me informed. I call on you as a fellow victim of the white power structure. We have to stick together."

"I'm not a victim."

"Not a victim? You sitting there with your yellow skin and slitty eyes and inscrutable manner swear to me on your fifteen-hundred SAT score and the bones of your ancestors that you're not a victim of racism?"

"You're really funny, Melba."

"I ain't bein' funny!"

"Oh, sorry. My bad."

"And what's with the ghetto talk? You rippin' off our language?"

"Melba, you have to calm down."

"I don't have to do nothin'! But let me tell you something, Jack Wong. There's a special place in media hell for reporters who make stuff up."

"Make stuff up? I didn't make anything up."

"Right. Next time you're stuck for a column idea, just call me, and I'll give you plenty."

"Relax, Melba. Look, I'll see you at Winstead's Christmas party Sunday night, won't I?"

"Well, I'll be there anyway. That's a command performance."

"We can talk there. I'll buy you a drink."

"Very funny, Jack. And after that column, you'd best make sure your invitation hasn't been revoked."

In the courtroom that afternoon, Gordon Moon called several security experts to underline the porous Baines Building security. Still, he was unable to place anyone else on the thirtieth floor the night of the murder. Eve again suggested they call Oswald as a witness. Duffy had nothing to say on the matter. Both Gordon and Vern dismissed the idea as foolish at best and dangerous at worst. Court was adjourned for the weekend.

CHAPTER THIRTY-TWO

Sunday, December 17

For the three years he had been in office, District Attorney Prentice Winstead had been throwing a huge party at his home the weekend before Christmas. Virtually the entire bar of the city was invited, and virtually the entire bar showed up, even including those who despised Winstead. The local media were also well represented, along with carefully selected political and social movers and shakers. The first year, Winstead had called it a Christmas party. The second year and this year, he had changed the designation to holiday party, in a spirit of inclusiveness or political correctness (depending on how you reacted to the change). Some who particularly loved Christmas, either as a specially honored religious holiday or a de facto secular holiday, had actually boycotted the party the previous year, but most of them had come creeping back this year. There were several reasons for this: along with peace on earth and good will toward personkind and putting aside our differences to jollify together and all that, the party provided a great opportunity for networking in the legal community. The food and the booze were remarkable for both quality and quantity. In short, the annual party was the legal social event of the year.

Eve and David had talked it over and decided it would be inadvisable for them to come to the party together, or even to acknowledge each other apart from a quick hello. They were both sorry.

Vern and Stacey had made much the same decision. They knew their relationship did nothing to affect their performance in the courtroom, but still it was best to avoid the appearance of evil. Stacey was sorry.

Agnes and Gordon, being married, were almost required to show up together, smile together, and pose for the official event photographer together. If either of them was sorry, they wouldn't admit it.

While Alison McCready was a prominent enough local personality to merit an invitation, neither she nor Prentice Winstead wanted their personal relationship to be generally known. They spent the evening in separate orbits, and clearly neither of them was sorry.

Winstead's enormous house had multiple large rooms with multiple open bars and a different colored Christmas . . . er, holiday, tree in every room. Holly and mistletoe were everywhere. As at most social occasions that season, no Santa Claus was in evidence. The malls and the street corners had to have them—for commerce, for the children, for charity, for tradition—but at big civic events that were geared to adults, it seemed in bad taste.

Eve met more lawyers that night than she had in her first three months in the city. The five-man combo playing seasonal music in Winstead's ballroom could handle rock, country, big band, or hymns with equal competence but not much inspiration. Eve danced a few times, once with her designated mentor.

"Vern, just how rich is Prentice Winstead anyway?" she asked him.

"Rich enough to buy the DA's office and make an offer on the governor's mansion."

"How did he make his money—or did he inherit it?"

"Inherited it. It goes back a few generations. I'm not sure just how his great grandfather stole it, but he got away with it."

Eve noticed Stacey Bamwanger across the room, standing alone and glaring—at her in particular, or at the room at large?

"Stacey's real intense, isn't she? She looks like she hates the opposition."

"Very competitive," Vern agreed.

The next time the dance turned her in Stacey's direction, Eve noticed that David Ketchum was talking to her. Doing his duty. He was such a good person.

Eve said, "How long is one expected to stay at these affairs?"

"I don't know," Vern said. "I'd say till he runs out of food and booze, but he never runs out of food or booze. Personally, it's my general practice to close the place, making sure I can still stand up when I leave. It's not good form to have to be carried out."

"I just feel I should be working every waking hour. I mean, we are in trial, aren't we?"

"You can't work all the time. Watch my sister and brother-in-law. When you see them heading for the exit, you might take that as a signal it's okay to leave. I won't, but you might."

As the evening wore on, Eve was never at a loss for someone to talk to, most but not all young males. She had a brief, cordial, but somewhat stiff conversation with Gordon and Agnes Moon. They struck her as an odd couple indeed, and she wondered how they managed to stay married. Her meeting with Prentice Winstead was kind of funny. While saying the appropriate hackneyed things you'd expect from a host, he managed to register subtle male lust, with which Eve was more than familiar, followed by clear though unspoken regret that she was far too unimportant to spend any time with, followed by a genteel brush-off.

She was somewhat surprised to see Duffy O'Gonigal among the guests. He greeted her with a wide smile, raised his glass, and said, "Tonic water." This couldn't be easy for him.

my career. But I'm gonna show 'em.'"

Melba noticed Eve looking stricken. "Don't worry, honey," she said. "That wasn't an *ex parte* discussion of the case. You have not been compromised in any way. But you need to know what kind of sharks you're swimming with in this city."

"And now I know," Eve said. "Thank you, Melba. I do appreciate that."

"You ever want a sister has your back, you call me, okay?"

"Sure."

Eve left Prentice Winstead's party still going strong. Waiting for the valet to bring her car around, she saw David Ketchum come up and hand in his ticket. With no one in earshot, he turned to her and said, "My place this evening?"

"No. I have work to do back at the office."

"After you're finished—"

"I don't know when I'll be finished. But we're finished."

"Uh, well, if you think we shouldn't see each other anymore until the trial is over—"

"That's not what I mean! We're finished for good!"

"But why?"

"If you don't know, I'm certainly not going to tell you."

Before he could remonstrate further, her car arrived and she sped down the Winstead driveway and headed for the Baines Building. She would lose herself in work.

Wilbur Ricketts, back to being assigned to nights, waved at her cordially.

"Good evening, miss. Going to burn some midnight oil? Haven't beamed anybody up to your floor tonight."

"It's the DA's Christmas party, Wilbur. Apparently all the business of the city stops for it. But I'm going to get some work done."

As she crossed toward the elevator, Oswald appeared suddenly at her elbow. "Miss Nyquist?"

Wilbur walked over from the security counter. "Don't bother Ms. Nyquist, Oswald," he said gently. "She has important work to do. She's helping Santa."

"I know that," Oswald said. "Why else would I want to talk to her?"

" 'Cause she's a pretty lady prob'ly," Wilbur said.

"It's all right, Wilbur," Eve said. "Oswald and I are friends." She managed to sound patient and cordial. No reason to blame either Wilbur or Oswald for the general sins of the male gender.

"I've heard that voice again," Oswald said. "The one coming out of the closet. Now I know who it was."

When she heard the name, Eve realized her colleagues must be right about the homeless man's mental state. He meant well, but what he claimed was beyond rational belief. She thanked Oswald gravely and asked him not to mention what he thought he'd heard to anyone else.

CHAPTER THIRTY-THREE

Monday, December 18

The next morning, Eve picked up her *Provincial Purveyor* and saw that Jack Wong had once again heard from his mysterious informant.

> *I'd about forgotten my friend Deep Snow, figuring he was a one-shot caller. Maybe he'd switched to a different tipple and expressed himself in some other creative way that didn't involve the Baines case. Well, I was wrong. Just before I took off for a big holiday party, which I'll get to in another column, I heard from him again.*
>
> *"Mr. Wong, this is Deep Snow. Remember me?"*
>
> *"I'm not likely to forget you, Deep. Or is it Mr. Snow?"*
>
> *"I'm glad you can be so light-hearted, but this is a serious business. Things are going badly for the Baines defense. I'm afraid an innocent man is going to be convicted in my place. I do believe I'd turn myself in, if I had the courage. But you do the job for me, Mr. Wong. You can send them to my door."*
>
> *"I can?"*
>
> *"Sure. I'm giving you all the clues. It's up to you to interpret them."*
>
> *"What clues? You're a raspy voice on the phone. You're no musician, that I can tell. But other than that, I'm in the dark. Just tell me who you are, or where you are, and I'll see to it the police come calling. I promise."*

Deep Snow didn't speak again. Instead he started that same off-tune humming. It was another Christmas carol, this time "We Three Kings."

Don't come caroling outside my window, Deep Snow. But do call again.

Eve put down the paper. What if this really was the murderer of Andrew Baines? No one else on the defense team was taking it seriously. She'd been cautioned not to call Jack Wong, and she wouldn't. But if she could figure out what the clues meant, maybe it would help. She hummed the two Christmas carols, one after the other, "Silent Night" from the first column, "We Three Kings" from this one. Then, in a sudden flash of insight, she put them together. She realized she knew who Deep Snow must be, and she wondered what she should do next.

She'd tell David. After all, the district attorney's office, unlike her side, was supposed to serve justice. But no, she couldn't tell David because she was never going to speak to David again. Anyway, she owed her allegiance to the defense team. She would call Gordon Moon.

"Gordon, I won't be in court today. I have a lead that might be very important."

"What is it, Eve?"

"I'll tell you if it pans out. You have to trust me on this. It may be the evidence that will save Charlie."

"Eve, as you know, we're about to the end of our case. We've called all our witnesses and presented all our evidence. I was planning to rest this morning. I don't know if Melba's going to put on rebuttal or not, but we could be looking at closing statements as early as this afternoon."

"Gordon, don't rest. You and Vern have to stall until you hear from me. Can you do that?"

"Eve, of course I can do that. Any trial lawyer worth his salt can burn up any amount of time advancing absolutely nothing.

But he can't do it without looking silly, and I don't like to look silly."

"Are you willing to look silly if it will save Charlie Baines?"

"Well, sure, but—"

"Then do it. I really do think I'm on to something. Have to go now."

David Ketchum didn't climb the steps of the courthouse that morning. It was a side-door kind of morning. Something had happened between him and Eve; he had no idea what it was; and he wanted nothing more than to avoid the world. When the security officer asked him if he was feeling okay, he offered a wan smile and said he was fine. On his way to his office, no fewer than three other people threw him worried looks, and his staunchly feminist secretary offered him coffee and a back rub.

"No, thanks, nothing. I just want to work in my office today. Lots of paper work to catch up on. Don't really want to deal with people if I can help it. Put off anybody you can."

"Sure, boss. But I can't put off the DA, now can I? Fawn told me he wants to see you as soon you come in."

David groaned. "That's all I need. With a little luck, maybe he just needs help picking a flower for his goddam buttonhole."

The uncharacteristic cynicism just made his secretary more worried. And when he entered the DA's outer office, Fawn Ambrosia said, "You look like hell, David."

"Thank you."

"Still recuperating from the boss's Christmas party?"

David sighed. "What ails me will last longer than any hangover."

"It can't be a death in the family, or you'd be taking compassionate leave. It must be the death of love."

"Fawn, you're reading romance novels again. If only it were the death of love, but my love lives on in confusion. What does the old man want to see me about?"

"I think it has something to do with Jack Wong's column this morning."

"Haven't seen it."

"Well, you'll hear about it."

Prentice Winstead wouldn't have noticed the map of misery on his chief deputy's face even on a good day, and this was decidedly not a good day. The DA looked out at the city through a window not as large as Gordon Moon's but impressive for the public sector, working his jaw, grinding his teeth, cracking his knuckles.

"Did you see Jack Wong's column?" he demanded.

David shook his head and found the metro section of the *ProPurv* thrust in his face. He read Wong's column quickly.

"Wong's a formidable adversary as always," Winstead said with a straight face.

On another day, David might have laughed, but today he could control any display of mirth or delight.

"We might as well call that informant of his Deep Shit," Winstead said, "because that's where he's putting us. Deep Shit. Damn that's clever. Wish I could use it in a speech. Could with the right audience. Men's service club maybe. Too negative, though. Reflects poorly on the office."

"I don't think you have to worry about Deep Snow, sir," David said. "He's just some crazy crank that Wong finds entertaining. He wouldn't do anything to hurt the office."

"And our evidence against Baines is strong, right?"

For the hundredth time, it seemed, David ticked off the points. "We have his DNA on a bloody Santa Claus beard found at the scene of the crime. We have his DNA on a used facial tissue found on the scene of the crime. He was the only one up there that night apart from Andrew Baines. The murder gun had his fingerprints on it. He had a motive. He fled the scene.

216

Gordon Moon's done his best to obfuscate things, but he doesn't really have any substantial defense. He's depending on the city's sentimental attachment to Baincs."

"Exactly. That's the problem. David, if we let the prosecution go ahead, we probably get a conviction, right?"

"Of course we let the prosecution go ahead. I don't see how we can miss."

"But in case it doesn't go our way, we need a fallback position."

"I don't understand."

"We can't come out of this thing looking foolish. I think Jack Wong might cooperate with us on this, if we broach it to him the right way."

Oh, yeah, Jack Wong might cooperate. "If we broach what, sir?"

"We might get some more media cooperation if we invite Alison McCready in on it, too."

"In on what, sir?"

"That's settled then. Ask Fawn to get Jack and Alison on the phone. We'll do a conference call."

"But what are we talking with them about, sir? It will help if I know."

"It's a simple plan. However this case ends, it will be just as the district attorney's office planned it." Winstead thought for a moment. "Unless there's a riot, of course. We're not planning on a riot."

"Uh, sir, whatever we do, we probably should let Melba Wooten in on it."

"Should we?"

"Oh, I think so."

"Do we care what happens to her?"

"Maybe not, but if the district attorney's office has some secret plan for her case that she hasn't been let in on, she might take it the wrong way."

"So?"

"She might make it difficult for us. In the media. She's been prone to talking a lot."

"Yes, I suppose you're right. But she's in court. After we talk to Jack and Alison, you can fill her in. On a need-to-know basis."

"Right," David said. *And I wish you'd fill me in on a need-to-know basis.*

Chapter Thirty-Four

"Do you really think Eve has something?" Vern asked when Gordon joined him and Charlie Baines at the defense table that morning shortly before court was to resume. "I mean we both know she has something but—"

"Save the jokes, Vern. Our performance today is going to provide enough comedy. Where's Duffy?"

"Hasn't shown up. Didn't he call you?"

"No, haven't heard from him."

"Think he's drunk again?"

"No, I don't. I know him better than you do. He's a great lawyer, and when he commits to something, he has a will of iron. He'd never come in on a case and go out on a bender. Till the case is over, that is. He'll have a good reason if he's not here."

"Right. At least Eve called."

"Look, I'm not sure where I'm going this morning, but I need some stuff from the law library. Before court's in session, get on your cell and have a paralegal fax some stuff over for us." Gordon scribbled some notes on his legal pad and handed it to Vern, who left the courtroom hurriedly.

"What's going on, Gordon?" Charlie Baines asked, not excessively concerned.

"Something good, I hope."

"All rise!" the bailiff roared, and the judge entered the courtroom.

"Good morning, ladies and gentlemen," Judge Estrada said. "Mr. Moon, you seem to be going it alone this morning. Have your colleagues deserted you?"

"No, Your Honor, and Mr. Wagstaff will be back in the courtroom presently. I'm ready to proceed."

"Very well. Are there any motions before we have the jury in?"

Both chief counsels offered a quick "No, Your Honor."

"My, my, aren't things going speedily? Bring in the jury."

When the jury had been seated and greeted, Gordon said, "Your Honor, the defense would like to recall Detective Richard Tracy."

"Take the stand, Detective Tracy. You are still under oath."

"Certainly, Your Honor," Tracy said. He managed to seem unruffled by the unexpected recall.

"Detective Tracy, I've been looking at some of your previous testimony. When we first spoke, I asked you what your goal was in an investigation, and you said it was to catch the suspect. Do you remember that?"

"Yes, certainly. That's what I said."

"Then do I take that to mean you invariably have a suspect at the outset of an investigation?"

"No, I didn't say that."

"But you said you want to catch the suspect."

"Isn't that obvious?"

"Well, how can you catch the suspect if you don't have a suspect?"

"Sometimes we don't know who the suspect is."

"You don't know—Detective, exactly what do you mean by the term suspect?"

"A person we believe committed the crime," Tracy said through clenched teeth. "A person we hope to charge and eventually see convicted of the crime in question."

"When you said your goal was to catch the suspect, it was at a stage of your investigation when you had no idea who the perpetrator of the crime might be. Why would you use the expression when you don't yet have an idea of who did it?"

"Counselor," Tracy said with exaggerated patience, "you know as well as I do that police officers have to be very careful in our terminology. So we use suspect when referring to the person we have reason to believe committed the crime."

"Even when you can't put a name or a face to that person?"

"It's safer that way, yes."

Melba Wooten was on her feet. "Your Honor, I object to this line of questioning as irrelevant to the matter at hand."

"Mr. Moon?"

"I have a right to show any bias in the witness, Your Honor. It's proper cross-examination."

"I'm inclined to give you some latitude. Objection overruled, but please don't belabor this, Mr. Moon."

"Detective, are you telling me in the police lexicon suspect is a synonym for perpetrator?"

"No, I didn't say that."

"If you can't put a name or a face to the person who committed the crime but still you call that person the suspect, I believe you did say that. And the implication is that you believe, or would have this jury believe, that suspicion equals guilt."

Tracy was red-faced and glaring. Melba tried again to rescue him.

"Objection, Your Honor. Counsel is not asking a question but improperly stating his opinion of the witness's testimony."

"Sustained. The jury will disregard counsel's statement."

"May I rephrase my statement in the form of a question, Your Honor?"

Judge Estrada sighed. "Come to the sidebar please, counselors."

When the lawyers had gathered, Judge Estrada said, "Mr. Moon, I think you've made your point. Is there any reason for this line of questioning to go any further?"

"Your Honor, I believe the investigating officer's very loose use of the term suspect is an indication of bias, and I want to make sure the jury understand that."

"Your Honor," Melba countered, "everyone knows how police use the word suspect. No reasonable person believes that the use of suspect in the way Detective Tracy used it implies any kind of prejudice or any kind of frame-up."

"Did I use the term frame-up, Ms. Wooten?" Gordon Moon said, a shocked expression on his face. "Do you know something I do not?"

"If counsel will stop sniping at each other," Judge Estrada said, "we can discuss this reasonably. I'll allow this line of questioning to continue, but you're on a short rein, Mr. Moon. Take your seats please."

When Melba had returned to the prosecution table, Agnes Moon whispered to her, "What's he up to? I thought he was in a hurry."

"You know him better than I do, girlfriend," Melba whispered back.

CHAPTER THIRTY-FIVE

Eve phoned the Majestic Theatre but was able to connect with no live human. The recorded message wished her a joyous holiday season and recited that evening's show times. Apparently there was no weekday matinee at the venerable movie house. A call to Sidney Monarca's home number reached a housekeeper, who confided that the old man spent most of his days working in his office at the theatre.

"I called there," Eve said, "and all I got was a recording."

"Oh, he won't answer his phone during the day."

"How do you reach him if there's an emergency?"

"I convinced him at his age he should carry a cell phone so he could call for help if he has to, but he hates it and never uses it. Is there some kind of emergency?"

"It's very important that I talk to him. Can I have his cell phone number?"

"No, ma'am, I'm sorry. I can't give you that information. And even if I could, I can't guarantee he'd answer it."

"Whereabouts in the theatre is his office located?"

"No idea, ma'am. I've never been there."

The only solution was to go to the Majestic and find Monarca.

"Detective Tracy," Gordon Moon said, "I will now read to you the definition of suspect in its noun form in *Webster's Third New International Dictionary:* 'one who is suspected; esp. one suspected of a crime or of being infected.' "

223

"Okay," said Tracy. "So?"

"Isn't the implication that one particular person is referred to, that in fact one could not be a suspect if one's identity is not known?"

"I don't see that."

"Now let me read you the definition from the second edition of the *Random House Unabridged Dictionary,* which you will find remarkably similar: 'a person who is suspected, esp. one suspected of a crime, offense, or the like.' Do you note once again that reference is made to a particular person, not a phantom person or an unidentified person?"

"Counselor, I don't know what you want me to say."

"Detective Tracy, the word suspect as a verb is defined by *Webster's Third* as follows: 'to imagine (one) to be guilty or culpable on slight evidence or without proof.' Does that accurately describe your case against Charles Baines?"

"Huh?"

"You heard the question, I think. Have you accused Charlie Baines on the basis of imaginary evidence?"

"No."

"Have you accused Charlie Baines without proof."

"No. There's plenty of proof. And that's not what suspect means."

"I'm simply quoting from a reputable authority on language, the language you and your partner Joe Friday are so careful about."

"It's Joseph Freedy!"

Melba Wooten rose to object and request another conference at the sidebar.

"Ladies and gentlemen of the jury," said Judge Estrada, "I know you just got here, but it appears we have some matters to discuss outside your presence, so consider this an early morning break."

"This is just really stupid," said Juror Number Four, a heavy-set retired building contractor, when the chosen twelve had filed into the jury room. "Don't they know we want to get out of here by Christmas?"

"We don't always understand why they're doing what they're doing," said Juror Number Nine, a short-statured accountant with a balding head. "This whole thing may have some importance we're not aware of."

Grandmotherly Juror Number Two said, "We have to remember we're not supposed to discuss the case among ourselves."

"Haven't you ever read a book about a trial?" snorted Juror Number One, a well-dressed advertising account executive. "Jurors never take that business about not discussing the case seriously. Nobody expects people to deny human nature."

"Anyway, who's discussing the case?" Number Four said. "All we're doing is venting our frustration. I still have to shop for presents for my wife's aunt and my worthless brother-in-law. Things were going along quickly, but now they're bringing everything to a halt over non-essentials."

"We've discussed the case in groups of twos and threes, sort of casually like," said Number Nine.

"I haven't!" insisted Number Two.

"Well, the rest of us have. And we traded information about literary agents and book contracts for after the case is over, but golly, they have to expect that. We've just never discussed the case as a group. That's what they told us not to do, isn't it? That and not reach any definite conclusion until we've heard all the evidence."

"I think we *should* discuss the case as a group," said Number

One. "Maybe not before, but at this stage of the game, it would be useful. We've heard all the important witnesses. We've seen all the damning evidence. We know it's almost over. Maybe it's time we talk it out, see which way the wind's blowing. Then, when they do give us the case, we can deliver a quick verdict and get that shopping done."

Number Four said, "I agree with my friend here. Now I know we don't like the idea of convicting Santa Claus for murder. But look at the evidence. The DNA on the beard and the tissue. The murder gun with his fingerprints. The clear motive and opportunity. And what do they offer to counter it? Smokescreens and red herrings. Do they deny the DNA evidence or the ballistics evidence? They can't. So what do they have? The possibility that somebody else was wandering around on the thirtieth floor that night. How likely is that, I ask you?"

Juror Number Five, a young receptionist with the appearance and demeanor of a high school cheerleader, said, "We have to ask ourselves, what is most in the spirit of Christmas?"

"What do you mean by that?" asked Juror Number Six, a hardware clerk who was the second youngest juror and whose interest in Number Five went beyond the intellectual.

"Well, Christmas is about being with family and friends, isn't it? If the evidence is overwhelming and we still take a long time to do a verdict, we're robbing our families and friends of our presence, taking away a lot of the joy of their Christmas. We owe it to the people we love to be there for them. I mean, I made lots of promises to be places on Christmas Eve and Christmas."

"We won't be working then, whatever happens," said Juror Number Twelve, a plumbing contractor.

"I know that, but there are a bunch of parties before Christmas that won't be the same without me, and there's special decorating I do that nobody else can do just the same way and everybody looks forward to every year. And I have special gifts that no one else can give. Like what I'm getting my mother this year: I'm having three of my tattoos removed, and I'm signing up for financial counseling. Who else can give her that gift if I'm stuck here on jury duty? I'll bet the rest of you can say the same. We owe our family and friends the gift of us at Christmas. And whether we think the old man is a nice old man or not, if we know he must have killed his brother, we have to find him guilty, and he wouldn't want us to deprive our friends and family of us by drawing it out. If he's really Santa Claus, that's what he'd want us to do. In the true spirit of Christmas. Do you see what I mean?"

"Exactly," said Number Six.

"And they call this younger generation selfish and narcissistic," said Number One. He put an avuncular arm around Number Five's shoulder and got a dirty look from Number Six. "I'm proud to serve on this jury with you, young lady. Look, all I'm asking for is this. We make an informal agreement that as of this point, Charlie Baines is guilty of murder and we have to convict him and we have to convict him fast. Not with joy, not with vindictiveness, but with due deliberate speed."

"We shouldn't be talking about this," Number Two insisted.

"Okay," said Number Four. "So what are you going to do, report us to the bailiff and ruin this trial for everybody?"

"No," Number Two mumbled. "I suppose not."

Number One said, "We won't take a formal ballot now. Don't want to leave a paper trail. We'll just make it an informal show of hands. How many for guilty?" Number One raised his own hand and watched the rest of the jury follow his lead one by one, some eagerly, some reluctantly, until twelve hands were raised.

Having parked her Toyota Corolla in the Majestic's rear lot, Eve walked around to the front of the cavernous old building. The central ticket booth and the large overhang area outside the doors were festooned with wreaths, tinsel, and colored lights. The ticket booth, as she expected, was closed and the doors into the lobby were locked. Through the glass, she could see the lobby decorations: a huge Christmas tree and a life-sized Santa (Charlie Baines could have posed for him) driving his sleigh, urging on a full complement of reindeer, including the non-canonical red-nosed leader. She stopped for a moment to look at the colorful old posters advertising the films in the Majestic's annual yuletide series. She remembered *The Preacher's Wife* with Denzel Washington playing an angel, but she had never seen *The Bishop's Wife* with Cary Grant in the part. She didn't care for John Wayne or westerns generally, but maybe *Three Godfathers* would be worth a look.

David would know. He knew all about old movies. Hah! Forget David. She would never speak to him again.

Eve moved on to the posters for *Meet Me in St. Louis* and *It's a Wonderful Life*. She had seen them a dozen times each of course, but she could always watch them again.

Right, Eve. Go home and turn on the TV, make some cocoa, eat a Santa Claus cookie, and find an old Christmas movie to watch. But you know you can't. You have more important things to do. You have to act like a lawyer. You have a duty to your client. You have to be brave, but above all, you have to be smart.

Walking around the building, she noticed a side door had been left slightly ajar. Someone must be working inside. She walked through and tentatively called, "Hello. Is anyone here?"

No answer. Entering the building, she found herself in an unlit corridor. She crept along cautiously until she came to another door. She pushed it open and peered into the massive auditorium, now dimly lit, its huge screen covered by a red curtain. She stepped inside and submerged herself in the majesty of the Majestic. One screen and all these rows and rows of seats. A balcony high above her. Were movie theatres ever really this big, this grand, this dignified? No wonder somebody like David—*can't you forget David?*—regarded these old movie houses almost like churches. But if Sidney Monarca was here, he wasn't working on his sermon.

Monarca had an office here somewhere. Where would it be? There were plenty of places to look. She walked along the worn carpet until she could look past the balcony to the projection room. Maybe the office was up there, but she saw no lights. She returned to the hallway, feeling her way along until she found another door. Behind it a narrow stairway, like one you might find in a lighthouse, spiraled downward into the cavernous bowels of the old building. It was dark at the top, but she could see a light at the bottom. Grasping the handrail, she carefully started down the steps.

Halfway down, she called, "Hello. Is anyone there?" resenting the quaver in her voice.

"Yes, who is it?" came a voice. Suddenly the light on the stairway was switched on. She wasn't sure whether the voice and the sudden light were more comforting or more frightening, but at least she could see her surroundings now. The walls on either side of her were decorated with framed lobby cards from an even earlier era than the Christmas movies the Majestic was advertising upstairs. She recognized Jean Harlow, Rudolph Valentino, Harold Lloyd.

"Is that you Mr. Monarca?"

"Yes. Come on down."

"Your Honor," Melba Wooten said, "Mr. Moon's entire argument seems to be based on whether the word suspect must refer to a known individual."

Gordon nodded. "Or at least one of which some kind of

description exists. Not a complete phantom."

With the jury sent out, both principal advocates were facing the bench but speaking loudly enough for the whole courtroom to hear them. Gordon went on, "When it is obvious a crime has been committed, but you don't know who committed it, you are looking for the perpetrator, not the suspect. When you find the person you believe to be the perpetrator, that person is properly called the suspect. By using the term suspect ambiguously, Detective Tracy and his colleagues hopelessly confuse the matter and little by little erase the important distinctions our society and our system of justice rightly draws between the accused and the convicted. The whole concept of presumed innocent until proven guilty rests on the proper use of words like suspect."

"Just wait a minute," Melba said. "Mr. Moon says it's obvious a crime has been committed. But is it so obvious? You agree don't you, Mr. Moon, that someone was there with Andrew Baines? For purposes of argument, not necessarily the defendant, but someone, right? I mean Baines didn't shoot himself, did he?"

Gordon said, "I'll give you that. Someone was there to shoot him. But it's still an unknown person. How can you call an unknown person a suspect?"

"You can call that unknown person a suspect because, until all the facts are known, we cannot say that a crime has been committed. Theoretically, Andrew Baines could have been shot in self-defense. I know he wasn't, but he might have been. We don't know why or how the unknown person did what he or she did, and therefore we don't know if it constitutes a crime. Given that fact, it's the word perpetrator that's prejudicial, not the word suspect. The person we call a suspect might in fact be a victim!"

At the prosecution table, Stacy Bamwanger whispered to

Agnes Moon, "Oh, my God, she said the 'v' word. Now we're off."

At the defense table, Vern Wagstaff whispered to Charlie Baines, "This is choice. Now she sounds more like a defense attorney than a DA. By the time she winds down, maybe we'll have heard from Eve."

As Eve reached the bottom of the stairway, she saw she had entered a massive basement that was being used as a combination storeroom and office. Several projectors of various ages lined the walls which were decorated with more movie posters and lobby cards. A bookcase on one wall was filled with what appeared to be motion picture reference books, and dusty cans of film were stacked in the corners. She saw Sidney Monarca rising creakily and walking toward her from a battered old wooden desk in the middle of the floor lit by a bare bulb hanging directly above it. Monarca's sleeves were rolled up, his jacket off and hung over the back of his chair. The old man wore a green visor and suspenders. An old-fashioned adding machine and a manual typewriter were barely visible among the stacks of paper covering his desk. No computer or fax was in evidence. The basement office mightn't have looked any different if it were 1940. No wonder he hated his cell phone.

Monarca peered at her. "Why, Miss Nyquist, to what do I owe the pleasure? Do sit down." He removed a stack of ancient exhibiters' trade journals from a chair to make good his hospitality. "I wish I could offer you something to eat or drink, but you took me by surprise."

"I'm sorry, Mr. Monarca, but I would not have barged in like this if it weren't very important. To my client."

"Naturally I'd do anything to help Charlie Baines." Monarca returned to the old swivel chair behind his desk and sat facing her.

231

"Naturally. Mr. Monarca, have you been reading Jack Wong's column in the *ProPurv*?"

The old man's eyes narrowed. "I read it occasionally."

"Then you have probably seen the columns about an anonymous source he calls Deep Snow."

"I have. Very amusing. Of course, you're too young to remember, but Deep Throat—"

"I've heard of Deep Throat, Mr. Monarca, but it's Deep Snow I'm concerned about."

"Wong is quite a creative young man, but his journalistic ethics may not be the best."

"What are you suggesting?"

"Merely that I smell a hoax. And even if Wong actually received those calls, Deep Snow is undoubtedly just a crank. I understand any big case brings them out of the woodwork."

"Perhaps, but assume for a moment Deep Snow is real and is telling the truth. In the middle of a trial for murder, I can't believe a reporter would do something so despicable as to make things up, and I can feel Deep Snow's anguish. Deep Snow is a man who committed a terrible crime, but he is also a man who has a heart, a conscience, who doesn't want to see an innocent man convicted for a crime he himself committed." Eve paused for a moment. Then, telling herself she'd talked around the subject long enough, she forged ahead. "Mr. Monarca, I want you to give yourself up."

"Give myself up? I don't understand."

"Yes, you do. You are Deep Snow. You killed Andrew Baines."

"Me? Why would you think that, young lady?"

"You wanted to be found out, Mr. Monarca. Criminals often do, especially criminals like Deep Snow who are racked with guilt but don't feel they have the courage to give themselves up. Each time you talked to Jack Wong, you gave him a clue to your identity. You hummed 'Silent Night.' One of the features of the

232

Majestic has been its nights of silent films."

"And that was a clue to me? Pretty far-fetched
do a lot of humming 'Silent Night' at this time of y

"But that's not all. The second tune Deep Snow
was 'We Three Kings.' Monarca means king in Italian,
it? And you started in business with two brothers. One Mc
plus two Monarcas equals three kings."

"Still pretty thin, I think."

"The first line of the carol goes 'We Three Kings of Orient
are . . .' Your first movie theatre was the Oriental, wasn't it?"

The old man sighed. "You've been very clever, Ms. Nyquist,
very clever indeed. Those clues could point to me, yes. But if
you think I'm a murderer, it was pretty silly of you to come
here alone, wasn't it?"

"Perhaps. But I don't think Deep Snow, motivated as he is by
a guilty conscience, would kill again."

Monarca sighed. "This is so much more complicated than
you believe." He reached into a drawer in his desk and pulled
out a handgun, showing it to her with a regretful look on his
face.

"What are you going to do?" Eve demanded, as coolly as she
could manage. "Kill me after all?"

"I'd prefer not to, but I don't think I have any choice at this
point, do you?"

"There's always a choice. You made those calls because you
didn't want to see an innocent man convicted. Now you're going to kill another innocent person, a lawyer trying to do her
best for her client, just to cover your tracks? I don't think Deep
Snow would do that."

Monarca raised the gun and pointed it at Eve. "Perhaps Deep
Snow wouldn't. You read me very wrong, Miss Nyquist. You've
made several false assumptions in coming here today. I will kill
you. If you try to scream, no one will hear you. If you think I

ght because I'm old and my hand is shaky, I
estimate me, not an unusual mistake for a young
you to make about a senior citizen, we who are
, marginalized by a youth-crazed society. And while
sider your options, let me make one more point. If you
run, I'll have to shoot you before I explain myself, and
 would be unsatisfactory for both of us. I feel a great need
o explain myself."

"Please do," Eve said softly.

"You're partly wrong and partly right in what you have claimed about me. I hated Andrew Baines because he was trying to cheat me. He and I had an agreement, one that of course had to be kept a secret, an agreement that would ultimately have benefited us both if he kept to his part of the bargain. Publicly I would oppose development of the Majestic, encouraging the preservationists and others who were out to save it, but our private agreement would guarantee me the most lucrative possible sale of the Majestic, which would permit me to share my love of classic film in a different venue while ensuring my own security for life. But I discovered Andrew was playing both ends against the middle, managing things in such a way that the only person enriched by any deal would be him. When I found him out, he upped the ante, so to speak: he claimed he had irrefutable evidence that I had burned down the Royal Theatre to collect the insurance. He also claimed he had proof I had murdered my brother Frank who found out I had burned the Royal and threatened to turn me in."

"And had you?" Eve asked. "Burned down the Royal and killed your brother?"

Monarca just smiled. His smile was chilling. Eve looked at the handgun—Angela Ramirez might have known the make and model of it, but who cared at the moment?—and was certain the old exhibitor wouldn't hesitate to pull the trigger.

"Shall I kill you now," he asked, "or should I go on￼ing?"

"Explain. Please."

"So Andrew Baines, with all his other attributes, wa￼ blackmailer. When I went to the Baines Building the night ￼ died, I didn't intend to confront him. I didn't even know he'd￼ be there. I hoped to search his office and find whatever evidence he had on me, plus something that proved how he was trying to cheat me on the Majestic deal. I had stolen a key, made a duplicate, and come to the building garbed as a cleaner. Yes, I hated Andrew Baines, and I had good reason. As for his brother Charlie, I always went along with the popular idea that our local would-be Santa was this wonderful civic-minded do-gooder, but I never really believed it. Charlie said he was on my side, but I know he was in with his brother, both of them cheating me. You see, I knew them as children. I know how close they were then. I know how the insidious little bastards used their family's influence to get those lobby cards."

"Was this all about the lobby cards?"

"Not all about them, no. I was willing to deal with the devil, that is, Andrew Baines, when I thought we had interests in common. But those lobby cards are no small matter. Can you imagine what some of those are worth today? And I loved them. I had started a collection of them, stashing them away when they weren't needed in the lobbies anymore. But I wasn't the only lobby card collector around, nosiree. Our manager at the Majestic was giving them away to the Baines kids, and I wanted it stopped. But my brothers—I was the kid of the family, just in my early twenties—my brothers said our manager at the Majestic was doing the right thing because the Baines brats had influential parents. I was in the business. I was an adult. They were children, collecting them on a whim. I should have understood. But there was something my brothers did not

…d. Collecting lobby cards was a passing fancy to the brothers. A week later, they'd be enthralled with some juvenile hobby. But I was a serious collector. Those lobby …s really meant something to me, and they still do.

"I knew those Baines boys as kids, and I watched them grow up. Andrew was the same grasping, avaricious, scheming person as an adult. But what about innocent, good-hearted Charlie? Could he have changed so much? I don't think so. If the two of them were so close as kids, I figured they were still a team now. So when I saw the opportunity to plant some evidence to point the finger at Charlie for the murder of his brother, I took it, and I'm not sorry. He'll be convicted on it. And do you know what?"

"What?" Eve said, her mouth dry.

"I even got some of his lobby cards. Stashed away there in his office." He gestured to a group on one wall. "A complete set for *Singin' in the Rain.*" He gestured to another area. "And another for *Mogambo,* around the same period. I took them with me when I left the building." Monarca sighed with pleasure, then returned his attention to his gun and the young woman he was pointing it at. "And now, Miss Nyquist, much as it pains me, you are going to have to exit the picture. Fade out, so to speak. I can't have you ruin me, you know."

"I'm not the only one who knows," Eve said, hearing the desperation in her voice.

"Yes, that's true. You refer to the person who made those calls to Jack Wong."

"Are you saying that wasn't you? You aren't Deep Snow?"

"Certainly not. Do you think I was trying to implicate myself? The conscience you attribute to Deep Snow has nothing to do with me. Now is there anything else you'd like me to explain before I kill you?"

Come on, Eve. Think of some way to keep this old man talking. You're a lawyer. You should be able to think of a question. "Your collection of lobby cards is really impressive. Which or most valuable?"

"Not about the lobby cards," Monarca said disdainful. know you're not really interested, and I can hardly hold you gunpoint and talk about my lobby cards before I kill you. D you think I'm stupid?"

"Certainly not. No, I don't think that." After a pause, she added with calculated nonchalance, "Oh, well, these lobby cards probably aren't all that valuable anyway."

"You don't think so? Did you see the one with Edward G. Robinson in *Little Caesar*? Or Lon Chaney in *The Unholy Three*, silent and sound versions? You'd be astonished at the prices . . ."

He was off. Now Eve could concentrate on thinking her way out of this. She knew she couldn't run or try to leap across the desk at him and take away the gun. Either way, her chances of getting shot were high. She might try to get her cell phone from her purse, but he'd be sure to see her. Was that circular stairway the only way to get to the basement office? Monarca was old and moved with difficulty. She couldn't imagine him climbing up and down those stairs every day. Surely there must be a hidden elevator here somewhere. That bookcase that held the reference books appeared to be on some sort of track. Maybe it opened and closed to reveal the elevator.

Or maybe it concealed something else. Something horrible.

Even if the bookcase gives access to the elevator, how can I get to it? Monarca and his gun are between me and the bookcase. Is there something I can use in the ceiling? She looked up. They had live shows here occasionally, didn't they? Maybe there was a trapdoor under the stage. But the ceiling was so high. She looked up and saw only a world of distant shadows. Every corner of the basement held its menace. Why had she come here alone? Why hadn't she arranged for some kind of backup?

It was hopeless. Eve would die here. As Monarca rattled on

s precious lobby cards, visions of her life began to flash
her eyes. Her parents. Her old golden retriever. Her
nood friends. Birthdays and Christmas mornings. Her
ior prom. Her law school professors and classmates. David.
Get out of my reverie, David. You aren't forgiven.) Duffy
O'Gonigal.

Duffy O'Gonigal? He was a nice enough old guy, but he
didn't really mean that much to her. Why was she hallucinating
him here in this den of death? Why was she seeing him emerg-
ing from the shadows behind Monarca's desk? Could it be—?

But it was impossible. Her mouth fell open. Monarca just
kept talking. He undoubtedly took her reaction for awed fascina-
tion at his lecture on the lobby cards.

Duffy O'Gonigal, his finger over his lips to silence her, crept
up behind Monarca, wrapped his arms around the old exhib-
iter, and wrested away his gun. Monarca glared hatred at the
lawyer, but he hadn't the strength for the struggle once his
equalizer had been taken from him.

"Duffy," Eve exclaimed, "where did you come from?"

Duffy winked. "The defense team has to stick together, and I
know this old place like the back of my hand."

"But how did you know I was here?"

"No time for that, honey. We have to get this murderer safely
in custody and then get to court. I'm sure you'll be happy to
testify, won't you, Sid."

"I'm an old man," Monarca said in a quavering, pathetic
voice. "I was just trying to scare her. You didn't really think I
was going to kill you, did you, Miss Nyquist?" Seeing no
sympathy in Eve's face, he turned back to Duffy. "She came
here unannounced. She was trespassing. I drew my gun in self-
defense." Duffy only looked vaguely amused. "I was crazy. I am
crazy. I'm legally insane. I want immunity from prosecution."

"Not usually possible in a murder case, Sid," Duffy said.

"And I can't speak for the district attorney's office. I make a deal with you."

"Yes! Yes! Anything!"

"If you go on trial for murder, I promise not to defend you

CHAPTER THIRTY-SIX

.nembers of the prosecution team sat looking ahead
ɔly. Charlie Baines and Vern Wagstaff sat at the defense
: looking vaguely amused. Gordon Moon stood facing the
ᴜᴇ₁ɪᴄh.

"Your Honor," he said, "with the court's indulgence—"

"Mr. Moon, you have had about enough of this court's
indulgence. The jury may thank you for an extra long morning
break, but I would like to wrap up this discussion before I have
to give them an early lunch. Whatever point you had to make
about the word suspect has been made."

"If I could quote just one more distinguished source, Your
Honor. Suspect, in its noun form, according to the *Oxford
English Dictionary*—"

Hearing a murmur from the spectators' gallery, Gordon
stopped and turned to the door at the back of the courtroom.
He saw Eve Nyquist rushing up the aisle to the defense table.
Hair disarranged, makeup askew, she had never looked more
beautiful.

"Your Honor, if I could beg a moment to consult with my
colleagues?" Gordon said.

"Only if you promise to halt this filibuster."

"Certainly, Your Honor. I agree with you. The point has been
made to my satisfaction, and I'm sure we'll be able to have the
jury rejoin us soon."

He spent a few moments in hurried conference with Eve and

Vern. Then he said, "Your Honor, the defense withdraws its last question about the term *suspect*. Indeed, we have no more questions for Detective Tracy. My next witness, however, is not on the witness list, and I beg the indulgence of my learned colleagues on the prosecution side to call her in the interest of justice."

"We're all interested in that here, Mr. Moon," Judge Estrada said. "Who is your witness?"

"The defense calls Eve Nyquist."

"Not so fast, counselor. You call her when I say you can call her. Do I understand that you intend to call a member of your defense team as a witness?"

"Yes, Your Honor."

"That's highly irregular, to put it mildly."

Melba Wooten rose to her feet. "We have no objection, Your Honor. Subject to cross-examination and rebuttal, of course."

"Of course," Gordon echoed.

"Bailiff, bring back the jury," Judge Estrada said wearily.

At the defense table, Gordon asked Eve one more question. "Where's Duffy?"

"He said he'd get here if he could."

"Good. He wasn't drunk when he rescued you?"

She smiled. "Nope, cold sober." Gordon glanced at Vern, a smirk of smug triumph on his face.

When the jurors had been reseated, Eve was called to the stand and sworn in.

"Ms. Nyquist," Gordon began, "the jury has grown accustomed to seeing you seated at the defense table throughout this trial. Why didn't you join Mr. Wagstaff and me there this morning?"

"I thought I had a possible lead that would prove our client innocent."

"And what was that?"

"Recently, the *Provincial Purveyor* has been running a series of columns by Jack Wong—"

Melba was on her feet. "Your Honor, the jurors have been admonished not to view or read media reports concerning this trial. I object to testimony concerning the content of such media reports."

"Sustained. Ms. Nyquist, you may tell us what you did as a result of those press reports without commenting on the specific nature of those press reports. Is that clear?"

"Yes, Your Honor."

"Ms. Nyquist," Gordon said, "what did you do as a result of reading those press reports?"

"I reached a possible conclusion as to who the subject of the columns was."

"And what did you do as a result of reaching this possible conclusion?"

"I went to the Majestic Theatre to talk to its owner, Sidney Monarca."

"The same Sidney Monarca who appeared as a witness in this trial?"

"The same."

"And what was the nature of your exchange with Mr. Monarca?"

"I accused him of the murder for which our client Charlie Baines is on trial."

"And what did Mr. Monarca do pursuant to this accusation?"

"He pulled a gun on me and threatened to kill me."

"And did he kill you?"

"No, he did not."

"Did he admit to having killed Andrew Baines?"

"Objection," Melba said. "Hearsay."

Everyone in the courtroom appeared exasperated by her

interruption, but the judge said, "Sustained. Yo
to what Mr. Monarca said."

"Ms. Nyquist," said Gordon, "as a result o
Monarca said, what was your conclusion?"

"That he had planted evidence to frame Charlie Ba
the murder of his brother."

"If Monarca pointed a gun at you and threatened to kill y
how do you account for your presence here, happily living an
breathing?"

"I was rather miraculously rescued by a colleague on the
defense team, Mr. Duffy O'Gonigal."

"And what occurred as a result of Mr. O'Gonigal's rescue of
you?"

"Mr. Monarca has been placed under arrest and charged
with assault."

"Not with murder?"

"No."

With a meaningful glance at the jury, Gordon said, "Not
yet." Then he turned to the prosecution table and said, "Your
witness."

Melba Wooten rose to her feet, smiled at the jury, seemed to
consider for a few moments, then shook her head disdainfully,
said, "No questions, Your Honor" and sat down.

"Do you have another witness, Mr. Moon?" Judge Estrada
asked.

"Yes, Your Honor. The defense would like to recall Sidney
Monarca."

Monarca, with officers on each arm, made his way totteringly
down the center aisle. He appeared a defeated man.

"Mr. Monarca," Judge Estrada said, "I have to advise you
that you cannot be compelled to testify against yourself."

"Yeah, yeah, I know that. But I'll tell the truth. I'm an old
man. What can you do to me?"

…nd you may seek the advice of counsel before
…ur testimony."

…thing I did was all that serious."

…on't think so?"

…arry on with your questioning, Mr. Moon."

Mr. Monarca, did you threaten to kill Ms. Nyquist, a
…member of the defense team?"

"No."

"You didn't?"

"Maybe I said something that gave her that idea, but I don't
know if I would have killed her. I mean, I know I would not
have killed her. Absolutely I would not have killed her. She
surprised me there, came on me without warning. She scared
me, and I guess I scared her a little bit in return. Waved a gun
at her. She and O'Gonigal took it all too seriously."

"Mr. Monarca, were you in fact on the thirtieth floor of the
Baines Building the night Andrew Baines was killed?"

"Uh, yes, I was there."

"And did you admit to Ms. Nyquist that you planted evidence
to frame my client for the murder of Andrew Baines?"

"Well, yes, I suppose I did."

"You were in Charlie Baines's office that night?"

"That's right."

"And did you also steal the lobby cards that Charlie Baines
was looking for in his office?"

"I didn't look upon it as stealing. I was taking something that
rightfully belonged to me. The lobby cards came from my
theatre."

"Fifty or more years ago?"

"Even so."

"Did you find an extra Santa Claus beard in the closet of
Charlie Baines's office and plant it on Andrew Baines's desk?"

"I did, yes."

"Did you also plant a facial tissue Charlie Baines into on Andrew Baines's desk?"

"Yes, I did."

"And did you move the murder gun from the scene and it in Charlie Baines's desk drawer?"

"Yeah, that was me, too. I was a little crazy, I guess. I was like a character in a movie."

"And did you make telephone calls to Jack Wong of the *Provincial Purveyor*, admitting to the crime and giving clues to your identity?"

"Now that little job somebody else did. But you have to smile at the irony. I frame Charlie Baines, and this caller, whoever he is, frames me."

"Do you mean framing you for a murder you actually committed, Mr. Monarca?"

"No, that's not what I mean at all. I didn't do it. He was already dead when I got there. I figured he must have killed his brother, but I knew people love him so much he might get away with it, so I just imported a little evidence to help make the case, that's all."

"Just a public spirited citizen, Mr. Monarca?"

"That's right. Just trying to serve justice."

"I'm sure. No more questions, Your Honor."

"Ms. Wooten, do you wish to cross-examine?"

"Yes, Your Honor. Mr. Monarca, are you taking some kind of medication?"

"Look at me, lady. I'm old and wobbly. I'm taking all sorts of medication."

"Did you make some sort of agreement with the defense to testify as you have?"

Monarca laughed. "What deal could the defense make with me? I thought it was you guys who could give people immunity."

one paid you for your testimony?"

s I'd notice."

said, "Your Honor, I have no more questions for the

r. Moon, does the defense wish to rest its case?"

Before Gordon could answer, Eve hissed in his ear, "No. tall. Break for lunch. Monarca didn't kill Andrew Baines."

"Then who did?"

"Break for lunch, Gordon, please."

Gordon said, "Your Honor, may I request a recess until this afternoon?"

Judge Estrada sighed. "We're coming near the lunch hour. We'll recess until two o'clock."

Back at the defense table, Charlie Baines was congratulating Eve on her detective work, but Gordon Moon returned to the table looking like a man lost and nearly ready to ask for directions.

When the jury had left, court had been adjourned, and Charlie Baines had been taken away, Gordon turned to Eve and said, "I don't know whether I should kiss you or strangle you. Are you okay?"

"I'm fine, Gordon."

"And where's Duffy? You said he'd meet us here."

"If he could. He said if he didn't make it to court, he'd meet us for lunch at Rumpole's."

"He's probably already there," Vern said, "celebrating his victory by buying drinks for the house."

"I've told you he wouldn't do that in the middle of trial," Gordon said.

Vern raised a conciliatory hand. "I said buy drinks, not drink drinks."

Gordon ignored him. "Okay, Eve. I give up. We're doing great there. Melba's ready to fold. Monarca is acting like a mental

case, but thanks to him the case against Charlie has coll.
What more is there for us to do? Where do we go from her

"To Rumpole's. I'm hungry."

Duffy O'Gonigal, cold sober, was waiting for them at a back booth at Rumpole's. He was finishing a club sandwich, with an astonishing glass of iced tea in front of him. He shook hands all around, accepted the congratulations of Gordon and Vern, and gave Eve a conspiratorial wink.

"So what about it, Duffy?" Gordon said. "Is she right? After all this, is Monarca innocent of murder?"

"If Eve says so, I think we should listen to her. You have a genius on your hands here, young fella. Hang onto her."

"So what do we do now?"

The question had been directed at Duffy, but Eve answered. "We call one more witness. I saw him earlier today, and I can have him in court and ready to testify this afternoon."

"Somebody on our witness list?"

"Oh, he's on there, but I don't think we ever expected to call him."

"Who is it?"

"Oswald Ogburn."

"Who the hell is that?"

"She means Oswald the fruitcake," Vern said. "You know him. He's around the Baines Building almost every day."

Gordon was incredulous. "We can't call that loony! It's suicidal! Who knows what he might say?"

"I know what he'll say. Something so fantastic, when he told me, I refused to believe him. But now it makes sense to me. Gordon, I told you when we had our first meeting that I wanted to serve justice. Well, it's an impulse I just can't overcome."

"Give it time," Vern muttered.

Eve went on, "I have done everything I can to save our client,

want to do more than that. I don't want to be the one to
. an innocent man to the gallows."

"We don't have a gallows in this state, Eve," Gordon said.
We don't even have lethal injection."

"You have to trust me, Gordon. Vern may call Oswald a
fruitcake, but this is one fruitcake that's going to be a most
welcome Christmas present."

"Are you saying that crumb Monarca is an innocent man?"

"Innocent, no. He had an underhanded deal with Andrew
Baines. He planted evidence to frame Charlie. He probably
burned down one of his theatres to collect the insurance, and
the police department's cold case unit should take a close look
at the death of his brother Frank. He threatened to kill me and
might have done it. But innocent of murdering Andrew Baines?
Yes."

Gordon Moon turned to his old mentor. "Duffy, what is all
this?"

"You've always trusted me, haven't you, Gordon, me lad? We
have to bring this to a proper conclusion. Do what Eve says.
She's on the right track."

"Can we order lunch?" Vern suggested.

"Eat and enjoy," Duffy roared. "Have Phil Etchebarren put it
on my tab. As for myself, I shall repair home to put on my law-
yering suit and join you in Judge Estrada's courtroom at the appointed hour."

Back in the courtroom, Gordon whispered to Eve, "He's here?"

"Out in the lobby, yes."

"Eve, this guy is your witness. You have to run with it. I have
no idea where this is all going, but Duffy told me I should trust
you and I will. That old gladiator has never steered me wrong
yet."

"Where is the old gladiator anyway?" Vern said.

"He'll be here. I'm sure he will."

The judge took the bench, the jury came in, and c
resumed.

"Over to you, Mr. Moon," Judge Estrada said wearily. "C:
your next witness."

"Ms. Nyquist will take the next witness, Your Honor."

Eve rose to her feet. She could read the surprise on the
judge's face, and suddenly she felt weak in the knees. *Get a hold
of yourself, Eve. You just escaped from a dark basement where you
were menaced by a crazed movie exhibitor. Why should the biggest
moment of your legal career make you nervous?* She cleared her
throat and said in an assertive voice, "Your Honor, the defense
calls Oswald Ogburn."

As Oswald, spiffily dressed by his standards in jeans and a
sweatshirt, was ushered into the courtroom, the members of the
prosecution team were looking at each other quizzically. Eve
imagined they were checking their witness list, making sure he
was on it, and it occurred to her if Gordon Moon had actually
been able to use the telephone book as a witness list, Oswald
wouldn't have qualified.

Eve knew her first few questions to Oswald wouldn't be help-
ful, but she had to get the damaging stuff out of the way on
direct examination, so the prosecution would have less opportunity to make anything of it on cross.

"Good morning, Mr. Ogburn," she said pleasantly.

"Good morning, Miss Nyquist. And call me Oswald, or I
might forget to answer you. I hear a lot of things I'm not supposed to answer, and I want to answer you, 'cause this is
important."

"Oswald, what is your occupation?"

"I don't really have an occupation."

"You're unemployed?"

"I don't have a regular job, so you might call me that, but I call me that. I find plenty to do."

"Where do you live?"

"In the city. All over the city. No particular place."

"You are homeless?"

"You might call me that, but I don't call me that. The city is my home."

"What is your favorite place in the city?"

"Baines Building, I guess. I have lots of friends there."

"Oswald, do you hear voices?"

"Yes, Miss Nyquist. I hear your voice right now."

"But do you hear other voices?"

"I hear lots of voices. All the time. It can be a problem."

"Are all the voices real?"

"They're real to me, so that makes them real, but other people don't hear them, so I guess they're not real to everybody. I mean everybody hears you now, I think, but other things I hear everybody doesn't hear. I'm crazy, you know. I think that may be my problem in adjusting to life. But I'm not totally crazy. I know lots of people crazier than me."

"Then you can tell the difference between my voice and the judge's voice and these other voices you hear that other people don't?"

"Sure, I can tell. They're my voices, and others don't hear them. I know the difference."

"Oswald, do you remember the night of July twenty-fourth of this year?"

"I do remember that. I mean I don't remember knowing that at the time because I don't always know what the date is, but I know that was the night Mr. Andrew Baines was killed, and I remember the night he was killed, and everybody says that was July twenty-fourth, so I guess that means I remember July twenty-fourth even though at the time, I didn't know it was July twenty-fourth."

Eve could sense amusement in the courtroom, as if tr
ties to the case, the press, and the spectators were all fir
Oswald sort of entertaining but didn't really expect anytl.
useful to come of his testimony. She was proud of how he w
doing. He hadn't really said anything insane or unreasonable.

"Were you in the Baines Building that night, Oswald?"

"Yes. Wilbur lets me sleep in the lobby sometimes when
nobody else is around. I was sleeping in the lobby and I woke
up when Santa Claus came. I mean, when Mr. Charlie Baines
came. I know he's not really Santa Claus. He just plays Santa
Claus. But he was dressed like Santa Claus that night, which
was funny because it wasn't around Christmas. I mean, if he
dressed like Santa Claus today, it would make sense, but he
isn't, but then he was, and it didn't."

"Did you visit any other floor of the Baines Building that
night, Oswald?"

"Yes, I did. I know I'm not supposed to, but I like to explore
that building at night, and there were always ways to get around.
I don't do it now, because they got more people to stop you,
but now sometimes I get invited. Like you invited me, Miss
Nyquist. I never used to get invited when Andrew Baines was
alive."

"What floor did you visit on the night of July twenty-fourth,
Oswald?"

"The thirtieth floor."

"That was the floor where Andrew Baines had his office?"

"Yes, it was."

"Did you go through the lobby to get to the thirtieth floor?"

"No, I said Wilbur would have stopped me. There's a side
door out in the alley that sometimes gets left propped open.
When it's like that, it's the easiest way to sneak in the building,
but if it's not, there are plenty of other ways."

"What did you see on the thirtieth floor that night?"

aw Santa Claus coming away from Mr. Andrew Baines's

You mean you saw Mr. Charlie Baines dressed as Santa
aus?"

"Yes."

"Did he see you?"

"Nobody sees me on the thirtieth floor because I know better than that. I'm not supposed to be there, so nobody sees me."

"And then did you look in Andrew Baines's office?"

"Yes. There was blood. It was bad. He was dead."

"Did you go into the office?"

"No. I wanted to get away from there. I walked along the hall, and then I heard a voice coming from a closet. An angry voice."

"And this was a real voice, Oswald? One I could hear if I'd been there?"

"Yes. One you could hear. But only if you'd been there."

"What did the voice say?"

"At first I thought he was talking about a car. I thought he said 'damned Subaru'! And then I thought it might be a Japanese person he was damning. It could have been a Japanese last name, or some kind of Japanese restaurant dish. That's what it sounded like."

"Did you remember later what the word was?"

"Yes. I went into Rumpole's one day. Phil, who works there, is a nice man. He sometimes gives me something to eat. And I heard somebody sitting at the bar with a newspaper in front of him and a pencil in his hand use that same word, and then I remembered where I heard it. It's the name for a puzzle people do."

"And what's that puzzle called, Oswald?"

"It's a Sudoku. I heard a man at the bar with a newspaper and yelling about a damned Sudoku. And I knew it was the same voice I'd heard that night on the thirtieth floor. I guess the man in the closet had finished killing Mr. Andrew Baines, then maybe heard somebody coming and hid in the closet, and now he was killing time doing a puzzle till he could get out of there."

"Don't tell me what you think might be true, Oswald, but tell me what you know. Whose voice was it you heard that night on the thirtieth floor and again in Rumpole's."

"Mr. Duffy O'Gonigal, that's who!"

The court erupted in noise. Judge Estrada banged her gavel. Hurried conferences took place at the defense and prosecution tables.

"We'll recess for ten minutes," the judge said. "Counsel will join me in my chambers."

Eve noticed Melba Wooten whip out her cell phone before coming to the judge's chambers and wondered whom she might be calling.

Gordon Moon was saying, "I can't believe it could have been Duffy. Can you believe it, Vern?"

"Well, he's not here, is he?"

"Oswald must have done the killing himself, and he's just trying to put the blame on Duffy."

"You think Oswald is that smart?" Vern asked.

"I think Oswald is very smart," Eve said gently. "And the judge is waiting for us."

When all the lawyers were gathered, Judge Estrada said, "Okay, where do we go from here, ladies and gentlemen? Do you have any more witnesses, Mr. Moon?"

"No, Your Honor, I don't think so."

"Are there any rebuttal witnesses, Ms. Wooten?"

"No, Your Honor."

"And do you intend to cross-examine the present witness?"

"What's to cross-examine?" Stacey Bamwanger said. "He's a homeless schizophrenic. I feel sorry for him. I wish he could get some help. But his testimony means nothing."

Judge Estrada looked at Melba Wooten. "I believe you are the lead prosecutor, Ms. Wooten. Would you like to answer my question?"

"I agree with my colleague that cross-examining Mr. Ogburn would gain us nothing."

"All right. Then let me ask you this. Is there any point in going to final arguments?"

"Of course we go to final arguments," Stacey Bamwanger said. "I mean this is all just blowing smoke. Isn't it? The defense hasn't really proved anything with its screwy last-minute witnesses. That old fart from the movie theatre is either nuts or he's been paid off by Charlie Baines. Duffy O'Gonigal is a red herring, a red herring that happens to be a member of the defense team. I can't believe this is happening."

"I'm going to let both sides huddle on this privately before we decide anything," said Judge Estrada. "But I should remind you that the defense has established that at least two and maybe three other people besides the defendant were on the thirtieth floor around the time of Andrew Baines's death. We have also heard testimony that Sidney Monarca planted the murder gun in Charles Baines's desk and planted the DNA evidence near the body. You need to consider whether, if we were to send the case to the jury, they would consider this reasonable doubt of Charles Baines's guilt."

"Your Honor," Melba Wooten said, "we don't need to huddle. The prosecution withdraws its case against Charles Baines. I've also asked Detective Tracy to locate Duffy O'Gonigal and bring him in for questioning."

"Duffy will be here any minute," Gordon Moon insisted. "He's not a fugitive."

"Then maybe Dick Tracy will be able to find him," Vern said.

"I can't believe this is happening," Stacey Bamwanger said

again. "I can't believe we're caving on this."

Melba, surprisingly unconcerned at Stacey's challenge to her authority, said, "You done your job, girlfriend. You done good." Turning to Agnes, she put a long arm on the shoulder of each of her colleagues and said, "We'll talk, girls. Everything will be fine."

When court resumed, Judge Estrada asked the jury for a directed verdict of not guilty. The jury delivered it without leaving the box. And court was adjourned a full week before Christmas.

Even as she was accepting congratulations from her defense colleagues and two surprisingly sporting members of the prosecution team, Eve overheard one reporter excitedly informing another that DA Prentice Winstead was on the steps of the courthouse setting up for a news conference with the statue of Justice in the background. TV stations went to a live cutaway of his appearance, and by that evening everyone in the city must have heard his astonishing announcement.

"Everybody ready?" Winstead said, checking his handkerchief and flower one last time. "Okay, let's go then." He cleared his throat as the video cameras rolled. "Ladies and gentlemen, I have an announcement that will lift a cloud from the sky over our city. Today—" A piece of masonry fell from the statue's blindfold, and Winstead leapt to one side just in time. "Who did that?" he said, looking up as if expecting to see a chimpanzee hanging from the statue. "Somebody is remote-control booby-trapping that statue, and I want to know who it is!" Then he looked back at the mass of faces and cameras, visibly took command of himself, smiled shakily, and said, "No problem, folks. I'm perfectly okay. Just a crazy thing that keeps happening with our statue. We try to fix it, but—Anyway, you won't use that footage, will you, fellas? Let's try it again, okay?"

An aide came to brush off the DA; the offending piece of

masonry was removed; and he resumed.

"My friends, I am happy to announce one of the proudest achievements of the district attorney's office since the voters placed their confidence in me and gave me this job. The acquittal of Charlie Baines is a victory for justice, and justice is what we are all about. But there is more to the story of the Charlie Baines prosecution and happy acquittal than anyone, outside of a select view, has known until this moment. And, as we give you back your Santa Claus as our Christmas present to the city, I will tell you that story . . ."

Even as the DA was speaking, a warrant was issued for the arrest of Duffy O'Gonigal. He was not to be found at his home, at Rumpole's, or anywhere in the city.

CHAPTER THIRTY-SEVEN

Tuesday, December 19

The next morning, Jack Wong's column told the story of the district attorney's triumph in the Charlie Baines case.

Now at last it can be told. Deep Snow has been identified, and Deep Snow apparently told your reporter at least part of the truth when he said he was the real murderer of Andrew Baines. But the most surprising part of the story is that the whole Baines prosecution was a daring and unprecedented act of jurisprudential wire walking by our brilliant District Attorney, Prentice Winstead. Like everyone else in the city, Winstead knew in his heart that the city Santa Claus, Charlie Baines, could not have been guilty of murder. But the planted evidence against him was so formidable that it appeared he might be wrongfully convicted. With the full knowledge and expert collaboration of chief trial deputy David Ketchum, Baines prosecutor Melba Wooten and her all-female team, and ace homicide detectives Richard (Dick) Tracy and Joseph Freedy, the DA staged the Baines trial to smoke the real murderer out of hiding. In short, it was all an act, possibly the finest act in an unparalleled career in public service. And Deep Snow took the bait, permitting the city to trot out the tinsel with a new spirit, mug under the mistletoe, and achieve Christmas closure.

Only one question remains to be answered. Where will the gifted Winstead go from here?

That evening, on the main floor of their Flicker Manor mc-mansion, with the sounds of children and nanny rising from the family room, Gordon said to Agnes, "You knew about this?"

"Oh, yes, certainly."

"And you couldn't tell me about it?"

"Gordon, dear, you had to concentrate on your job. If you had known we were all on the same team, as it were, you couldn't have handled the defense any better, could you? Maybe you would have relaxed too much if you had known. Maybe the trial would have finished too fast. Maybe it would have ended before the real killer revealed himself. It was best to handle it the way we did." She looked at him soulfully. "I really am concerned with justice, you know. You were a hero, Gordon, dragging out the trial as you did over the definition of suspect. It was brilliant."

"And the one time you thought I was doing the right thing, fighting on the right side, you couldn't even tell me?"

"But I'm telling you now," she said.

And in that moment, their frayed relationship achieved its warmest, closest, most loving point in several years.

"David," Eve Nyquist said, "I was never going to speak to you again. Melba Wooten told me you and Prentice Winstead set her up to fail in giving her the Baines prosecution. Was that all part of the plan?"

"Uh, yes, sure, of course, all part of the plan."

"Then you didn't throw Melba to the wolves to save your own skin?"

"You thought I would do that?"

"She thought so herself."

"She had to say that."

"But why?"

"So that our relationship wouldn't ruin the case."

"How could our relationship ruin the case?"

"Because I love you so much."

Eve didn't quite get that but liked it anyway. She gazed into his eyes and said, "I've misjudged you terribly. But couldn't you have told me?"

"Eve, if I had told you, would you have been able to walk into the Majestic and terrible danger with no thought for yourself? Would you have been able to interpret the clues put out by Deep Snow? Duffy O'Gonigal wasn't in on the plot, you know, and we didn't even know he did it. In short, if you had known what we were up to, would you have been able to solve the case almost single-handedly?"

"I don't know," she said.

"Well, I do know. It's not always best to know everything." *And,* he added to himself, *I hope for the sake of my own future happiness you never find out everything.*

"Stacey," said Vern Wagstaff, "I never figured you for such a sentimental gesture as going along with a sham prosecution to save Christmas."

"There are sides to me you have never discovered, Vern. You may learn more as time goes by, but you will never know all of me. I am woman. I am eternal mystery." Certainly the tightly wound version of a Mona Lisa smile on Stacey's face was mysterious enough.

"You were so convincingly outraged in the judge's chambers, I still find it hard to believe you were part of the plan the whole time. And, of course, you couldn't have let me know what was going on, could you?"

"Would you have believed me?"

"Well, no, I suppose not."

"Maybe you can believe this," Stacey said, with a sudden anger blazing in her eyes. "It's a pack of lies. The whole prosecution team wasn't in on this grand plan to trap the real murderer, and I don't know how anybody could believe we were. By the time Agnes and I got clued in by Melba, Winstead was already out on the courthouse steps doing his song and dance. Dick Tracy and Joe Freedy didn't know anything about it either, though they're pathetically eager to pretend they did. Melba told us all to keep our mouths shut and unspecified rewards would follow. As far as I can understand, the only parties to it were the DA, Dave Ketchum, Melba, and the DA's personal media lap dogs, Wong and McCready. They figure we won't tell anybody because it would just make us look ridiculous, and as it is, we land on the winning side. All very neat."

"I should have known," said Vern admiringly. "Then you were breathing fire in the judge's chambers for real."

"Being phony doesn't come easy to me, Vern. I have to be me. You need to know that." Stacey sighed and seemed to deflate. "But Winstead's charade is bigger than any of us, and I have to go along with it. You won't tell anybody, will you?"

"Who would I tell? My brother-in-law? And I'd have to tell him about our relationship."

"So what? Is there something wrong with our relationship?"

"Well, you're a prosecutor and I'm a defense attorney. We were on opposing sides."

"So what? What about your sister and Gordon Moon?"

"Doesn't count. They're married. Everybody knew about them going in."

"Okay. But don't you know Dave Ketchum is screwing Eve Nyquist?"

"No, I didn't know that."

"Hah! I'll bet. The only defense-prosecution relationship that's really a secret is ours. Why is that, Vern? Are you ashamed of me?"

"So do you *want* me to tell my brother-in-law the truth?"

"No, but I want you to not tell him for the right reasons. Because you're loyal to me, not because you're ashamed of keeping company with such an ugly broad, okay?"

"You're not an ugly broad, Stacey."

"I'm not?"

"No." Vern almost added "not really," but he knew that would have ruined it. "But, Stacey, what about the judge? Was she in on it? And if she was, how did they get her to agree to it?"

Stacey glared at him. "How should I know? You know her better than I do, don't you?"

"Years ago I did. Not now. I have trouble buying her press quotes. All she said was she played it straight down the middle, didn't know about the prosecution's plan, was glad ultimate justice had been done, and if Charlie Baines didn't have a problem with it, she didn't either. But aren't there all kinds of ethical issues involved here?"

"Do you think about ethics, Vicious Vern? Do you think about ethics while you're raping and pillaging? I guess I have a lot to discover about you, too. You are man. You are mystery."

"Put *Stagecoach* on the DVD. I'm ready to ride."

"I don't understand any of this," Agnes Moon said into the phone.

"Look, girlfriend, just be glad we're landing on our feet, okay?" Melba said.

"At least you tipped me off before Gordon started asking questions. I had to tell him I knew all along because that was the story Winstead gave the press, but who could possibly believe it? How did Winstead get the judge to go along with this? That's what I want to know."

"She didn't know about it until the case was over."

"And Tracy and Freedy?"

"Same with them."

"And can we trust them to keep their mouths shut?"

"Let's just say everyone will be rewarded, all right, girlfriend?"

Agnes heard a masculine voice from below calling, "Agnes, come see what Wimmy and Westy made for Waggy!"

"I'm coming dear!" Agnes called back. "Have to go, Melba."

CHAPTER THIRTY-EIGHT

Sunday, December 24

On Christmas Eve, Prentice Winstead threw another party, for a smaller and more select group: everyone involved in the Baines prosecution, including lawyers on both sides. (Duffy O'Gonigal's invitation had proved undeliverable.) Even the very surprised jury had been invited, and about half of them showed up, some with husbands, wives, or significant others accompanying. Judge Estrada, the guests were told, had been invited but politely declined.

"Didn't you tell me you already had a party to go to on Christmas Eve?" Juror Number Six said to Juror Number Five.

"Yes, I did," Number Five replied. "But I had to come to this one. I don't want to deprive my friends and family of hearing how I went to a party at the home of Prentice Winstead. Telling them about the experience, letting them share it, will be my Christmas present to them, don't you see?"

Number Six said in mock outrage, "I thought announcing our engagement was your present to your family and friends."

"I don't have to limit myself to one present, do I?"

"You're so generous."

The two young jurors were not the only ones celebrating an engagement. Prentice Winstead announced that Alison Mc-Cready had consented to be his bride, while hinting that his run for governor the following year was all but certain. The only members of the media present were his intended wife and the ubiquitous Jack Wong, but Winstead, no more than half as stupid as he looked, was always on. His whole life was a press release, accompanied, he hoped, by a photo op.

"So who's going to be the next DA?" Jack Wong asked the room at large.

"I can think of no finer candidate than my chief trial deputy David Ketchum," the DA said, "and he will certainly have my support."

David, with a secretive grin, said he would not be a candidate but would support Melba Wooten, if she chose to seek the job. Melba looked surprised and pleased at his endorsement but said nothing.

When everyone had drinks in hand and had gathered around the largest of the Christmas trees in the largest of the district attorney's rooms, the host said archly, "Say, wait a minute. Where's the guest of honor?"

And that was the cue for Charlie Baines, in full Santa Claus regalia and carrying a small canvas bag in his hand rather than a back-breakingly heavy one over his shoulder, to enter the room. The gathering broke into spontaneous applause to which Charlie responded with soft-spoken thanks.

"We always knew you were innocent," said Juror Number Four, whose beaming wife was on his arm. "Didn't we, kids?" Numbers Five and Six nodded in agreement.

"We never would have convicted Santa Claus," said Number One, who had been enjoying more of Winstead's alcoholic refreshments than anyone else in the room.

"I owe all of you my sincerest thanks," said Charlie Baines. "I never doubted the spirit of Christmas or the infallibility of American justice for a moment. Now I will offer you some small tokens of my gratitude. Merry Christmas, one and all!"

The presents that emerged from Santa's canvas bag were small in size but large in impact. When he handed a manila

envelope to Melba Wooten, she looked at it so̤
ciously, as if she doubted his forgiveness and fea̤
bomb or at least a practical joke. But when sh̤
suspicions aside, opened it, pulled out a document and
its contents, her mouth opened wide, and she said, "Oh,
Claus, this is too much." Then she turned to Agnes Moon
said, "I won't be running for DA, either. Over to you, girlfrienc

"What will you be doing?" Agnes asked.

"I am the new player-coach of the Hummingbirds." When all
faces in the room looked blank, she said, "Ain't you heard of
the Hummingbirds? It's only the city's new WNBA team, that's
all. How did you manage that, Charlie, er, Santa?"

"The owner can hire the coach. Once I got out of jail, I
wanted nothing more than to spend my money. So I bought the
team. Understand, I want a winner."

"You'll have one, don't worry." She paused a moment as if
considering her next words carefully. "You know, I don't often
talk about this, but it was a white Santa Claus that gave me my
first basketball, all those years ago, when I was in grade school.
Up to then, my height was only an embarrassment. But once I
got that ball in my hands, I was a changed kid."

"Was that you?" Charlie said. "Were you the tall little girl I
gave that basketball to?"

"Sure, that was me. You mean that was you?" She impulsively
embraced Charlie to applause from the group.

"Does this make you feel less like a victim?" David asked.
When Melba turned on him, he decided it had been the wrong
thing to say.

"Hell, no," she said, scowling first but then smiling. "But this
case showed me anybody can be a victim. Even Santa Claus can
be a victim. So we victims just have to help each other out,
that's all."

Charlie continued to pass out gifts, some designated to

_e_, others more generic, with a supply of extras to ___ unexpected guest would be left out. When David ___ opened his envelope and read the contents, he was ___ y not surprised but mouthed a misty-eyed "Thank you."

___ aarlie," Vern Wagstaff said, "you've been busy. How'd you ___ age to put all this together in the six days since you got out jail?"

Charlie said, "Who but Santa Claus knows how to organize his time in this season of the year?"

Eve and David were no longer hiding their relationship. Prentice Winstead came over to them and said softly, "If there were any misunderstandings as a result of our rather elaborate plot, I hope they can be smoothed over."

Eve found herself looking at David. He looked back at her. They locked eyes. She said, "They're smoothed over. They're very smooth."

"Aren't you going to ask me why I'm quitting the DA's office?" David said to Eve when Winstead had drifted away.

"Well, yes, I have been wondering."

"Charlie bought the Majestic when his funds got freed up. He just handed me a very generous contract to manage it. It's the perfect job for me. And it includes health insurance better than the city's. It covers dependents," he added meaningfully.

In another corner of the room, Agnes Moon said, "Will they ever catch up with Duffy, I wonder."

"Probably not," Gordon said. "I hope not." Later he would tell his wife about the letter he'd received earlier that day, the letter that was now in his jacket pocket. But the reason for sharing it with her had nothing to do with the likelihood of her being the next DA

Santa's presents to Agnes Moon and Vern Wagstaff consisted not of envelopes but two small, wrapped packages, and he said they came not from him but from Judge Estrada. They opened

them simultaneously, and each found one-half of that tra॒
radio they had broken as children. Each was accompanied
short note in which Marisol Estrada congratulated them
finally landing on the same side in a cause.

"Can I see your half for a second?" Vern asked.

"No, you can't," said Agnes. "I may never see it again."

"Let a neutral party look at both halves," said Charlie.

Vern shrugged. "Well, if you can't trust Santa Claus . . ."

They both handed over the parts, which Charlie fit together
with a little duct tape from his jacket pocket. "Always carry it,"
he explained. He took two AAA batteries from the same pocket
and put them in the radio. "This is the part of the gift from
me," he said.

Charlie switched on the radio, and the assembled group heard
the tinny voice of a disc jockey saying, "And here is the winner
of the poll for worst ever Christmas song," followed by the
voice of Frank Sinatra singing, "Oh by gosh, by golly, it's time
for mistletoe and holly."

Marisol Estrada's sentimental gesture resulted in a rapproche-
ment between the two siblings that would last almost through
New Year's.

Many things would change in the months to come. Prentice
Winstead was elected governor, made Jack Wong his press
secretary, and immediately began running for his party's
nomination for President. Dick Tracy and Joe Freedy headed
the governor's security force. Alison McCready flourished as
first lady, until a sex scandal threatened to retire the whole Winstead team from public life. Stacey Bamwanger opposed Agnes
Wagstaff Moon for District Attorney, guaranteeing a woman in
the office, but lost in a landslide and retired from the DA's office to become a radio talk-show host. Melba (Jumping Jack)
Wooten's bad knees shortened her stint as player-coach, but she
guided the Hummingbirds to a winning record. David Ketchum

a success of the revitalized Majestic and of his marriage
ve, who saw him through innumerable crises and traumas
n of his dramatic past. Sidney Monarca died before he could
e prosecuted for the assault on Eve or his brother's long-ago
murder. Oswald became a peer counselor in a mental health
clinic. An investigation of the late Andrew Baines's complicated
affairs revealed his treachery in getting Phil Etchebarren's law
license revoked. Charlie Baines resumed his career as the city's
official Santa Claus. Gordon Moon, husband of the new DA,
always carried his last letter from Duffy O'Gonigal with him
and frequently pulled it out for inspiration.

December 24

Dear Gordon,

*This is the last "lesson" you'll get from your old mentor, so
listen up. First off, this may look like a suicide note, but it ain't.
I have too much residue of my Catholic upbringing for that. I
can hear you saying, yeah, Duff, murder didn't bother you, but
you draw the line at suicide. Fair enough, but murder did bother
me. A little. Not as much as some other things bothered me. If I
work up enough regret and remorse, I'll find a priest somewhere
and confess to him. For now, I'll just confess to you.*

*Though this is not a suicide note, it might as well be. The
sawbones told me last June my veritable buffet of life-shortening
medical conditions threatened to do me in within months unless
I change my ways, which I was not about to do. My legal career
was over, so why would I want to sacrifice my drinking career?
Not seeing much point in spending my remaining days on trial
for murder, I've arranged to disappear. The Keystone Kops and
Prentice Winstead's corps of Keystone prosecutors can look for
me all they want, and you can share this confession far and
wide. I won't be found, and that's that.*

*My idea was not an original one, I'll admit. I got it from
Trial and Error, an old British detective novel by Anthony*

Berkeley, in which a man named Mr. Todhunter was in the same position I was. Like the guy in the novel, I asked myself, what good deed can I do before I go that will make up for all the years of sitting on my can in Rumpole's and other watering holes bemoaning my alcoholic fate?

I killed Andrew Baines, not because of the threat to that old Majestic movie house, much as I loved it, but because of a whole series of things he did to hurt this city, including the dirty deal that got my pal Phil Etchebarren disbarred. Of course, I had no idea Charlie Baines would be in the building at the time and that he would be charged with the murder of his brother. I couldn't believe it was happening, though I should have seen it coming. The same thing happened to Mr. Todhunter.

When I was hiding in the maintenance closet on the thirtieth floor that night, doing my puzzles, talking to them a little too vocally as I found out later, and waiting for all the traffic to pass through—God, it was like Victory Street at rush hour up there, wasn't it?—I had seen that pious old fraud Sid Monarca, snooping around for who the hell knew what reason. Then when I heard about the DNA evidence on the tissue and the beard and the transportation of the gun I used from Andrew's office to Charlie's, I realized that somebody was deliberately framing Charlie for the murder. I knew I hadn't framed Charlie. I knew the cleaning lady hadn't framed Charlie. So even though I still wasn't sure why Sid was up there to begin with—it wasn't to kill Andrew, unless he came to do it and found somebody had got to it first—I knew he had to be the one doing the framing.

About that gun, by the way. No, I didn't personally burgle Clarabelle Algonquin. I got that handsome weapon several hands down the line through untraceable and unsavory sources, about which enough said. Clarabelle's name intrigued me so much, though, that I felt I had to meet her. She's a widow and we hit *it off immediately. To make a long story short, don't look for her either.*

At the point Charlie got charged, I wasn't quite brave enough to give myself up, but I was crafty enough for another good deed. I'd seen Monarca, but he hadn't seen me. If Monarca could frame Charlie, why couldn't I pay it forward, so to speak, and frame Monarca? Sid's love for old movies was genuine enough, but that didn't mean he wasn't a lousy crook. I always figured he burned down the Royal himself to collect the insurance money, maybe killed his brother Frank to cover his tracks, and as you know by now, he was in cahoots with Andrew on a plot to shake down the investors in that development plan by running up the price on the Majestic, not knowing that old Andrew was playing both ends against the middle in his best entrepreneurial style. At the very least, by redirecting suspicion to Sid Monarca, I could create some reasonable doubt, and I figured in this town, it wouldn't take much of that for a jury to let Santa Claus off the hook.

So I started calling Jack Wong with my Deep Snow act. I made the clues as broad as I could, but none of the dunderheads in this town seemed able to read them properly. Except for our very own—Eve Nyquist, who went to beard the lion in his nostalgic den. Fortunately, I was watching events closely, and I was able to get her out of it. From my days as an usher there, I knew a couple of ways to get down to his basement office, so I was able to surprise him.

Anyhow, now the trial is over. You wanted a Christmas story, Gordon, and you got one. But a Christmas story demands happy endings all around—which mine is, believe it or not, in its own perverse way. (Clarabelle is quite a woman!) Take the opportunity to tie up the loose ends.

The main thing I'd do is start paying more attention to those kids. I don't want you to retire from the law and become a house husband but, God, Gordon, with the money you've made and the money your wife already has, you could cut back your schedule and trust your associates more and maybe get home a little earlier. And if getting home before Agnes lays the guilt trip on her that she's been trying to lay on you—well, she's a mother. It's more likely to work on her. Maybe you'll become a family again. Just a suggestion.

Anyway, have a Merry Christmas. And as you continue in your distinguished career, just remember this: the law is like a holly bush, and the lawyer is a magpie that steals the berries off it and ruins your Christmas. And sometimes, when a bird is pest, you just have to shoot it.

No, on second thought, this is about happy endings. Don't shoot that magpie. Just clap your hands and chase it away.

Your proud mentor,
Duffy O'Gonigal

ABOUT THE AUTHOR

Jon L. Breen is the author of seven previous novels, most recently *Eye of God;* three short story collections, most recently *Kill the Umpire: The Calls of Ed Gorgon;* three reference volumes on mystery and detective fiction, including two Edgar Award winners; and more articles and book reviews than he can count. He contributes review columns to *Ellery Queen's Mystery Magazine* and *Mystery Scene* and has edited or co-edited several anthologies. A longtime trial buff, he won one of his two Edgars for the 1984 first edition of *Novel Verdicts: A Guide to Courtroom Fiction,* research for which prepared him well for his own contribution to Big Trial fiction. He lives in Fountain Valley, California, with his wife Rita.